LETTERS FROM SPAIN

BY

CLIVE ANNING

Published 2006 by arima publishing

www.arimapublishing.com

ISBN 1 84549 113 0

© Clive Anning 2006

Printed and bound in the United Kingdom

Typeset in Garamond 11/16

Swirl is an imprint of arima publishing.

arima publishing
ASK House, Northgate Avenue
Bury St Edmunds, Suffolk IP32 6BB
t: (+44) 01284 700321

www.arimapublishing.com

Chapter 1

She sat on the wooden slatted seat with its curled wrought iron supports; it was the same seat her nanny had sat on so many years ago when she had cradled her in her arms. Little had changed in this part of the garden during that time; the seat had always been there. Of course some of the timbers had been replaced and it had been repainted several times. Green, always green. It was probably there when her mother had moved in. She had been far too young to remember, but somehow coming to this unchanged almost natural area beyond the formality of the privet hedges, structured flower borders and manicured lawns gave her a sense of security and comfort that she found hard to find elsewhere, even in her own bedroom. A relatively small area in the south-western corner, it was enclosed by thick laurel bushes on the three sides bordering the garden with just a small opening to squeeze through from the crazy paved path that led down from the house to this far end of the garden. The perimeter fence, a height of nearly two metres down either side of the property, was reduced at this point to an open low wooden post affair with wide mesh galvanised wire nailed to the lower half. The seat, back to the garden, faced out to afford an uninterrupted view across the fields of Surrey to the Weald of Kent beyond.

It was late afternoon and as the hazy sun began to recede behind the tall poplars on the corner of the adjacent wood, the reality of the early spring sent its tentacles around her back and shoulders. She shivered involuntarily though she did not notice.

The view was little changed also since she moved here with mother all those years ago, apart from the M25 London orbital motorway that now cut a great swathe across the valley floor below the North Downs escarpment where she now sat. She could remember as a child watching the construction with fascination from this high vantage point. The gigantic earthmovers digging a huge white furrow of chalk across the plain from east to west, the great swirls of dust as lorries hurried to and fro with their cargoes full of soil and rock, concrete and tarmacadam. Children from her primary school would do almost anything to gain her favour and be invited round. No one else had a garden with such a grand view or indeed such a large house. 'Your Ma and Pa must have loads of money,' one of the village boys used to constantly say. She never let on that her father was dead, that she had never known him, that her mother was reluctant to talk about him and had always turned the conversation away from the subject as soon as she could. This was something she did not want to share, dared not share for fear of the emotions that might well up and overwhelm her. Why was her father shrouded in mystery? Why did her mother keep no picture or memory of him around the house? She remembered going to Katherine's house for tea one day and seeing family photographs on the sideboard and mantle piece. 'Everyone has those, silly,' said Katherine dismissively when Emma had naively remarked about them.

In the car going home she had asked her mother innocently why they did not have a picture of daddy or of the three of them like Katherine had. Mother had became angry, 'Your father is dead and that's all there is to it, we don't need pictures to remind us,' she shouted enough to startle Emma into believing she had been very wrong even to mention it. With that the subject was closed and the rest of the journey carried in frosty silence.

She used to revel in the popularity that this unique vantage point of the motorway afforded. She did not make friends easily; even then she had inexplicable mood swings that made her peers uncertain of her. It was good while it lasted she had often told herself. But now all signs of the great scars of construction effort inflicted on the landscape were gone. Trees had matured, concrete weathered, fences and hedges set. It might have always been there. Now the intrusion was more bearable to the eye but far less so to the ear. Where in times past she had revelled in the beauty of the silence interrupted only by the chatter of starlings or the cry of the rook; now there was a constant drum as vehicle chased vehicle in a never ending plight like ants in a frenzy along a well-trodden path.

The shouting of children caught her attention. Over to the west, just on the edge of her vision the footpath of the North Downs Way emerged from the wood beyond the boundary of their garden. Many a hiker would pause here to take in the view before the path was again swallowed up by the coppice a little further down the hill. She turned her head and saw two children both dressed in brightly coloured anoraks pointing animatedly at the scene below and calling to their parents who were just emerging from the trees. The distance was too great to catch what they were saying and the wind was snatching at their sounds making them appear even stranger to the ear. As she returned her head, a movement just on the edge of the wood caught her attention. It was in shadow and difficult to determine. Was she mistaken? No, a man, she could not tell any of his features at this distance, was standing there. He had both arms up to his face; she could just decipher the shape of his bent elbows. She tightened her eyes in concentration and saw he was holding a pair of binoculars and, she was sure, pointing them straight at her. Instinctively she turned away but then looked straight back. Only the dark shadows of the trees filled the spot where she thought she had seen him. Was she imagining things she asked herself? It was not the first time in recent weeks she had thought she was being watched.

+++++++++

The man lowered the glasses quickly and moved deftly back through the trees and further along the path. The family hadn't seen him of that he was sure, but what about the girl, had she? He had been watching her for several minutes but she had hardly moved and all that was visible was a three-quarter view from behind her right shoulder. The children too momentarily distracted him but then he had seen her turn. He only had the opportunity to view her full face for a split second but he was sure this was the girl he was looking for. About twenty-six or -seven, slim faced and from what he could see slim body as well. Medium length jet-black hair falling straight at first but then curling outwards gently as it brushed her shoulders, she had thin lips, a small button sort of nose and large dark eyes. She was not model girl material but also not unattractive. He had noted all this in a split second because he knew what he was looking for. The hairstyle was different, but the face, he knew the face. His searching was surely over.

+++++++++

The outline of the South Downs in the distance was slowly merging with the darkening sky. The angled roof of a large building on the industrial estate just south of Broadhurst reflected a deep orange like a brightly glowing ember as it caught the lowering sun. She shivered again. There were sheep and cattle in many of the fields, three horses quietly grazing over at Miles Farm, a farmer spraying a crop that was just pushing through the soil. A thousand and one other things on which to focus the eye if one was so inclined, but Emma was lost deep in thought, her eye seeing, her mind not registering; she could have been anywhere for all that was happening below her. Yet she found great comfort in this little corner of the garden. Perhaps it was because it never changed. Nanny had always called it Emma's corner because she was so often to be found there. Whatever the reason she somehow felt safe here; she could, here of all places try and discover herself, try and understand why she so often felt as she did. Yet for as many answers, if they were answers, she seemed to pose herself more questions.

+++++++++

Ray Brooks steered his pride and joy through the thinning traffic of Chartwood. He had been on duty since 8am. It had been a quieter than usual day, a couple of businessmen to Heathrow to catch the morning flight to Hong Kong. He had often taken them to the airport, either one or other of them or both. 'They must have flown more miles than I've had hot dinners he would joke to Kirsty in the office. Truth was, he was probably right; still they tipped quite well. Then back to Chartwood for a few local shopping trips for some of the regulars. The 'old girls' as he called them, a family to the railway station for a birthday treat in London and plenty of time in between at the offices of Chippam Taxis to run the leather once again over the paintwork. His boss John Chippam told him he would be down to the bare metal soon. But he didn't mind, he enjoyed his work and he loved his albeit second hand two-point-eight litre midnight blue Rover Sterling. Another few months and he would clear the finance and the car would be his, he felt a warm glow of satisfaction as he contemplated the thought. His day was nearly over but he enjoyed this last trip. It had become a regular run for the last few weeks every Saturday afternoon to take Jane Dennington the new hairdresser up *Silver Lane* to the big house at the end. She had arrived in the town about three months back and rather than work from a salon had built up a small business calling on people in their own homes. The lady in *Silver Lane*, Mrs Bertram he thought her name was, was one of her first customers. He quite fancied Jane and she had even let him buy her a drink in the bar of The Bricklayers Arms a week ago last Friday. It was a nice pub, a warm and homely atmosphere; not as rowdy as the two in the centre of the town. The landlord Mike was into 60's music and had set up a professional music system in one corner. He quite fancied himself as a 'pilot of the airwaves' and was actually quite good at it, his wife Brenda regularly joked that she should have let him join Radio Caroline out in the North Sea all those years ago when she had the chance!

Jane had recognised Ray instantly and invited him to join her. She had been having a drink with her lodgers, a young business couple in their thirties but they were now leaving to baby sit for some friends and she was glad of the company. He was discovering how she seemed to have the ability to be at ease with everyone and there was a quiet confidence about her that attracted him and began to touch emotions that he didn't know he had.

He turned into Ravenswood Close and pulled up outside her lodgings, a 1930's semi-detached house. This was in the older part of town, not quite as groomed as the newer estates on the outskirts that had birthed so quickly in the boom of the seventies and eighties but for all that they were well kept and there was an air of maturity about this area that was a long way from reaching the edges of town. Jane was waiting and he put the dryer and her bag in the boot. As he climbed back into the car she was already fastening her seatbelt. He was immediately conscious of the sweet smell of her perfume and the ease with which she made conversation. He slipped the car into gear and headed west for the eight-minute drive to the far end of *Silver Lane.*

As they turned into the bottom end of the lane and began the ascent up past the old brick worker's cottages Ray was a very contented man. Jane had agreed to a date next Wednesday at the cinema in Beckworth followed by an Italian meal at *Giardini's* in *North Street.* He knew it would set him back quite a bit but he was confident it would be worth it. He could hardly suppress his excitement at the prospect. He didn't know why but he felt like a school kid fixing his first date.

The thickening clouds were bringing a premature darkness, which was accentuated in the lane by the thick hedgerow and evergreen trees that lined this part of the road. At one time it had been the boundary of the Brookman estate but the manor house had fallen into disrepair years ago and the land sold off to pay for the double blow of upkeep and death duties. Ray turned on his lights. They had left the last of the houses a quarter of a mile behind now and the lane narrowed here and became more pitted and uneven. As he turned the wheel and dropped down into second gear to take the sharp right hand bend a dark blur raced towards him from the blind spot at the edge of the windscreen. Instinctively he swung the wheel to the left and stood on the brake but he was already well into the right hand turn and the back of the car gave way on the mud that had washed down the hill following the previous night's rain. The dark blur thumped into the offside of the Rover just behind the driver's door and pushed it off the road and into a hawthorn bush before it came to a halt. Ray leapt out, raised his fist and swore at the receding car still hurtling down the lane at reckless speed and with no lights showing. He found himself shaking with rage as he surveyed the damaged car lying there at a drunken angle, the two nearside wheels lodged in the shallow drainage ditch. Suddenly, embarrassed for forgetting her, he remembered Jane and rushed back to his door. She was all right, saved from any serious injury by her seat belt but clearly shaken and her face had gone very white. Ray grabbed the microphone of his radio and tried to call base, Ted would still be there and could get a call to the police; he was not going to let this drop. All he got was a lot of static noise and no response; this part of *Silver Lane* must be in a dead spot shielded by the hill behind them he realised. Frustrated he threw the mike down into the well behind the gear column and swore again. Jane tried to calm him and touched his arm. She suggested they go on up to Mrs Bertram's house and ask to use the phone from there. Ray agreed and gently eased the car back onto the road but not before it and the hawthorn had vented their anger at each other with a further scraping cry of pain that Ray could hardly bear to hear. It was all he could do to suppress his anger and feelings of hurt that his beloved car had been damaged like this.

At the top of the lane he pulled through the stone pillars and into the impressive sweeping stone chipped drive of *Tall Trees*. The drive was bordered with rhododendron bushes on either side for some twenty metres before it opened out to reveal the impressive Victorian house and manicured lawn that swept across the front of it in a great arc. Rising majestically and erect from every part of the grounds, tall trees of every description pointed heavenward almost dwarfing the house with their regal presence. The property was aptly named. As Ray switched off the engine so a sense of unease swept over them both, the sky was quite dark by now and there were no lights showing anywhere in the house yet they could see through the gloom that the front door was wide open. They alighted from the car and made towards it. Ringing the bell they instinctively called out "Mrs Bertram!" There was no sound save for the moaning in the high trees as the wind lifted with the threatening storm. They stepped carefully inside neither daring to speak to the other somehow knowing that all was not well. The door to the dining room at the front of the house was open slightly, Ray pushed it back gently; he could feel Jane's quickened breath on the back of his neck. The room was in a mess; draws had been pulled out of the dresser, their contents spilled out all over the floor and several small pictures and ornaments smashed and trodden into the thick pile carpet along with a carriage clock.

+++++++++

Emma shivered again and this time became more aware of her surroundings. The dark clouds rolling in from behind the hill to the northwest looked menacing. She realised how dark it had got, lights were appearing on the gloomy landscape and the vehicle movement on the motorway below looked like a picture of a fibre-optic cable she had seen in a magazine advertisement recently. As she looked up at the stirring poplar trees she felt the first drops of cold rain upon her face. It was time to go and face her mother. She made her way through the narrow gap in the laurel, round the old tool shed and started her way up the path to the house. Although still some way from the house; she could see from the security light above the French windows that the door was still open. Her mother had opened it earlier in the afternoon when the sun was up to let the fresh air, and scent of the hyacinth bed now in full bloom nearby, waft into the lounge and remove some of its mustiness. There was no other light on in the house and she guessed her mother must be in the front bedroom perhaps sorting out her spring clothes from last year and deciding how much of a new wardrobe she needed to have. Mother was not short of money and though generally she was careful with it, clothes and perfumes were her one weakness.

Emma was nearing the open doors now as the rain and wind began to increase in unison. She started to hurry her head bowed against the weather. There was a flash of lightning that brilliantly lit all her surroundings in stark relief, and then a moment's pause as her senses tensed for the inevitable crash of thunder which came soon after. Then as it receded and she placed her right foot on the doorstep to enter the lounge a loud and long piercing scream from somewhere inside the house drowned out every other sound.

Chapter 2

The red fluid was warm and sticky and she was covered in it. It poured out of her mother's chest like a great fountain that could not be stopped and flowed down her pale blue sweater onto the top of her denim trousers. Her mother was screaming, 'Stop the blood, stop the blood!' Emma tried desperately but as she placed her hand over the wound it deflected the warm liquid into her face and hair. Emma screamed and shook, tears coursing down her cheeks. She held her hands out and stared at them. Hardly an area of the pale skin was untouched, she watched in horror as it trickled down her inner arms and dripped onto the carpet below. Hands grasped her shoulders; had they come back for her? She struggled in blind panic. Then through the mix of her own screams and that of her mother's she heard a softer voice,

'It's all right Emma, It's all right, I'm here'.

Her eyes, that had been open, but not seeing slowly focussed on the silhouette bending over her. Emma slowly became aware of her surroundings, she was shaking and in a cold sweat, her hair matted against her forehead, her eyes damp with tears of fear, the bed a tangled mess with sheet and duvet twisted and creased below and about her. She reached up and threw her arms around the ample figure of Valerie Marcheson who shifted more fully onto the bed and cradling her shoulders with her left arm stroked Emma's head and pulled it towards her ample bosom with her right hand.

Emma sobbed, 'When will they end, Valerie, when will they end?'

'Soon, my love, very soon,' she replied staring ahead at the cameo of their reflection in the dressing table mirror, knowing she was only saying what Emma wanted, no needed to hear. Though she did not believe it, nor she suspected did Emma who was far too bright to know that such trauma would not leave them in peace that easily. She glanced at the radio alarm clock on the bedside table. The red numbers mocked back 02:17, another four hours and more before the first signs of daylight. The nightmare had come just eleven minutes later than last night but earlier than the previous one to that. She knew it would be a long time before uninterrupted sleep returned into Emma's life.

'Would you like a cup of tea love,' Valerie Marcheson offered.

Emma drew back her head, the tears had left a large wet patch on Valerie's night-gown but she did not seem to notice or care. She pushed her hair back with her left hand and stretched for her handkerchief from under the pillow.

Sniffing and blowing her nose she said, 'I'll come with you, I don't want to be alone just now.'

With that Emma reached for her dressing gown and the two women made for the stairs and the kitchen below.

+++++++++

Nearly a week had passed since the nightmare of that Saturday evening. To Emma one day had seemed to blur into the next as police and forensic experts had invaded the house. The detective in charge of the murder enquiry, for murder it surely was, was a Detective Inspector Smurdon, called in by the local station from Kent Police headquarters at Maidstone. He was a stern looking man in his late forties with an angular face and receding hairline. He had arrived just after 8pm that evening dressed in an ill-fitting dinner jacket; his presence at the Bearstead Rotarians annual dinner-dance interrupted somewhat to his relief. He had surveyed the scene and barked his various orders though much of his requirement for doctor, photographer, and a forensic team had already been put in hand by Detective Constable Higton who had arrived a good hour before the Inspector.

Preliminary statements had been taken from Ray Brooks and Jane Dennington but they were not able to offer much information. Ray was certain that there were two men in the car. One, the driver, perhaps in his early twenties, the other older, maybe forties or older and both wearing dark clothes but he could not give any fuller description. Jane thought both the men looked young but when pressed said she was unsure. Ray was also certain the car had been a BMW 5-series, black or dark blue but could offer nothing more. They had then been allowed to leave but much to Ray's annoyance his car was impounded for forensic tests on the paintwork. His boss John Chippam came to take them both home.

Emma had been taken to a local hotel that night accompanied by a woman detective constable but she had been quite distraught and her doctor had been summoned. He prescribed some sleeping tablets and Emma had eventually subsided into a fitful sleep. Inspector Smurdon had enquired whom they might contact in the way of relatives but Emma had replied that there was no one. Her father, Barry Bertram was dead, she was an only child and neither of her parents had any brothers or sisters that she was aware of, although she knew little of her mother's side of the family and nothing of her father's. Jane Dennington who had come to know Emma through her recent regular hair dressing trips was able to confirm that an address and telephone number in Norwich found on a note by Constable Higton in the kitchen was that of Valerie Marcheson's sister. She had told Jane on her last visit that she was planning to go and stay there this weekend. Valerie Marcheson had been Doreen Bertram's live in housekeeper and cook for the last eleven years and had returned late on the Sunday evening following a call from the local police in Norwich. She was a plump round-faced woman with greying hair, a very homely woman, the sort who never looked fully dressed or comfortable unless they had an apron tied around their waist. She was probably in her mid fifties though she never mentioned her birthday and never as far as Emma could remember received any cards during the year. Even at Christmas she preferred to stay with Emma and her mother, rarely took any time off and simply visited her sister in Norfolk for a couple of long weekends every year. She was as much a mystery to Emma as her mother was; perhaps that's why the two got along so well. Emma could never recall Valerie talking about her background or childhood and like her mother would always steer the subject away if it were broached. Valerie was clearly shocked by Mrs Bertram's death but almost equally upset by the mess made by the intruders and little less so by the constant intrusion of the police and their experts. It was a time consuming task as they sifted through the debris and checked everywhere for fingerprints and signs of any material foreign to the scene. Human hairs, skin tissue, fibre from clothing and so on. Much annoyed that she could not tidy up straight away she constantly harassed the police, not that it made any difference, until their crime scene investigation was completed.

On the Wednesday she had been given the all clear and Jane had taken Emma out for a drive and walk on the North Downs while Valerie set to and tried to erase all evidence of the event, although she knew of course that would not be possible. Several porcelain ornaments and a carriage clock that had stood on the sideboard were smashed to pieces and well beyond repair. The violent scene would no doubt return to Emma in her mind and in her nightmares for many a month to come. As it had indeed every night so far without fail as she had thrashed around in her bed denied the sleep her body so desperately needed.

To everyone's surprise Emma had insisted on returning to the house as soon as possible. At the hotel she had felt isolated, fearful and very unsettled and couldn't get away from it quickly enough. The thought that the violence had happened here in this house was tempered by the fact that she would be in familiar surroundings, in her own bed in her own room and with the ever-comforting presence of Valerie Marcheson not far away.

On Thursday morning at eleven the inspector called to go over Emma's statement with her. For a man no doubt hardened by many encounters with heinous crimes over some twenty years of service his approach was gentle, yet also thorough.

'Would you mind going over everything again for me, from the time you left... where was it.... in the garden?'

'The bottom corner, the seat overlooking the valley,' she said quietly. She gripped the arms of the chair tightly not wanting to let go lest her nerves betrayed her.

They were in the lounge. Emma had taken a high back, rather hard chair with carved mahogany arms in the corner to the left of the French doors. She sat with her back to the window hoping the brightness of the day would mask her looks. Her face was pale and drawn from the lack of sleep and the redness in her eyes betrayed the fact that she still shed many tears. The inspector sat uncomfortably on the low settee by the fireplace. He looked around the room. It was large by modern standards and he guessed that the house had been built in the mid to late 1800's. The large open fireplace was the central feature, but the old grate had been removed and an imitation coal gas fire had replaced it. It was that that now popped away, the gas barely igniting but providing enough warmth to take the early spring chill off the room. There was a chest of drawers against one of the inner walls, its polished mahogany gleaming in the morning sun. The inspector noticed its typical 18th century style and remembered his ex-wife's fascination with all things antique. He had learnt a lot about the trade, how to recognise certain features, how to tell genuine from fake. His mind wandered for a moment, even after six years he still missed her. They had just drifted apart, her with the antiques business, him with working his way up through the ranks.

He shook himself out of the reverie; Emma was recounting again every detail as she could remember it. Events prior to hearing Jane Dennington scream had been blurred. She had returned up the garden by the usual path, deep in thought, it was an automatic journey. No, she had not seen or heard anything unusual, no, she could not recall the sound of a car in the lane at any time that afternoon. When the inspector pressed on this point she told him that the house and tall trees not only acted as a visual screen but were good at keeping the sounds out too. Besides she

CLIVE ANNING

had been at the bottom end of the garden for at least an hour and a half.

For the next forty-five minutes the inspector gently questioned Emma. Had she noticed or seen anything or anyone unusual recently? Had there been any callers to the house, any unusual telephone calls, mail or deliveries? Could she think of anyone that mother had had a disagreement or dispute with recently? Was she certain that nothing was missing?

She had answered all the questions in the negative. Everything had been normal, nothing unusual had happened. She was just considering if she should mention the feeling she was being watched, but then dismissed it from her mind as nonsense when Inspector Smurdon asked:

'Can you possibly think of anyone who might mean her harm?'

The question came as a shock. Until then she had assumed it was an attempted burglary that had gone horribly wrong.

'I...I don't understand Inspector, are you suggesting it was deliberate? You can't possibly mean that. No, there is no one. We live... lived quiet lives here, a very predictable existence, twice a week to Westerham for shopping, once a month to Knightsbridge and Harrods on the train, that sort of thing. Some would call us dull Inspector, many I think might envy us,' Emma paused, surprised by her growing confidence. 'Why do you ask Inspector?'

'I've been a policeman a long time Miss, things just don't add up, no money taken, in fact nothing taken at all according to your statement, although some quite expensive items were there for the taking. Several valuable porcelain pieces broken, an expensive getaway car, do you know anyone with a black BMW Miss Bertram?'

The Inspector had shifted forward on the settee, was leaning in her direction and staring straight at her.

'What... sorry...I, no I don't.'

The question had come as a surprise; the inspector was unnerving her, was she under suspicion, where were these questions leading?

'The lab have confirmed the paint samples taken from the taxi driver's car came from a black BMW Miss, just thought you might know someone who had a car like that?'

The questioning went on. Did her mother have any business associates, what was her business; was she in debt, where did her income come from? The directness of the questions unsettled Emma even more and she became agitated, but before the Inspector could press for an answer, Valerie Marcheson who had been sitting quietly in the corner until now intervened.

Rising out of her seat and advancing toward him she said, 'Really Inspector that is quite enough! This poor child has just lost her mother in the most appalling circumstances and you seem to be treating her more like a criminal than a victim.'

The Inspector looked at Emma who now clasped a small cotton handkerchief to her mouth, her fist so tight that the knuckles were ivory white. He paused and then rose, 'Well thank you Miss Bertram, you will let us know if anything comes to mind won't you? I'm sorry to have distressed you.'

He made his way to the door, 'Don't get up I'll see myself out,' he paused and turned to face Emma again, 'Tell me, do you think your mother would have let a couple of strangers into the house?'

'I don't know,' Emma replied quietly, her head now bowed.

'Hmm.' said the Inspector and turned to go.

Yet as the Inspector closed the door behind him Emma knew that Mother had been very security conscious, she would have looked through the spyglass in the front door before opening it. If she did not recognise the caller, she would not have opened the door without the security chain being engaged. So why did she let them in, and who were they? So little made any sense. As she thought about it she realised just how little she knew about her mother, the woman who had raised her and with whom she had lived for all these years.

+++++++++

Constable Higton was standing in the dining room doorway and caught the Inspector's eye as he approached.

'Wouldn't think anything had happened here, would you,' he said, surveying the crime scene now all neat and tidy, the scent of rich furniture polish still heavy in the air.

The Inspector said, 'Knock that plate off the dresser there and onto the floor.'

'What?' Higton looked puzzled.

'Just do it!'

'But...'

The Inspector muttered under his breath and stepped smartly past Higton. With one quick sweep of his arm the plate was airborne and despite the panicky lunge of Higton as if he was in the slips for England at Lord's Cricket Ground, the plate fell quickly to the carpet.

'What was all that about?' Higton asked, his heart skipping a beat. 'Thank God the plate didn't break!' He placed it carefully back on its stand.

'Exactly,' said the Inspector. 'See how thick that carpet is? Those plates must have been smashed down and stamped on to break them up into so many pieces. And that carriage clock likewise. No, this was no ordinary burglary gone wrong, this was something very carefully planned of that I am sure. They were looking for something, either in fact or in information and somehow I don't think they've found it yet.'

'But what?' asked Higton.

'If we knew that, we would know why Doreen Bertram was killed,' he paused, 'Maybe she wasn't meant to die, maybe they were just trying to extract information and it all went horribly wrong. Look at the facts, as far as we know they weren't disturbed once they had killed her. Emma Bertram was at the bottom of the garden if her story is to be believed and the taxi was still at the bottom of the lane, so why leave? I think they either panicked because they had killed her, or knew that the source of the information they had come for was now dead and there was no point in staying.'

'And Emma Bertram, what can she tell us about it all?'

'Not as much as she knows, of that I am sure,' replied the Inspector. 'Come on let's get back to the station.'

As they returned to their car the driver was on the radio and they heard the end of the conversation.

'...Right, okay, I'll tell the Inspector, Lima two-five out.'

'What?' demanded Smurdon.

'A black BMW with damage to the offside front wing has been found burnt out on a piece of wasteland near Sevenoaks. It's quite a remote spot but it wasn't there last Saturday morning,' the driver told him.

'Right, get Forensic down there fast to check it out. Let's hope they can give us the breakthrough we need, there's plenty to this case that just doesn't add up.'

+++++++++

In the dingy basement office of a dingy warehouse now converted into an even more dingy club at the back of Woolworths in dingy Peacock Street, Limehouse in the East End of London, Robbie Wilson was bordering on a heart attack. Years of neglect, too much consumption of alcohol and forty cigarettes a day made the fifty-five year old look more like sixty-five.

'Bloody fools!' he screamed. 'All this work, years of piecing it all together and the first contact is screwed up by you two worms.'

'But boss...'

'Shut up!' Wilson shouted. 'It's taken me a long time to find her. Go and ask questions I said, tread carefully I said. Bloody hell!' He stopped pacing the threadbare carpet to lean on the edge of the battered filing cabinet by the door. His face was alarmingly bright red and flushed, great beads of sweat oozed from his forehead and fat neck, his blood shot eyes looked like they would pop from his skull at any moment.

The older man dared to speak. 'Look Boss we're really sorry we messed up, but she just went berserk and lunged at us. Darren was only holding the knife as a frightener. We thought that braking a few of her precious possessions would ease her tongue but when we mentioned Barry Masters she went white as a sheet and came at us in a fury, she slipped on the broken pottery and fell on the knife. It all happened so quickly, that's the honest truth.'

Wilson flopped his ample frame into the swivel chair behind the battered desk and dabbed a dirty handkerchief across his brow and round his neck. 'What about evidence?'

'There won't be any Boss, we wore gloves the whole time and the motor's been torched down at Sevenoaks. There's nothing to connect us.' said the older man.

'Any witnesses?'

'No dad, look no one saw us; we got out clean and fast. I don't know why you are making so much fuss, the old bat deserved it,' said the younger man.

In two amazing strides Robbie Wilson was out of the chair, across the room and had smashed the back of his hand across the face of the younger man propelling him with tremendous force into the filing cabinet.

'When I say you've fouled up, then you've fouled up! Don't you ever answer me back boy!' Wilson turned to the older man, 'Get that worm of a son of mine out of here.'

Darren Wilson could taste the blood in his mouth, could feel it dripping from his nose as John Peters eased him to his feet and led him out of the room. He glanced in his father's direction, his look bore pure hatred. Yet again his father had humiliated him in front of someone. Soon he would do it no more; soon his own son would see to that he promised himself.

For the second time that afternoon, Robbie Wilson slumped into the swivel chair exhausted. What now? Could the girl provide any clues? And where did she fit into it all? He knew Doreen very well thirty years ago and in a conversation one day, he remembered, she had revealed to him that she couldn't have children, something to do with an inherited genetic disorder. Yet he had little doubt now that Doreen Bertram was the woman he had been looking for.

Chapter 3

'Man born of a woman has but a short time to live. Like a flower he blossoms and then withers; like a shadow he flees and never stays'.

Emma's mind had been wandering when she caught the Vicar's words. It seemed so inappropriate to refer to 'man' when it was her mother lying there in the coffin at the front of the crematorium chapel. Was that really her mother there in that small wooden box? In life her mother's presence could fill a room, command a hushed audience, although she kept her interests to a very small circle of friends and seemed, Emma reflected, to prefer a life lived in semi-seclusion.

And now she was reduced to a small wooden box. A single spray of flowers, white and purple, lilies and iris lay on the top of the polished oak. She found herself again staring at the coffin, sharply in focus while everything else appeared a blur to her eyes. She did not notice the low April sun casting a strange coloured pattern on the panelled wall to the left of the coffin as it shone through the stained glass window above the blue and gold curtains at the front of the chapel.

'In the midst of life we are in death; to whom can we turn for help, but to you, Lord, who are justly angered by our sins?'

Sins, did mother commit any? Did she commit any more or less than anyone else gathered there that Friday afternoon? Emma wondered. Heaven or hell, if there were such places, what would be in store for those still unknown who had committed this atrocity, for those who had brought about an abrupt end to their quiet and secluded lifestyle that had forced her into territory unknown?

She stole a glance to her left. Valerie Marcheson, in the row behind was dabbing her face with a small white handkerchief. Behind her two other ladies in dark winter coats stood stony faced staring ahead. Beside her on her right was Jane Dennington and Emma was grateful for her companionship. She had called at the house or telephoned every day since the tragedy. It was as if their shared experience that fateful Saturday afternoon nearly three weeks ago had somehow bonded them in a special relationship. One which Emma was glad to encourage, it gave her a strength she desperately needed just now and Jane had become a good friend and listener. Valerie Marcheson too was glad to see Emma finding friendship with someone of her own age. Too long had she lived in isolation, too long in her own world. Now more than ever she needed to be taken out of herself.

The vicar moved his hand to the side of the lectern and pressed a button. A click and quiet whirring started the coffin on its descent into the bowel of the podium on which it had rested.

'...*earth to earth, ashes to ashes, dust to dust: in sure and certain hope of the resurrection to eternal life through our Lord Jesus Christ, who died, was buried, and rose again for us. To him be glory for ever and ever. Amen.*'

As the organ intoned the strains of the hymn, *Abide with me*, the Usher materialised at her left elbow and gently guided Emma to the door. It was over.

+++++++++

Doreen Bertram's body had been released the previous Tuesday. The police surgeon having reported the findings of the autopsy to the Coroner that she had died of a heart attack following a massive loss of blood caused by the penetration of a steel blade some six to eight inches long into the main artery. Inspector Smurdon had told the court that the police were following a number of lines of enquiry but they had little to go on. The Coroner had recorded a verdict of death by person or persons unknown.

Emma had not attended and was glad that she had spared herself the ordeal. There had been a large press attendance and no doubt they would have wanted an interview. Inspector Smurdon had already had to place a constable at the house to fend off unwelcome press, photographers and sightseers and Valerie Marcheson had taken to leaving the telephone off the hook. Jane had purchased a mobile phone for Emma and they were using that to communicate with each other and the police.

Arrangements for the funeral had been undertaken with military precision by George Cowdrey, a retired army major and the Bertram's nearest neighbour down the lane. When Emma was younger she had often spent an evening sitting with his wife Judith while he was away on active duty somewhere in the world. In the earlier days, the Major had taken his wife with him on his postings abroad and young Emma sat enthralled as Judith related stories and events from far flung places and different cultures. What Emma had only read about in books was suddenly brought alive and exciting and she longed that one day she too might have the courage to break free of her sheltered lifestyle and venture to such distant and exotic places. Yet to step outside of the world in which she was cocooned gave her even then a sense of foreboding. The Major's wife was also very talented and Emma learnt to embroider, do cross-stitch, quilting and other crafts which she enjoyed greatly. Just after Emma's sixteenth birthday Judith Cowdrey was diagnosed with cancer of the bowel and was dead within six months. Emma found it very hard to take and became depressed for many weeks following. The Major on the other hand had coped remarkably well with his wife's death and had become a regular caller at *Tall Trees* though there was nothing more than a neighbourly friendship between him and Doreen Bertram.

+++++++++

The inspector had been delayed at the police station when the funeral service was due to start but now parked his car in the crematorium car park and spotted Higton standing alone away from the mourners who were now exiting the chapel. The vicar was in deep conversation with two ladies at the door whilst most of the others were standing sombre faced in small groups while others stooped to read the labels on the various floral tributes.

'Seen anything or anyone interesting?' he said as he approached Higton.

'There are several people I don't recognise but I think they must all be neighbours, and friends. Thankfully the press have kept away as requested. No one looks out of place and the service went as normal as these things do.' Higton replied. 'They've all been invited back to the house afterwards, the vicar made an announcement.'

The April sun was now dipping behind the trees on the perimeter of the crematorium grounds and the temperature began to drop. The Inspector surveyed the scene again. Most of the funeral party were making their way back to the cars now. 'Oh well, we can check up on any we need to back at the house. I've just had the report from forensic on that BMW. The engine and chassis numbers confirm it was stolen in Soho about a month ago, the paint and damage matches the knock with our taxi, it's our car alright but they can't come up with any other forensic evidence.'

'What about licence plates?' Higton asked.

'Taken off before they torched the car; these guys are very professional which gives this case a worrying edge, and I doubt they used anything other than false plates.' Smurdon said. 'Anyway I'm having a check made on the video footage for the last month since the car was stolen from the security cameras in Chartwell high street - it's a long shot but it might turn up something.' He paused, 'What do you make of that?

Over there on the left hand edge of the rose garden.' Higton casually followed the direction of the inspector's slight nod. A young man, probably in his mid to late twenties, his features hidden in the lengthening shadows appeared to be showing interest in the plaques placed among the rose bushes but was glancing up regularly and watching the funeral party as they stood in the car park. The car for Emma, Jane and Valerie Marcheson was parked further away from the rest and it was there that his interest seemed to lie.

'I'm sure it's the same man I saw earlier,' Higton said, 'I thought he was with the previous group. There was a funeral for a 23 year-old motor cyclist killed in a road traffic accident on the motorway about ten days ago. He was milling around then, but come to think of it I didn't see him speaking to any of them.'

'Right, go find out what he's up to. I'm going to catch Miss Bertram before they go and just check it's still okay to call up at the house this afternoon. I'll meet you up there later.'

+++++++++

Inspector Smurdon surveyed the scene. He felt awkward standing there alone in the corner of the lounge by the French windows. The funeral had been the last at the crematorium that day and as he looked out on the back garden of the house it was already becoming quite dark. He could barely see as far as the end of the first hedge that separated the lawn and flower borders from the fruit trees beyond. Exactly where Emma's corner lay he could only guess.

He turned back into the room. He was glad to note that the door to the dining room remained firmly closed. The furniture in the lounge had been moved back to make more room for those gathered and a gate-leg table had been set up at one end on which was laid a spread more fitting a celebration banquet than a funeral he thought.

Valerie Marcheson and a young girl he had not seen before were busy fussing around the guests with trays of tea and plates of sandwiches. Miss Bertram he noticed was talking to three ladies with Jane Dennington standing along side. Jane had not in fact left Emma's side the whole day.

Several women and a few men were standing or sitting in groups and he could catch snatches of their conversation. The words, 'dreadful, frightening, horrific' and 'sorely missed' carried across to him. Every so often he was aware of sideways glances towards him when someone muttered the word 'police'.

A man in his early sixties detached himself from a nearby group and headed towards him. He was dressed in a dark grey suit and Smurdon recognised him as the chairman of the magistrates' bench at Sevenoaks.

He spoke. 'I understand you are the policeman in charge of the investigation of this shameful affair. Got any leads have you? Trust you will apprehend these perpetrators quickly Inspector. I was only discussing it with your chief constable two evenings ago over dinner. We meet quite regularly you know. This sort of thing just doesn't happen in Chartwood. It needs to be sorted Inspector, it needs to be sorted!' All this in one breath without much of a pause. He was about to continue when Constable Higton appeared in the doorway and signalled to the Inspector. Smurdon was glad to have a reason to excuse himself from what looked to be a torturously one-sided conversation. Smurdon reached Higton, 'What have you got?'

'Not much,' Higton replied, 'He saw me coming and did a runner behind the crematorium. I gave chase but lost sight of him near the gates. Then I heard a car revving loudly just round the corner in Whitely Road. By the time I got to the corner the car had taken off at a fair pace, but I'm sure the driver was the same man.'

'Car details?' asked Smurdon.

'Y reg. Ford Focus, light blue with an 85 in the number,' he paused, 'sorry, that's all I got.'

'Hmm…,' said the Inspector, 'it may be nothing, it may be something, get back to the station, log the details and get someone checking on that registration. I'm nearly finished here; I just want to talk to the Major who made the funeral arrangements. I'll see you later.'

Smurdon began to make his way back across the room when a lady in a strangely patterned ill-fitting green dress that seemed most inappropriate for the occasion accosted him. He eyed her up and down. About fifty-five and not particularly well groomed, Smurdon felt she seemed more than a little out of place among the other guests. If she had been at the crematorium earlier he hadn't noticed her.

'You are the police, aren't you?' she said, 'Betty Weston, Mill West Farm. I hope you've checked out that Gypsy site over at Fairford Lane. They back onto my land you know and I've had a lot of damage done with fences being broken and chickens being stolen. I wouldn't be at all surprised if they weren't into the stealing and got caught in the act. Mark my words; it'll be two of them. You should arrest the lot of them and clear them all off that site.'

Smurdon promised he would look into it and moved quickly on. He found the Major talking to an elderly couple, but they moved away as he approached.

'Major, Inspector Smurdon, Kent Police,' he said. 'I'm sure Miss Bertram will be very grateful for your help in arranging all of this for her.'

'Happy to oblige, just so sad it had to be for this occasion. She's a lovely girl you know, but she can have mood swings and you really just don't know where you are with her sometimes,' he replied. 'I just hope she can cope on her own, her mother was such a very strong character.'

'Tell me Major,' Smurdon said, 'Doreen Bertram seems to have been a very private person. No one knows very much about her. I know you've been interviewed but you were probably the closest person to her apart from the housekeeper, Valerie Marcheson and of course Miss Bertram, can you shed any more light for us, we really seem to be up a blind alley on this one?'

'No, I've thought of little else since your man came to see me,' he replied, 'Mrs Bertram was very pleasant but as you say Inspector she kept herself to herself, a very private woman. In all the conversations I had with her, she never talked about her background and if I ever probed, in an interested sort of way you understand, she steered the conversation away. She wanted to keep it private so I respected that.'

'Did she ever talk about Mr Bertram?' asked Smurdon.

'No, simply told me on one occasion that he had died a long time ago and that that chapter in her life was closed. You know inspector, she didn't have a photograph or anything around the house to remind her of him as far as I could see. What that has done to young Emma,' he paused, 'well, who knows? Still not my place to speculate, what?'

The Major paused to take a bite from a piece of fruit cake. 'Mmm, good cook that Valerie Marcheson, I wonder what she will do now?' he paused, 'Ah tell me Inspector, found your black BMW yet? You know I'm sure if it had been around the area or up the lane before that Saturday someone would have seen it. We just don't get many strangers around here; in fact I've only seen one strange car in the last month in the lane and that was pale blue not black.'

The inspectors ears pricked up, 'Tell me about it.'

'Well it would have been the week before the murder, on the Wednesday; it was parked at the bottom of the lane just this side of the bricklayers' cottages in that small lay-by. It was there when I drove down at about 10.45am, I did a bit of shopping and then had an appointment with my accountant in Westerham at 11.15am so it must have been getting on for one o'clock when I came back and it was still there.'

'Was there anyone in it?'

Yes, a young man. I slowed right down on the way back and had a good look at him; made sure he knew that I had seen him. I'm quite security conscious you know, young people that hang about these days are usually up to no good. Bring back conscription and all that, what!'

'Can you describe him?' asked Smurdon.

'Can't tell his height of course but short dark brown or black hair, clean shaven, tidy appearance, quite dark skinned but white - like he had a good suntan but wrong time of year for that though.'

'What about the car? Make, model, registration number?' pressed the Inspector.

I did make a mental note of the number and was going to write it down when I got home but Miss Blanchard, that's my neighbour on the other side down the lane.' He paused, 'That's her over there with the navy blue coat talking to Emma Bertram. She stopped me for a chat and I had clean forgotten about it by the time I got in. But it was a modern car, a new shape, four doors, pale blue, Vauxhall or Ford maybe. Sorry I'm not very good on cars. But you could ask that Miss Dennington, the hairdresser.'

'Why?' queried the Inspector.

'Well I saw the car again on the Friday in Chartwood High Street outside Peter's the newsagent at about two thirty in the afternoon, same driver,' said the Major, 'And Miss Dennington was leaning in the window talking to him.'

+++++++++

At last they were all gone. Some had left quite quickly but others had seemed to want to linger and Emma was now feeling very tired although it was only early evening. Valerie Marcheson had insisted that Emma was not to help with any of the clearing up and that she and Joanne could manage quite well. Emma retired to the day room to keep out of the way and was glad for the solitude. The ordeal of the funeral had left her mentally and physically drained. Jane had offered to stay but Emma had encouraged her to go back to her lodgings and catch up on some of the things she needed to do. She was worried that Jane's hairdressing business must be suffering for all the time she was giving to Emma.

She clutched a mug of sweet tea between both hands and stood by the window. The curtains had not been drawn but all that was discernible outside was the dark shape of the trees on the edge of the top lawn just showing against a slightly lighter but rapidly darkening sky. She had not turned the light on preferring to stand in the gloom. The events of the day had taken their toll and she felt totally drained. The light from the hallway shone through the slightly open door of the room casting a pale but strange reflection on the window that for a split second made Emma think that her mother was standing behind her. Her heart skipped a beat and she turned. Her eyes were moist. The enormity of what had happened began to weigh heavily upon her. She was on her own now. Mistress of the house, how would she cope?

'Oh mother,' she whispered out loud and then the tears she had kept at bay could be held no longer. She slumped without thinking, not into her own chair, but into mother's favourite armchair and cried her heart out.

It was some minutes before the sobbing subsided and she lifted her head from where it had been buried in her hands. She dried her eyes and shifted more comfortably back into the armchair and reached for the table lamp beside her and switched it on. She looked up as the light illuminated the familiar scene. So many of her mother's things, no more than that, her mother's very presence was there in that room. She could not eradicate that, nor did she want to. It was something that somehow gave her comfort.

She picked up the book mother had been reading. *Defying Gravity*, poems by Roger McGough. Mother had loved poetry but usually opted for the classics of Shelley and Keats. She slowly turned the pages and read snippets of the text but her mind could not concentrate and she returned the book to the table. As she did so an envelope fell out onto the carpet. She picked it up. It was an airmail envelope postmarked two months ago and addressed to Emma in very neat handwriting. It had already been slit open and Emma reached inside. It was empty. Who had sent it, what had it contained and more importantly why had Mother not passed it on as it was addressed to her she wondered? She searched the table and nearby writing desk but there was no sign of a letter or anything that might have been the contents of the envelope. She looked at it again, particularly the stamp and the postmark. Mother had said nothing about having received it and Emma knew of no one who lived in Denia, a place in Spain she had never heard of. Mystified, she sat there clutching the envelope and quietly mouthed the words, "Oh Mother" as more tears welled in her eyes.

Chapter 4

Emma stood on the pavement of Marshall Street next to a telephone box and surveyed the drab Victorian terraced block opposite her. She tried to imagine it as the modern plush offices they apparently once were when this area of Westerham was developed in the late 1800's. It was not easy. Now the street was just a rat run from the industrial estate through to the trunk road and then on to the motorway network, and never built to take the size and volume of traffic. She closed her eyes as another giant articulated lorry thundered by sending up swirls of dust, grit and rubbish. The hot diesel fumes lunged at her nostrils while sharp specks of dirt crept between her eyelashes making her eyes smart and water. Down the street children played in the doorway of an empty shop. One ran his hand along the filthy glass and peeling paintwork shouting to his friends above the noise of traffic. The poorly scribbled *'Everything must go'* sign hanging by one corner on the inside of the glass seemed to sum up the dereliction of the area. A lot had already left this place and most of its dignity with it.

Arriving early in the town she had parked her car in the slip road just along from the triangular green where the statues of a reclining Winston Churchill and Major-General James Wolfe stand guard over the passing inhabitants. She had plucked up courage to enter the *Copper Kettle* tea rooms on her own and took a window seat where she could occupy her time alone less conspicuously and watch the comings and goings of everyday life in this small country town. Here she had a good view of the green and enjoyed watching mothers out shopping with their young children, businessmen with their cases of samples and mobile phones in their hands and delivery drivers restocking the local shops with product and produce of every kind. Despite the coming of the motorway that had taken a lot of the through traffic away, it was still a busy place.

She sipped her coffee and watched as two women stood chatting, their children running around the green happily lost in a world of play. She thought how lovely it would be to be back at that age again. Not having a care in the world, not having to make decisions about the future, not having to cope with the pressures and complexities that adult life thrusts upon you without giving a choice in the matter.

Her thoughts were interrupted by a blast from the horn of a delivery van approaching the café. A young man with a Mediterranean looking skin and wearing a bright blue anorak had stepped off the pavement right in front of the shop to allow a mother with her pram to pass and was nearly hit from behind by the van. A few choice words from the driver leaning out of his window turned several heads and the young man looking suitably embarrassed quickly stepped back onto the pavement. For a brief moment their eyes met through the shop window and then he was gone. It was just a brief encounter but it caused Emma's heart to skip a beat. It seemed somehow not a casual meeting of the eyes; it was as if they had tried to communicate something in that fleeting moment. Emma felt as if his eyes had pierced right through, and it unnerved her.

Sitting there alone she reflected that for many years she had hardly ever gone out without her mother and it seemed very strange and unnatural to be alone. Her unpredictable mood swings and times of depression had led to a solitary existence. She didn't much care for the modern approach to life enjoyed by many of her contemporaries and had quite happily retreated into the cloistered world of *Tall Trees* filling her time when able with the embroidery and other skills that Judith Cowdrey had taught her. She had actually become quite good at it and sold several items through one of the shops in the town. Although her relationship with Mother had not been as close as she would have liked, they had an unspoken code where each knew the agreed boundaries of the relationship and they would each accept the other's company in a companionable way. There was so much she did not know about her mother, her background, her family, and her upbringing. Questions years ago had brought the same icy response time and again that she had stopped asking them. For some reason that she could not or would not explain, Doreen Bertram was determined to keep her past a well kept secret even from her daughter. A past that would now perhaps remain locked up forever.

As Emma sat by the window she was thankful she had not seen anyone she knew and was glad not to have to answer the inevitable questions of kindly but enquiring minds. The national newspapers had of course covered the story quite fully but with lack of any new information from the police they had soon moved on to other news. To the local *Westerham and District Daily Press* however it was news item of the year thus far. They seemed to cover every angle of the story they possibly could with endless articles but even they could only speculate about the past of a woman who lived a very private life. Emma had overheard

Valerie Marcheson say to Jane as they studied the morning paper yesterday, 'They'll be interviewing Mrs Maunders cat next!'

She drained the last dregs of the coffee and sighed. Despite all that had happened, she felt remarkably well and did not feel the tentacles of depression that would so often grip her at times like this. She remembered how depressed she had become when Judith Cowdrey had died and yet this time despite everything she actually felt very positive. She prayed it would last.

The wail of a police siren on the main road jolted her thoughts. She looked again at her watch; it was time. She crossed the road and surveyed the dirty brass plaque on the door to number seventeen. *Curtis, Forsythe & Ptns. Solicitors and Commissioners for Oaths (First Floor).* It took nearly all her strength to push open the large oak door. It was on a strong spring and it hammered shut as soon as she released it sending a loud echo up the dingy stone stairwell.

Emma paused to accustom herself to the dim surroundings of the entrance lobby. A low powered bulb hung from the yellowed ceiling. The walls were of similar colour at the top and then a deep green from about chest height down. They were dirty and badly scuffed by the passing of time. The air of dereliction did not stop outside the door. To the left of the door was a ledge where the postman left the mail. Several unopened circulars were scattered along it and a couple lay on the floor, torn and trampled. She climbed the stairs to the first floor and entered a small lobby where a brown threadbare and much stained carpet greeted her. Two well-worn armchairs and a low glass topped coffee table that was covered in coffee cup rings and a few long out-dated magazines were the only items of furniture. The whole place had a depressing air of finality about it, as if no one cared any more. The small narrow window on the far wall let in scant light. Emma was unsure if this was because it clearly had not been cleaned for a long time or if it was that the window looked out onto a small compact courtyard where the two floors above shut out most of the natural light.

She had never been here before and found herself puzzling why her mother had chosen this solicitor. As far as she knew Mr Curtis had dealt with their affairs for as long as she could remember and she had expected a plusher office altogether. On one wall a small aperture had been cut to allow a sliding glass door to be inserted about three feet above the floor. To one side was a plastic sign '*Enquiries*' and a bell push beside it. Emma reached out and pressed the button. A dull thrum echoed on the other side of the wall and the glass door slid back to reveal a young blond woman with brightly painted nails.

'Yes?' she asked rather curtly.

'I've come to see Mr Curtis, I have an appointment,' Emma replied.

'Name?' Clearly a woman of few words.

'Emma Bertram,' Emma responded, keeping her reply similarly short and turned immediately to take a seat on one of the faded chairs before the blond could command her to 'sit' like she might a dog. She glanced at the magazines on the coffee table. They were well worn and torn; the most recent appeared to be a six-month old copy of *Homes and Gardens*. As she flicked through its pages the door in the wall adjacent to the enquiry window opened and a young man dressed in a grey suit emerged. About 22 years old he had a fresh complexion and his hair was a startling wavy dark brown, a little untidy for the sombre suit he was wearing. He carried a bundle of papers in manila folders tied together with green ribbon. He smiled and spoke.

'You must be Miss Bertram, I'm sure Mr Curtis won't be long.' He hesitated as if to say more but then just broadened his smile and made for the stairs.

The door opened again to reveal the blond girl.

'He'll see you now - this way.'

Emma followed her through the inner office that she noted was cluttered with filing cabinets and steel racks. Every inch of space appeared to be filled with files and papers and the room had a mustiness mixed with a smell of stale tobacco. She doubted they ever employed a cleaner and again found herself puzzling over her mother's choice of lawyer.

'Come in Miss Bertram, do come in and take a seat, I'm Charles Curtis.'

The man who ushered her to the broad leather upright armchair in front of his desk was about fifty-five, bald across the crown but with a good shock of grey hair around the sides and back of his head. His expensive but ill-fitting dark grey suit did little to enhance his portly frame that strained at the buttons of his waistcoat. He flopped back into his chair behind the desk and let out a deep sigh as if the effort of just getting up from the desk was the equivalent for any one else of running a hundred yards. The desk was littered with papers and legal folders tied in bundles by various coloured ribbons. A cigarette burned on an over full ashtray on one side of the desk and sent a plume of blue smoke winding up to join the already smog filled room.

Emma could already feel her throat tightening and hoped the meeting would not take long.

The secretary of few words exited from the room and as soon as the door was closed, Charles Curtis gathered some papers in his nicotine stained hands and looked up from his desk. His eyes were small for the size of his face and very close to his nose. He peered at Emma over wire framed half glasses and smiled slightly.

'It came as a great shock to us all Miss Bertram, to learn of your mother's sad demise and in such awful circumstances.' He paused.

'I understand the police are somewhat mystified by the event, no money taken?' he said more as a statement than a question.

'No,' replied Emma, seeing in her mind yet again the scene of devastation in the front dining room of their house. 'Mother always kept her cash in the second drawer of the bureau, the burglars had clearly gone through the desk but as far as I can tell nothing was taken.'

'And she apparently let them in, no forced entry.' Again a statement rather than a question.

'Yes, but....'

'And the police have no clue to their identity?'

'No'.

'Hmm...' He hesitated as if he was going to say more on the subject but then changed his mind. He shuffled through the papers in his hand as if he was looking for the right sheet. He looked up.

'Your mother has left you very well provided for, apart from a small sum of £5,000 for Mrs Marcheson, your housekeeper, she has left the balance of her estate to you which of course includes the house *Tall Trees*. There is no mortgage on the property and there are several sound investments bringing in more than you are ever likely to need unless you develop some exceptionally expensive tastes.' He paused to smile at his words, but then thought better of it.

'I will arrange for a sum of say £2,000 to be transferred into your bank account on the first of each month, if you ever need any more just let me know.'

He put the papers in a folder and began to rise from his seat, the meeting as far as he was concerned was over, but Emma remained seated.

'Mr Curtis, where did my mother's money come from?' she asked.

He sank back into the chair, 'As I said she, now you, have substantial investments, your income will come from that.'

'That's not what I meant.' Emma replied. 'I've never really thought about it before, but mother has never worked as long as I can remember, so where did all this money come from?'

He looked a little harried, 'I really can't say, she's had it a long time and it's just grown into a considerable sum over the years.' He hesitated and fiddled with the papers in the folder as if consulting some figures, 'Yes, ah, that's it, careful investment over the years.'

'But where did the original monies come from and how much was it?' Emma persisted, 'There must still have been a substantial sum to start with, where did that come from and when. Was there a relative that I don't know about? She told me once that she was fostered but didn't want to talk about it, she said she never knew who her real parents were so she could never have had anything from them...'

'Questions, questions, so many questions,' Curtis replied in a rather condescending manner.

He paused and smiled. 'I suggest you leave all the worries of that sort of thing to our investment company and us. Not the sort of thing for a pretty young head like yours to worry about, eh?'

'You'll be well provided for, that's all you need to know!' With that he was out from behind his desk at a startling speed that surprised Emma. He gently touched the back of her chair and then opened the door to the general office.

'My condolences again, Miss Bertram, do give me a call if I can help in any way at all.'

He held the door and gave a slight bow as Emma swept past ignoring his proffered handshake. She was seething inside. Nothing riled her more than a man that treated her like a stupid child. She took the stairs two at a time and snatched at the front door. As she did so the young man she had seen in the office earlier was just putting his weight against the door to come in. He flew passed her and crashed onto the bottom step, papers flying everywhere.

Her last memory as she left was of seeing him sprawled on the bottom stairs and rubbing his elbow, a frightened startled look upon his face but she was too angry to stop and apologise.

+++++++++

Across the street another young man standing in the telephone box had watched Emma storm up the road, her face clearly flushed with anger. He noted which doorway she had just come from and made an entry in a little pocket book before leaving to walk back to his hire car which was parked around the next corner. He was glad to be back in the comparative warmth of the car. It had become quite cold standing there in the telephone box and he wished he had been wearing his coat. But he knew that after the unfortunate incident outside the tearooms earlier that morning his blue anorak would have to go and he would need to find something less conspicuous.

+++++++++

As Emma had swept down the stairs, Charles Curtis shouted that he was not to be disturbed and slammed his office door shut. He realised that his hands were shaking and he grabbed the ever available packet of strong French cigarettes from his desk and hurriedly lit one. He slumped into his chair and drew deeply on the cigarette. He knew that he had handled it badly. Emma Bertram was not to be the push over he was led to believe she would be. She would keep asking questions until she received satisfactory answers. He could no doubt find some for her, but would she accept them, would she believe them? She was bright and intelligent. It was not going to be easy.

He leaned forward and rested his left elbow on the desk and in turn rested his jaw in his hand. He pondered the situation for a while and then decided what he must do. He picked up the telephone and dialled an international number. It was a number he knew off by heart, a number that you would not find written down anywhere, not in his office or in his home - a number that to all intents and purposes did not exist.

Chapter 5

Jane Dennington entered *Tall Trees* by the back door. She knew it was usually unlocked if Valerie Marcheson was in and it saved her from having to come through the house to answer the front door.

'Hello love,' greeted Valerie from the kitchen, 'You look nice this morning, in fact you look stunning, you'd better watch out for the boys in the village, they'll all be after you!' she smiled, 'I'm just making coffee, would you like one?'

Jane was dressed in fawn slacks with a simple white tee shirt under a fawn coloured v-neck sweater. Her long blond hair reached down to her shoulder blades and with her slim but shapely figure she did indeed look stunning. 'Yes please Valerie,' she said, 'where's Emma?'

'She must be up in her bedroom; I've not seen her for a while. Here you are; you can take the tray up.'

Jane climbed to the top of the stairs, crossed the landing and tapped gently on Emma's door as she entered. 'Coffee up!' she said cheerfully but as she pushed open the door she saw that the room was empty. She stood listening for a moment and looked back into the corridor. The door to the bathroom was slightly ajar but there was no sound from there.

She decided Emma must be down in the lounge or the day room and returned to the top of the stairs with the intention of going back down when she heard a noise from somewhere above. She paused, listened and heard it again. Someone was moving things around on the floor above. Valerie had once told her that the top floor had been shut up for years. Even she had a bedroom on the same floor as Emma and her mother.

Jane quietly put the coffee tray down on the small table at the top of the stairs and made her way to the end of the landing. Here the passageway narrowed and turned at right angles to reveal a smaller stairway that led up to what must have been the servants' quarters when the house was originally built. She had never been to this end of the corridor before and noticed that the plush decor of the landing finished at the turn of the stairs. Pausing again she listened. There it was again, a shuffling noise of something being dragged across the floor above. She could feel the quickening beat of her heart, every muscle in her body felt tense. She carefully trod the well-worn and faded carpet until she could peer over the top step. The door at the end of the short corridor was open with the key still inserted in the lock. It occurred to her that she could shut the door on the intruder and lock in whoever it was, and then call for help. A shaft of sunlight filled with hundreds of particles of dust drew her attention to the window from which it came. The window was in the far wall of the small landing and was slightly open. From where she stood she could see that it exited onto a flat part of the roof in the middle of the building but could not see if the lock on the window had been forced. She also had no idea if that part of the roof could be accessed from the ground.

The noise was still coming from beyond the open door but had changed now to the sound of a shuffling of paper. Jane crept up the final treads, moved quietly forward and slowly peered round the open door not realising that the sun would cast her shadow into the open room. The occupant of the room was startled by the reflected movement and turned. 'Oh, you gave me a fright!' said Emma. 'What are you doing creeping up on me,' she jokingly remonstrated.

'Oh, it's you, thank God, What are you doing up here? I thought this floor was all shut off, I thought you were an intruder!' Jane let out a sigh of relief.

'I found the key in Mother's bedside drawer; I've not been up here for years. There's lots of papers in boxes, they all seem to do with the house but I was hoping....,' Emma paused, 'Well I don't know, hoping I might find something that would tell me more about her. That Mr Curtis, the solicitor, was holding back from me I know, but why? Why is Mother's past so shrouded in mystery? And who was my father? Why and when did he die? Why do I know so little?' said Emma sighing as she sank into a dusty old armchair clutching a sheaf of papers.

Jane could see the tears welling up in Emma's eyes and recognised the signs. She had got to know her a lot over these last few weeks and found that Emma could quite unexpectedly change her mood dramatically. At first she put it down to the trauma of the death of her mother but Valerie had shared with her privately that it was often like this.

'Why don't we go downstairs, there's a cup of coffee on the landing that will be getting cold if we don't drink it soon,' Jane encouraged.

But Emma shook herself out of the mood and seemed to brighten. 'No thanks, could you bring it up here? Now I've started on this lot I want to keep going until I find something.' She paused, taking in Jane's clothes for the first time, 'And if you are going to join me you'd better borrow an overall from Valerie, it's very dusty up here.'

The house had been built in the mid-1860's and the entire top floor had been storerooms and servants quarters originally. Now they were no longer used, the distemper faded and peeling, the floor gathering the dust of many years.

The room they were in was one of the larger ones and still contained some of the old furniture including the washstand with its large white bowl and jug. A faded picture of some country scene hung on the wall above it. An old bed was pushed up on its side against one wall and everything was shrouded in a thick layer of dust and spiders web. There were several large cardboard boxes piled in the centre of the room and it was these that Emma was working her way through. For the next hour they continued in near silence as they sifted through piles of papers and magazines, just occasionally commenting on a find. Doreen Bertram seemed to have kept every estimate, receipt and invoice relating to the house for many years. Gas and electric, rates and repair bills, even details of the gardener's wages going back for nearly twenty years. There were piles of old gardening and country life magazines together with several copies of the local paper.

'You know, for a woman who kept the past such a secret it seems odd that she retained so much detail of her life since she moved to *Tall Trees*,' commented Jane.

Emma sat back and blew a strand of hair from her face that had dislodged from the grip she had placed it in earlier. 'Are we ever going to find anything?' she said.

Jane looked up, 'Well it's all pretty consistent. Lots about everything except the people and the past that we need to know.' She paused and sipped the last of the now cold coffee. 'What's in there?' she said, pointing the mug at an old oak dresser in the corner of the room. It had several drawers but most were obscured by a roll of carpet that had been placed across a couple of upright chairs in front of it.

Jane put down her cup and together they heaved on the carpet and dragged it and the chairs forward far enough to be able to get the drawers partially open. Most of them appeared empty. In fact all of them at first looked empty until Jane rolled up her sleeve and reached in. At the back of the top right hand drawer she dislodged a small bundle held in a perished elastic band that broke as she pulled the package out. She handed it to Emma who leafed slowly through the contents. There were letters, a couple of postcards, a sepia studio photograph of a young lady in twenties style costume with the name *'Millie'* on the back, and a black and white photograph of three young men in their early twenties grinning at the camera. As soon as Jane saw it she snatched it out of Emma's hand.

'Let me see,' her eyes widened as she stared at the photograph. She guessed by the cut of their clothes and their hairstyles that it was probably taken in the nineteen sixties. The three men were standing by the corner of a wall near a road junction and she could see there was a row of shops out of focus on the other side of the street. Emma took it back and turned it over. In what she was sure was her mother's hand, was written, *'John, Barry and Robert 1967'*. She stared at the grinning man in the centre. Was that Barry, her father now dead? The father she had never set eyes on and had never known?

+++++++++

Constable Higton entered the Inspector's office to find Smurdon leaning back in his seat behind the desk. His legs and size eleven boots crossed and up on the corner of the table. His face was very thoughtful.

'Penny for them?' said Higton.

'Oh, I've never known so many dead ends on a case. There's no word on the street, no one seems to know anything, not a whisper,' Smurdon said. 'The London Police can't offer any connections and the Super wants us to put it down to a burglary gone wrong and wrap it up! No doubt he's got his eye on the budgets.'

'What about the hairdresser, Jane Dennington?' asked Higton.

'She denies ever speaking to a man in a pale blue car in the high street, says the Major must be mistaken, got quite indignant when I pushed the point. I'm not convinced she's telling the truth though.' He paused. 'What do we really know about Doreen Bertram? Next to nothing. She lived a quiet life and kept herself to herself is all anyone will tell us! There's got to be more.'

And then he made his decision. 'I don't care what the Super says about budgets; there's more to this than a burglary gone wrong. Find out all you can about Doreen Bertram, where did she come from before moving into Chartwood, what was her maiden name, who did she marry and when did he die, get a copy of her birth and marriage certificate. I want a file that thick,' he indicated a two inch span with his hand, 'I want to know more about Doreen Bertram than she knew herself!'

+++++++++

Jane and Emma knelt on the floor piecing together the snippets of information they had gathered from the bundle of letters and papers they had found in the attic room. Millie it appeared was an older sister of Doreen Bertram. From the few letters they had it was clear that their relationship was somewhat distant. Most of the correspondence wished a polite birthday greeting or enquired after Doreen's health. Emma had been mentioned twice in the letters and she remembered visiting an 'Aunt Millie' near Bristol a few times when she was a child. At the time she just thought she was a friend of her mother's, nothing had been made of the fact that they were related and Emma was stunned by the discovery. The last letter was dated 1995 and the handwriting was noticeably shaky. Of reference to her father Barry Bertram there was none other than the assumed photo.

There was a torn receipt from a jewellers made out to a B Masters and two other photographs. One a faded and clearly old wedding picture of a couple standing on the steps of a church somewhere, and one of the same couple a little older, with two young girls in the back garden of a two up, two down terrace house. On the back of the latter was written '*M & me 1948*'.

Was she also seeing a picture of her grandparents for the first time? It seemed the only explanation, but as she so often found, what she had discovered today only served to raise more questions. Who were her grandparents and did they become rich after this photograph had been taken and is that where her mother's money came from? The setting was certainly a modest house in 1948. And why was this all that her mother had kept? And yet none of this made any sense if as mother had said she was brought up in a foster home and didn't know her parents? There were no other photographs of her mother in her teens or twenties and no wedding photographs. She did not even know if the smiling face that seemed somehow to reach out to her was her father. And what of Millie? Why did she not keep in touch more with her only sister? And was Aunt Millie still alive?

Suddenly Emma felt overwhelmed. Tears welled up in her eyes again and began to run down in streaks across her dusty cheeks, the sun still streaming through the small window highlighted the anguish in her face. Jane watched, wanting to say something but dared not speak. The emotion of the moment hung heavy in the air like the mustiness and cobwebs surrounding them. All was silent for a long moment; then Emma let out a deep sigh. She raised and pushed back her bent shoulders and as if some new force had entered her body. Emma was determined that the answer to these and many other questions that were flooding her mind would be found. Once and for all she was going to get to the bottom of the mystery. She stood up, looked resolutely at Jane and said. 'I am going to find the answer, I *must* know why!'

The decision had been made and she felt better than she had for months. She had set a new purpose in life now and soon she was determined that she would know the answer to the mystery.

+++++++++

'Are you sure?' said Robbie Wilson.

'Yer, it's got to be' said Peters, 'Greg Johnson said he went out with her for a while, then after the war she married a bloke from the merchant navy called Ted Lutterington and they moved out of town down to the south coast somewhere near Eastbourne. They were there for several years then he heard they had suddenly upped sticks and moved west to a place near Bristol. The name and age fits and there's only one Lutterington in the electoral roll down there, I checked. It's a pretty uncommon name ain't it?'

'We can't be certain,' said Wilson, 'look, go down there on your own and take a look around. Ask some very discreet questions and then report back to me. Don't do anything and don't take Darren with you, don't even tell him where you are going, okay.'

When Peters had left the room, Robbie Wilson sat back and considered the situation. Could the sister and her husband, if he was still alive, throw any light on his quest he wondered? It was interesting, indeed perhaps significant that they had lived on the south coast of England for a time. Also that the husband was a navy man, and a navy man could easily have had access to a boat.

+++++++++

It was early evening in Charles Curtis office. His secretary and the other staff had gone home for the day and he was alone. He switched on his computer and activated the e-mail. There were a number of messages relating to his legal business but they would wait until the morning. He switched to his private file and entered the password that only he knew. There was one message waiting for him, one that he had expected. He read the contents carefully. He didn't like the nature of the questions being asked, he would have preferred to ignore them but knew that he dare not. He read the message again carefully and then deleted it. Switching off the computer he lifted the telephone handset and dialled a London number. He needed information and he needed it quickly.

Chapter 6

Jane Dennington looked out of the window as the car sped along the M4 motorway heading west out of London. They had left the dirty and unkempt look of the sprawling city behind, had passed through suburbia with its tree lined avenues and car cluttered roads and were now passing the last of the 'new' estates. Here houses were packed with alarming density into tiny areas on the edge of the urban spread. The open countryside lay ahead and there was a freshness in the vista after the damp and dreary weeks of winter. Trees were now showing new leaf, fields were being sown and tended and she could see birds collecting material for their nests. They passed a small coppice that opened out onto a field full of sheep and new lambs dancing in the warmth of the spring sunshine. She closed her eyes and took a deep breath. The smell of the freshness of the countryside had found its way through the car ventilator system and she savoured the sense. She was feeling very pleased with herself that she had persuaded Emma to let her help with solving the mystery of her family background. She hadn't told anyone but she found the hairdressing business boring. Going to the homes of the over rich and the over ripe as she had referred to them when speaking on the telephone to a friend even nauseated her and she found it hard at times to be civil and not treat them with disdain. They lived in a world that was just a fantasy to her, one that was so far removed from her tough upbringing in the inner city and one that she was never likely to attain nor indeed wished to. She was glad to be doing something else.

She had roped Ray in as well, and she turned to watch him now as he drove them west towards Bristol in his released but still dented car. She studied his features. A thin face with a slightly pointed nose, his chin stuck out a little too much and had a small dimple in the centre. His build was altogether wiry which accentuated his height. She had been out with more handsome looking men for sure, but Ray had a caring depth, very often just in the little things, that she had not seen in a man before which she found very alluring, yet she knew their relationship could not last.

In the back of the car Emma had dozed. Although it was now six weeks since her mother's death she was still finding it hard to sleep at night. She too had watched the changing vista from city to countryside and realised how little of England she had seen. Her mother had not been keen to go on holiday very much and they had only been abroad twice, once to the south of France and another time to Italy. Mother didn't like flying and she refused ever to go on a boat. Even on those holidays they had not joined in the various tours on offer preferring to stay in the hotel grounds. At the time she had not questioned it but now began to feel that mother's lifestyle, and consequently hers, was almost reclusive. She had listened for a while to Ray and Jane talking. Of the latest films and music, of pop singers and groups, of nightclubs and dance crazes, and of fashions and styles, the majority of which was to her as from another world and only went to reinforce the feeling of isolation that her life with mother at *Tall Trees* had inflicted on her up till now.

In Doreen Bertram's address book they had found an address for 'Millie' at a place just south of Bristol called Failand and Emma recognised the name, but there was no telephone number and so she had decided with encouragement from Jane to take a trip down to the area to see if Millie still lived there.

They stopped for morning coffee at Membury Services and Jane insisted on going over the detail once more. How they would approach Millie, what they would say to her and so on. She checked again that Emma had got the photographs with her and once more asked if Emma had found anything else in the house relating to the mystery. Emma was grateful for Jane's help but felt somehow uneasy that Jane seemed to be taking over what she knew must be for her to find out.

Jane finished her coffee and made an excuse to go to the Ladies. Emma had not spoken much to Ray and found herself feeling a little uneasy sitting there with him. Ray sensed this and proffered small talk, chatting about the traffic on the road, the views of the countryside and the lambs in the fields and so on. Emma began to feel more at ease; she had been looking down at her cup but now looked up at him. He smiled at her, a warm kind smile.

'Everything will be okay,' he said, 'you'll find the answers, I know you will.'

'Thank you,' she said and smiled back, 'I am very grateful to you both,' she paused, 'Jane must be held up in a queue or she should have been back by now.' she said looking toward the entrance. As she did so she saw Jane replacing the receiver on a payphone in the lobby and head back towards the restaurant.

'Sorry to be so long, what a crowd, they never make these places big enough do they? Well I'm ready, let's go shall we?'

They changed roads and joined the motorway that was the main arterial route to the south west of England and the holiday resorts of Devon and Cornwall. This initially ran south and skirted the western edge of the city of Bristol and Emma could just remember a little about her trips with mother to the city. They would take the express train from Paddington into Bristol Temple Meads Station and then hire a taxi out to Millie's place. She seemed to recall that the taxi journey was quite long and couldn't understand why the train did not go further. Mother had explained that Aunt Millie lived out in the country where the trains did not go. She wondered if she would recognise it. Ray had bought a map and it showed the village of Failand to be very close to the motorway but that of course was not there when she had visited as a child.

Ray turned off the motorway at junction twenty and followed the secondary road through the straggling village of Tickenham, then changing to a lower gear he steered the car up the long steep hill towards Failand.

'Not long now,' he said.

Emma looked out of the window as Ray pulled up at a garage to ask directions. Nothing looked familiar at all, but from the animated conversation on the forecourt across the road she could tell that Ray was getting his instructions. He climbed back in.

'Little more than a mile and a half now,' he said and turned to give Emma a reassuring smile. Emma felt a sudden tightening in her stomach. The realisation that they were nearly there made her tense. What would Millie's reaction be? How would she take to three people turning up unannounced? Millie was older than Doreen, but by how much? They had guessed it could be as much as ten years, which would put her into her late sixties even seventies. She sensed that Jane was tense too; her head kept turning from one side of the car to the other as if she was looking for something, but Emma could not see her eyes.

Ray turned up a narrow lane that wound past a field of cows, then into a dip with some old farm buildings bordering the road. He had to stop to let a tractor by and Emma, looking at the buildings, caught her breath and said,

'*Hillside Farm*', exactly at the same time as Jane, who being in the front seat, could see and read the notice on the gate. Just up the hill were two stone cottages with slate roofs next to each other. They had presumably been built at the same time and were identical in construction and exterior layout. The gardens were also much the same size but there the similarity ended. For one cottage was freshly painted and had neat curtains at the windows. The garden was well stocked and neatly kept. Large camellia bushes either side of the front door had already burst into bloom, below the front hedge on the bank that edged the lane a splendid display of daffodils greeted the traveller and a neatly kept vegetable patch could be seen to the side of the cottage through the wooden gate. The other cottage was the opposite, paint peeled from the window frames; drab net curtains covered the bottom half of most of the windows that looked as if they had not been cleaned in months. The garden was overgrown, the path to the front door just about passable through the mass of decaying vegetation. The barely visible name on the rotting wooden gate indicated that they had arrived.

Ray pulled the car into a lay-by opposite the gate and Emma got out. It was all coming back to her now. She remembered the cottage with the strange little porch, the tree in the garden she had swung from, the gate with its wooden arch. Yet all was so different. The noise of the nearby motorway, the air of neglect. Clearly little had been done for years to stem the decay of this place. The garden and greenhouse could not have been touched in years. Without thinking she had closed her eyes and could picture herself standing there by the pond as a little girl watching the frogs bathing at the waters edge. It was the first time she had seen a real frog and she had been fascinated.

She was brought sharply out of her reverie by the sound of a thud and a curse from Jane who had dropped her bag as she got out of the car. The contents had spilled out on the grass verge and her mobile phone had spun off under the car. Ray retrieved it and wiped it on a cloth from the car for her.

All three approached the cottage although it was agreed that Ray would wait by the gate. Jane and Emma pushed open the outer door of the porch and entered. The constant drum of the nearby motorway was quieter here and as Emma rapped the iron knocker it sounded very loud in the confined space. They waited but all was silent inside. Emma found herself whispering; 'Perhaps she's sleeping,' Jane shrugged and hammered the door again more louder and longer this time that made Emma wince, but the result was the same. Nothing.

As they exited the porch Ray joined them and suggested they take a look around the back. They tried the back door but it was locked, they peered in the side window but the dinginess and dirt precluded them from seeing much although strangely enough what they were able to see argued with the exterior of the cottage. For inside the furniture appeared neat and orderly. The table immediately inside the window was covered in a lace cloth and had several fine ornaments neatly arranged on it. They could also just discern a tidy and orderly bookcase on the wall to the left.

They were debating what to do next when a voice called out:

'Can I help you?'

A plump middle aged woman with trowel in hand was standing in the garden of the neighbouring cottage just where there was a break in the hedge.

'We are looking for Mrs Millie Lutterington,' said Jane, 'But we can't seem to get a reply.'

The neighbour eyed them suspiciously and looked them up and down for a long moment. 'Who wants her?' She asked with some concern.

'I'm Emma Bertram, her niece,' Emma replied stepping forward with a smile, 'I used to come here as a child with my mother sometimes, and my friends and I were just passing this way so we thought we would call in.'

The woman stared at Emma and moved closer to the fence.

'Oh, my poor love, yes I recognise your picture from the newspaper now... your poor mother. I had no idea she was related to Millie until that detective came here from London yesterday morning.'

'Can you tell us where Millie is now?' asked Jane.

'Like I told the policeman, she was taken queer about two weeks ago and went into a nursing home at Clevedon until she got better. Poor love, she's had these turns before and always come back, but this time I'm not so sure, she didn't look so good when I saw her on Monday. I try to get in to see her twice a week when my husband is not using the car. I thought I was the only friend she had, I had no idea she had a sister, she never mentioned her.'

'No,' said Emma feeling rather embarrassed, 'I don't think my mother and Millie got on very well, I don't know why. I've only just found her address amongst my mother's things.'

'Well it's good that you'll be visiting her,' replied the neighbour, 'my husband and I are going away in the morning for a few days to visit our son up north and we won't be back till Wednesday. I did tell her when I saw her last.'

'Can you tell us the name of the nursing home please?' interrupted Jane.

+++++++++

'So what have you got?' asked Smurdon.

Higton had entered the room a sheaf of papers in his hand.

'Well so far not as much as you would like I'm sure,' said the constable. 'This woman just doesn't seem to have existed before 1973. No details before she moved to Chartwood. No previous address, no relatives we can find, no marriage certificate, nothing!' The daughter's birth was registered in Sevenoaks on the 4th June 1973. Mother Doreen Bertram, Father Barry Bertram listed as an entertainments manager. Of him we can find no trace either. I'm getting the names and details of all missing persons around that time.

According to the neighbours when she moved here there was just the baby girl Emma a few weeks old, no husband.' He paused, 'We've spoken at length to the housekeeper and she says Mrs Bertram never spoke of her husband other than to say he was dead. When she had broached the subject once she was told in no uncertain terms that that chapter of her life was over and never to mention it again.'

'What about a previous housekeeper?' Smurdon asked.

'There wasn't one; Valerie Marcheson was employed when Mrs Bertram got back trouble about eleven years ago. There was a Nanny when Miss Bertram was a baby but she died a couple of years ago in that nursing home at the end of Chartwood Lane.'

'So,' said Smurdon, 'We have a woman in her early thirties who suddenly appears with a young baby girl, purchases an expensive house in a select area, never as far as we know goes out to work and is clearly financially well off.'

He paused, 'What about an accountant?'

'It was all handled through her solicitor, Curtis Forsythe in Westerham, not the sort of solicitor you would expect to be handling that kind of client. They had a practice in Bermondsey, south east London originally. I've had a word with the London police and they tell me they were linked with some of the more dubious characters of that area but nothing was proved. We've interviewed Charles Curtis who waffled client confidentiality and all that. When we pressed him he simply said that the lady arrived with substantial investments but he is unable to say where the monies originated from.'

'Do you believe him?' asked Smurdon.

'No,' replied Higton, 'I've no doubt he knows more.'

'All right, keep delving, and keep me posted if anything else comes up.'

+++++++++

Rest Haven was an imposing Victorian building at the end of a winding tree lined drive on rising ground at the northern edge of the town of

Clevedon. As they drove through the gates they could see that the grounds were neatly kept. The smell of freshly mown grass invaded their nostrils and they could see the gardener making what looked like the first cut of the season as his ride on mower painted contrasting stripes across the wide lawn. The head of the drive opened out into wide gravel area in front of the house where a number of cars and a van were parked.

Emma, Jane and Ray got out and looked back the way they had come. From this elevated position they could see through the tops of the trees across the town to the Bristol Channel estuary beyond. A bulk car transporter was heading downstream against the backdrop of a misty South Wales coastline. Some features were just discernible such as the industrial dockside area of Swansea where wisps of smoke hung in the air above like a plume of feathers in a strange hat.

The gravelled car park was bordered with a stone balustrade on two sides and beyond that the ground dropped away sharply to two large borders full of winter pansies which gave a bright splash of colour to the scene.

Just then a door banged behind them. A young man in overalls walked from the front door carrying a box of tools and some copper piping and started loading them into the white van parked nearby. The door opened again and an older man, also in overalls, appeared with a middle-aged woman. They exchanged a few brief words before the men got into the van and drove off down the drive. The woman stood there, her eyes closed, and appeared to be taking in deep breaths as if she was glad to be out in the fresh air.

Jane moved forward, her feet crunching on the gravel, which caused the woman to start. Up to now she had been unaware of their presence and a frown swept across her face.

'Can I help you?' she enquired.

All three had moved nearer now and Emma could see that she was in her early fifties, a stern face that could at one time have been beautiful but now showed the lines of stress and ageing. Her shoulders hung low and forward making her back rounded while her chest hung limp over a plump figure. She was dressed quite smartly in a grey suit over a white blouse, the lapel of the suit held a badge announcing, *Grace Dowling, Matron, DI Group*.

'We have come to visit Mrs Lutterington,' said Emma.

The Matron eyed them suspiciously, 'Oh you have, have you? And who are you, the Press I suppose. Well you can't see her. She's not well enough to see anyone, especially not you.'

Emma looked puzzled, 'The Press? No we are not from the newspapers; whatever gave you that idea? I am Emma Bertram, her niece, my mother and Mrs Lutterington, Millie were sisters.'

Emma paused, and then added, 'they were not very close, but I remember visiting her at Failand when I was a child, -- my mother died recently.' her voice tailing off.

Grace Dowling didn't say anything but looked from one to the other of them as if uncertain what to do. Finally she said, 'You two had better come into my office,' and looking directly at Ray said, 'You can wait in your car if you like, there's not enough room for three.'

With that she turned towards the door and Emma and Jane followed the Matron into the house. The door from the porch opened into a large square hall with a broad staircase sweeping up to a landing immediately in front of them. Above the front door the light of the midday sun entering through a deep stained glass window cast a scatter of multi-coloured droplets across the rich burgundy carpet. To the right a lift had been installed, but was neatly encased in mahogany panelling which all but disguised its presence. On the left a large polished desk was situated above which a sign saying *Reception* was hung.

Grace Dowling led them behind the right hand side of the desk into a small room that was clearly the office. The room was spartan but business like. She sat down behind the larger of the two desks in the room and motioned to Emma and Jane to draw up the chairs that were in the far corner by the filing cabinet.

'Now, first of all I think I had better have some form of identification from you.' she said quite sternly.

Emma handed the photographs and the letters she had found in the attic rooms across the desk. 'I'm sorry it's not much, but it's all I have,' said Emma. 'I only realised my mother and Millie were related when I was clearing her things out after she died.'

Emma paused, 'I don't know why she kept this from me, but... well my mother was secretive about a lot of things,' said Emma, her voice trailing away.

Grace Dowling studied the photograph for a long time and inspected the inscription on the back.

'Millie Lutterington is a frail old lady,' she began, 'She came here about two weeks ago after a small stroke. Her speech is somewhat impaired and she is also in the early stages of Alzheimer's. She had been improving until that detective came yesterday about this time.' she paused, still uncertain that they were who they said they were, 'why do you want to see her?'

'Look,' said Jane rather impatiently, 'Emma here just wants to find out more about her mother. For some reason she kept a lot of her past locked up and hidden from her. Now that she has discovered she had a sister she wants to try and understand why.'

Grace Dowling was silent for a while; her eyes fixed on the two brown photographs, which she held one in each hand. 'Was you mothers name, Doreen?' she asked Emma.

'Yes, that's right, what can you tell us,' said Emma sensing there was more, 'And why did you think we were from the Press?'

The Matron hesitated and then said, 'Mrs Lutterington was doing very well up to yesterday considering her age and frailty. As I said she had had a mild stroke and was a little confused from time to time, but we could understand her and she was no trouble. In fact she was an ideal patient in many ways. We were expecting that she might want to go home again, we've had her here before and she can be very independent. Then yesterday this policeman came. He said he had an urgent confidential matter to discuss with her and that I should be warned that the Press might be round and it would be better if I didn't let them speak to her. It all seemed very strange, but you don't question a policeman do you? I took him up to her room and left them alone. I don't know what time he left, no one saw him go, but one of my nurses found Millie in a very distressed state about half past four when she took her a cup of tea.'

She paused, 'I'm sorry but I cannot allow any visitor today, that's completely out of the question, we had to sedate her for fear that she would have another stroke.'

+++++++++

Ray's car was parked on the sea front at Clevedon not far from the newly restored Victorian pier. They had purchased fish and chips and were munching their way half-heartedly through them as they went over the events of the day. Swirls of dark cloud were rolling in from the west bringing the first drops of rain of the storm that would inevitably follow. The South Wales coastline had long disappeared from view and as the quickening wind began to snatch at the car Emma reflected that the miserable weather mirrored her own feelings of despair. They had come all this way and achieved nothing, and yet as dusk began to settle around them she also felt a sense of unease. Something had happened today that made her feel unsettled, something wasn't right, yet she couldn't put her finger on it.

'How did that Inspector Smurdon find out about Millie?' said Jane more as a statement than a question. 'You certainly didn't tell him did you?' she turned towards Emma questioningly.

'No, I didn't know myself until a couple of days ago. I wonder how he found out and why he didn't tell me.' replied Emma.

'And why frighten the old lady, and the Matron for that matter – telling them the press would be round.' offered Ray. 'What was the point of that?'

The two women were quiet for a while, each lost in their own thoughts while Ray fidgeted and glanced at his watch a couple of times.

Emma broke the silence. 'I've decided to stay here the night and go back to *Rest Haven* in the morning and see if Millie is any better, I can't come all this way without knowing. There's a hotel further along the front, I saw it earlier, I can stay there.'

Jane turned, taken aback by her statement and studied Emma who now began to realise the enormity of the decision she had made. Many young women stayed in hotels on their own no doubt these days but she had never done anything like this before, but she had made the decision and was determined to stick by it.

Jane protested, 'But you can't stay, I mean, you've got nothing with you.'

'I have actually,' said Emma, 'I don't know why but I put a few things in this bag this morning, and I shall be fine thank you. I can get a taxi in the morning and once I have seen Aunt Millie I can come back on the train.'

'No, I must stay with you,' persisted Jane, 'You must not be on your own, you need someone with you. I can telephone my lodger and ask her to cancel my appointments for tomorrow, they'll understand....'

'Jane, I've made up my mind.' said Emma interrupting, 'You've been more than generous with your time over the last few weeks and I can't possible take anymore of it.'

Turning to Ray she said, 'Now Ray take this young lady of yours home now before it gets any later, you'll not be in Chartwood much before midnight as it is. You can drop me at the hotel on the way.'

Jane continued her persistence about staying right up to the moment that Ray pulled up outside the hotel and became quite agitated when Emma got out of the car but Ray was eager to get going. He had a long drive ahead of him and was beginning to feel tired from the day already. As soon as Emma was on the kerb he put his foot down and was away round the corner.

'Why didn't you back me up,' Jane screamed at him, 'I needed to be there with Emma,' she fumed.

Although Ray had turned the heater on as they sped back up the motorway the atmosphere in the car was far from warm and little was said between them for the entire journey.

Chapter 7

Emma had enjoyed the new experience. The hotel was only three-star and probably not very special but it was a novelty to her and although she had stayed with mother in hotels abroad before now, this somehow seemed very different being on her own. She was quite enjoying the attention she now received from the young waiter who was serving her breakfast in the dining room. She could see through the large windows overlooking the estuary that the storm had passed during the night and the sun was beginning to break through the thin mist. Several fishermen were already at the end of the pier; their lines reaching down into the brown swirling waters. Quite a large boat, she did not know what type it was, was making its way downstream into the Bristol Channel. She could see sparrows and a blackbird gathering material for their nests from the short garden that led down steeply to the waters edge. It promised to be another warm spring day.

Earlier she had decided against using a taxi and opted to hire a car instead. She did not know when or if Aunt Millie would be able to see her and rather than wait around at the home she had reasoned with herself that she could be more flexible with a car. Perhaps look around the area or go back to the home for a second visit later if necessary.

The hotel had arranged for a car to be delivered at 10am. She was pleased with herself that she felt so well. The uncertain feelings of the night before and of the decision she had made to stay had not lasted long. As she sat there sipping her coffee she reflected in fact that she had not had a depressive turn for quite some time. Her resolve to get to the bottom of the secrets of Doreen Bertram had given her a new impetus in life and she was glad of it.

The hire car was ready and waiting and it didn't take her long to get used to it as she negotiated the short journey to the nursing home. She parked in the drive and entered the familiar entrance hall. She could hear voices in the building and footsteps on the floor above but no one was visible. She waited by the reception desk and looked around at the imposing wood panelling and large portraits of stern looking men that hung at intervals in their heavy gilt frames. She found herself wondering who had built the house and who these nameless people were that looked down from the past in silent gaze on each passing day.

An audible 'ding' from across the hall indicated that the lift had descended. The door opened and a nurse in smart white uniform approached.

She smiled and said, 'Can I help you?'

'I've come to visit Mrs Lutterington if she's well enough, I'm her niece.' Emma replied.

The smile disappeared from the nurse's face. 'You'd better wait in the office,' she said, 'I'll find the matron for you.'

She ushered Emma into the room and quickly turned towards a door leading to a corridor. As she pushed through it Emma heard her calling, 'Mrs Dowling, Mrs Dowling.'

Emma sat in silence and looked around. All the trappings of a small office were about her. Files lay scattered; there was a blotter and notepad next to a telephone on each of the two desks and a fax machine on a table by a large grey filing cabinet. Her eye was drawn to the bookshelf behind the matron's desk. Bold titles leapt back at her. *Mental Depression in the Elderly, Caring for the Carers, Care Home Manual 1999*, and so on. Outside through the small window she could see the corner of the rear garden, which was just now being clipped by the morning sun.

There was a noise at the door and Grace Dowling entered. She looked tired and drawn and let out a great sigh as she leaned forward onto her desk.

'I'm sorry to have kept you,' she said, 'I didn't expect to see you again today.'

'How is my aunt, Mrs Dowling, can I see her today please, I would dearly love to?' enquired Emma.

'My dear child, I'm so very sorry, there's no easy way to put this but your aunt passed away in the night. We didn't expect it, I should have let you see her yesterday, I'm so sorry.' With that she slumped into the chair behind her desk.

Emma just sat there; it was the last thing she had expected to hear. She had come all this way. The only lead she had to her mothers past, the only living relative that she knew of was now dead. She wanted to cry but simply felt numbed by the shock.

The Matron made an effort to rise and came round to the other side of the desk and sat next to Emma. She put her arm around her. 'I'm so sorry my dear; you lost your mother recently didn't you. I realised you were all over the newspapers a few weeks ago weren't you. I didn't connect it until after you had gone yesterday.'

She paused and stifled a yawn. 'I'm sorry; I've been up half the night what with your aunt and another lady that has been very unwell.'

Just then the door opened and a young woman in a kitchen overall came in with a tray of tea and biscuits and put them on the desk in front of them and then exited the room.

'Excuse me,' the matron said, but I need this, would you like one.

Emma nodded slightly and whispered a thank you as the matron proceeded to pour two cups of tea. She handed one to Emma and offered her the biscuits but Emma refused.

Grace Dowling took a large gulp of tea and then rested the cup on her desk, 'There is much I must tell you,' she began, 'while it is still fresh in my memory. A while after you left yesterday I went to see how Millie was. She had rested well during the afternoon and the sedative had worn off so she was quite improved on the previous day. We chatted for a bit and I decided that as she seemed so much better I would mention that you had called. She asked so much about you, asked me to describe you, to tell her what you had said. She knew that your mother had been killed and somehow I think expected you to have contacted her sooner or later. She kept saying something like 'that's good, she must know now', but it didn't really make any sense. Then she asked for her handbag and gave me these.'

Grace Dowling reached across her desk and opened the top drawer. She lifted out a key ring and a small sealed brown envelope and handed them to Emma. 'She said I was to ensure that you got these, that the policeman wasn't to be told about them and that you must look in the fireplace. She was very insistent that I learnt the message accurately and it wasn't until I had repeated it back to her several times that she seemed to relax. I was to ensure that you got these keys, that I wasn't to tell anyone, especially the policeman and that you must look in the fireplace,' she repeated. She paused and then added, 'I don't know if that makes any sense to you; it certainly doesn't to me. I thought at first that it was the Alzheimer's confusing her but she was very lucid about it.'

Emma looked down at the envelope and key ring in her hand and shook her head, 'Not really, no.' she said. 'How did my aunt die then?' She questioned quietly.

'After she had made me promise to give you this message she said she wanted to rest. I helped her to get comfortable and left her to sleep. She was woken for the evening meal but didn't want anything. The nurses checked on her regularly through the evening and into the night and she was resting quite peacefully. Nurse Dawkin called me at about 2am when she realised something was wrong; your aunt had just slipped away quietly. The doctor has been and on initial examination believes it was a heart attack. There will be a post mortem of course.'

She paused, 'I suppose you are the only living relative, she had you listed as her next of kin on her admission form you know. Will you be arranging the funeral?'

Emma spoke quietly, 'Yes, yes of course.... I think I would like to go now.... I will contact you later in the week when I get back to Kent.'

+++++++++

Emma sat in the hire car. It was parked against the gate of a field in a quiet lane not far from the nursing home. She could not remember anything of the drive or how she got there. She sat clasping the two items in her hand, a faded leather key fob on a ring with two keys. One was a Yale type, the other a larger one, the sort that might open an older lock. They were both well worn. The small brown envelope was almost 'polished' as if perhaps Millie had kept it in her handbag unopened for many years. Emma stared at the items. The events of the morning had come as such a great shock and she still could not take it all in. Why had Millie died when she was so close to meeting her again? Why had she passed on these two items and what was the meaning of the mysterious message? Who was the policeman who had visited her and why did he cause Millie to become so distressed?

She put the keys down on the passenger seat and carefully opened the envelope. Inside was an old photograph, taken she could see in Aunt Millie's garden. Two women were standing looking at the camera and one was holding a baby in her arms. She could tell that although the picture was almost thirty years old there was no mistaking that it was Millie standing next to her mother who was holding the baby. She turned the photograph over. Pencilled on the back were the words: *Doreen and her little 'nene' delivered at last. The bargain has been kept'.*

She stared at the picture and again at the words on the back. None of this made any sense, what did *'nene'* mean? A teardrop fell on the photograph, and then another and suddenly the floodgates opened, 'Oh Millie,' she whispered.

While the warm spring sunshine shone down on the fields north of Clevedon; while the birds sang their happy chorus and the lambs played joyfully in the field beyond the gate, Emma Bertram cried out to God to give her the strength that she so desperately needed just now.

+++++++++

'We've got a breakthrough in the Bertram case, though I'm not sure of its significance yet,' said Higton as he entered the Inspector's office. 'I've just had that Jane Dennington on the telephone. She was demanding to know what we were doing by upsetting Emma Bertram's Aunt. I didn't let on that I hadn't a clue what she was talking about, just let her ramble on. Apparently she, Miss Bertram and that taxi driver went down to a place near Bristol yesterday to see Doreen Bertram's sister. She was in a nursing home there and had been visited by a policeman on Tuesday who it seems upset her and caused her a lot of distress. I've been on to the local boys in Bristol to find out what their enquiries were about. I'm waiting for their reply now.'

'Emma Bertram was very clear in her statement that she had no living relatives.' said Smurdon, 'So what's she up to?'

'I've tried to contact her this morning but it seems she stayed down there over night.' replied Higton.

'Right, as soon as she is back go and question her. Remind her, that mother or not, this is a murder enquiry we are dealing with and we expect to be given all the facts. Find out why she lied to us.'

++++++++++

Emma stood by the gate and looked again at the peeling paintwork of the cottage and then turned to survey the garden. Despite the many weeds that choked the borders, daffodils and crocus still pushed through in many places and Emma closed her eyes remembering again her visits as a child which had now so clearly returned to her memory. She pushed open the porch door and stepped inside. Despite the fact that Aunt Millie had given her the keys, for surely they were of the cottage and nowhere else, she felt an intruder and found herself glancing around to see if anyone was watching. Of the neighbours there was no sign.

She pushed the larger key into the lock of the front door and turned it. It unlocked with ease and she felt the door give a little. She inserted the other key and pushed the door slightly. It opened about six inches and then stuck firm. She tried to push it harder but found it wouldn't budge. She bent down and reached around the door. There was something blocking its path. It felt like the leg of a chair. She gave it a pull and managed to move it so that the door released. As the door swung open she gasped in horror at what she saw.

The house was in a mess, the contents of drawers were strewn across the floor, furniture was upended, the cushions from two armchairs had been ripped open, and ornaments were on the floor smashed in pieces. Emma made her way carefully through to the kitchen. Cupboards here had been opened and their contents spilled out, the back door that they had tried the day before was open, a glass panel shattered next to the lock. Emma climbed the narrow stairs and peered into the first bedroom. That likewise had been ransacked, books from the bookshelves scattered across the bed and floor, clothes strewn across the bed. Emma moved towards the other bedroom but just as she did so the door of the bathroom opened with great force knocking her backwards onto the bed in the first room. She was just aware of a dark coated person pushing hurriedly past her. She tried to grab the side of a wardrobe to steady herself but as she did so it began to move with her. As she fell backwards onto the bed so the wardrobe fell on top of her catching the side of her head just above the right eye. She felt a searing pain and then everything went dark.

+++++++++

Emma began to come to. Her head hurt and she could only see clearly out of one eye. The wardrobe was pressing on her right arm but she managed to shift it with her left hand sufficiently to be able to ease herself gingerly out from under it. She sat on the floor and held her head in her hands while the pain marginally subsided. As the throbbing eased she listened. She could hear nothing but the rapid beating of her own heart. She stood slowly and crept towards the bathroom where the door still stood out across the landing. She took hold of the handle and carefully peered round the door but there was no one there. The only other room off the small landing was another bedroom and Emma could see that this room had received the same treatment, but of the intruder there was no sign. She went to the bathroom and studied herself in the mirror. A large bruise was already forming across the corner of her right eye and she found some *witch hazel* in the medicine cabinet and dabbed it on the bruise with a tissue.

Moving cautiously back downstairs and carrying an umbrella for self-defence that she had found in the bedroom she checked the other rooms but the intruder had fled. She locked the front door and dragged the heavy kitchen table over against the back door so that it could not be opened easily from the outside. The sun was beginning to weaken in the sky and she realised she must have been knocked out for some time. She sat in the living room on the chair she had righted and stared ahead wondering what to do next and then it came to her, she was staring at the fireplace. What had the message said, *'I must look at the fireplace'*.

Emma rose slowly and looked at the litter of ornaments and papers on the mantle shelf. She worked her way through them one by one but they were nothing more than bills and circulars. Either side of the hearth, which was full of ash from the remains of a fire, was a bucket of logs one side and a poker and tongs on the other. She moved them and looked under the logs but there was nothing, she tried pressing the knobs that protruded slightly in the carved design of the surround but realised how ridiculous she was. She sat back in the chair and thought again. None of this made any sense. *I must look on the fireplace*, No, *I must look in the fireplace*, that was the message. She moved forward and bent down peering as best she could up the chimney. It was dark but she could see a ledge of some sort just before the opening narrowed into the chimney proper. She pulled her sleeve up and reached into the void running her hand slowly around the ledge. By the time she had finished her hand and the cuff of her blouse were filthy and she had found nothing other than years of soot and dust. She cursed herself for having put a decent outfit on but had wanted to look smart for her visit to Millie. This is crazy she thought to herself as she washed her hands at the kitchen sink, who would hide anything up a chimney where there was a fire burning every day. And then it struck her, there was another smaller fireplace in the first bedroom she had entered and that had an arrangement of artificial flowers in it, it was not used to light a fire. She went upstairs again, climbed over the fallen wardrobe and knelt down in front of it and removed the flowers. As before she reached up, yes there was a similar ledge and as she moved her hand around she soon struck something. It felt like a small package tied with string and she carefully extracted it from the chimney. In her hand she held what felt like a small bundle of papers about an inch thick neatly wrapped in brown paper and tied with string. Was this what the intruder had been looking for? She blew the dust off and started to pull at the knot.

Just then a loud scraping noise came from below. Someone was trying to get in the back door pushing against the heavy table. She grabbed her shoulder bag and stuffed the package inside it as she heard the table screech again across the kitchen floor. She heard heavy footsteps, had the intruder not left but been watching from outside, had he now returned to finish the job and perhaps her? The intruder was now at the bottom of the stairs; she could hear his heavy breathing from the exertion of opening the door. If perhaps she could hide he may not see her; she cursed herself for leaving the umbrella in the kitchen. She looked across at the wardrobe still balanced at an angle across the bed, if she could get under this side of it she would not be seen from the door. She slithered on her side across the room and eased herself quietly under the edge of the wardrobe but as she did so she dislodged some books that she had not seen on the other side of the bed and they fell to the floor with a thump.

Emma laid there, every muscle in her body tense with fear; her hands up to her face in a ready act of defence for the blow she was sure would come. The footsteps were at the door now and she sensed a shadow moving across the room.

'Can you tell me what you think you are doing here please Miss?' said a deep voice. Emma raised her head slowly and looked out from her hiding place. A uniformed policeman stood hand on hips staring down at her.

Chapter 8

Emma lay on the hotel bed fully clothed and exhausted. She had spent over two hours in the local police station explaining her presence at Millie's cottage and giving what scant details she had of the intruder. A call to the nursing home had confirmed her identity. The policeman who found her was brother to the next door neighbour and was just checking that his sister's cottage was secure when he noticed the broken pane of glass in the kitchen door of the adjoining cottage. No, he had not seen or passed any strangers on his way up the lane.

She looked at the bedside clock; she must have dosed for it was now past eight in the evening. She forced herself off the bed and telephoned down to reception for a light supper to be sent up to her room while she showered and changed. The food arrived, a mushroom omelette with salad garnish and at the first smell she realised how hungry she was. She devoured it quickly, but all the time she ate her eyes did not stray far from the soot-smeared package that now lay on the table in front of her. Of this discovery she had not told the police, and only now having been physically refreshed did she feel able to open it. She tugged cautiously at the string, somehow sensing that this would take her further into the unknown, along a path that would reveal more about the mystery of Doreen Bertram. For all her desire for the truth, she sensed a foreboding. Was she now opening a door that had been shut for a purpose, and was it a door best left closed?

More soot and dust fell out of the folds of the thick brown paper as she carefully unfolded it. Inside was an old cardboard envelope, the sort that photographs used to be supplied in when they were collected from the chemist. She opened it gently. It contained a number of papers and several photographs. The pictures, all of which were in black and white, caught her attention first. There was a duplicate of the picture she had been given at the nursing home but this one had no inscription on the back. There was a closer shot of the baby in her mother's arms. This one had '*Emma 6 months old and mine*' written in pencil on the back but Emma was uncertain if it was in her mother's handwriting. There was one other picture of the same baby; a close up of it cradled in a man's arms. They were strong tanned arms with the sleeves rolled up high showing bulging muscles and hairy forearms. The hands were of a man used to manual work yet the photo somehow conveyed that there was gentleness in the way in which the baby was held. But whose were they? Were these the arms of the father she had never known, or perhaps Millie's husband? There was no way of telling.

Another picture was of four men standing on a fishing boat. Two of the men were clearly fishermen by their dress, but of the others Emma was less certain. There were three more photographs in all, each picturing a man and a woman. The same people, Emma was sure, but taken over a period of several years and in different locations. In one they were standing in front of a very large ship and the man had a naval uniform on. He stood proud and erect, and Millie instead of facing the camera was looking at her man full of admiration.

Emma studied the pictures. The woman in the three was undoubtedly Millie, and the man was one of the two other men in the fishing boat picture. Millie's husband she presumed. She looked again at the fishing boat. It was a good size, about fifty feet long she guessed judging by the scale and it must have been moored to a buoy close to the shore for a beach with fishing huts was clearly visible if a little out of focus in the background. She studied again the fourth man, he had his hand up near his face as if he were shielding his eyes from the sun yet there were no other shadows to suggest that was the reason. Was he shielding his face to avoid his identity being revealed? It was impossible to tell. Emma studied the picture until her eyes began to smart; could this last man be the Barry from the photo that she had found in the attic? Was this again another picture of her unknown father? She was uncertain, yet somehow a sixth sense told her it was.

Emma turned her attention to the papers that accompanied the photographs. She unfolded a piece of thin paper that was stained along each fold. It opened out to about ten by eight inches. It was a hand drawn map, sketched roughly with several roads or lanes and what looked like a pub and a church marked by a crossroads. A few further buildings were drawn and two of the roads were marked, 'Fairlight Road' and 'Ore Lane' together with 'Placketts Farm' shown about halfway along Ore Lane. Of its whereabouts there was no indication. The names were English enough but they meant nothing to Emma.

Also in the envelope were two receipts from a chandlery in Eastbourne Sussex for various items of what Emma took to be fishing or navigational gear and boat parts. The total was for over three thousand pounds which must have been a lot of money in May 1973, the date of the receipts and the year of her birth. They were made out to a Joseph Hewetson of Hastings, a seaside and fishing resort just a few miles east of Eastbourne, but no more definitive an address.

The remaining items were envelopes containing letters between Millie and her husband Ted. They had been sent from ports around the world and judging by the postmark dates he had been in the merchant navy for many years. Emma glanced at a couple but they were clearly of an intimate nature and she put them down quickly feeling an uncomfortable intruder. She noted that most of them, the more recent ones had been sent to an address in Pevensey Bay that she knew to be a costal village between Eastbourne and Hastings.

One last envelope, different from the rest, contained three items, Millie's marriage certificate dated April 1956 and her husband Ted's death certificate which recorded his death as accidental. The remaining piece was a single newspaper cutting from page six of the *Bristol Evening Post* dated 17th January 1979.

Emma stared at the headline:

HIT AND RUN CARNAGE ON THE B3128- Mystery caller at the Pub.

EXCLUSIVE interview with Publican Mike Carter.

The body of local man Edward Lutterington was found by the roadside early yesterday morning on the B3128 half a mile from the Portbury turn off. His injuries were consistent with being struck by a vehicle at high speed. Police believe his body was carried some 150 yards from the point of impact.

Ted Lutterington, a retired merchant seaman was a regular at the Shire Horses in Failand. His usual routine was to drink and socialise with the regulars most evenings from around 8pm until 10pm and then walk the quarter mile to his cottage in Briar Lane. According to landlord, Mike Carter, last night a stranger appeared at the pub and met with Mr Lutterington. They were deep in conversation and at times their voices were raised. Both men left the pub together at around 9pm looking grim.

A police spokesman stated that they had a description but as yet no trace of the mystery caller or any car he may have been driving. Their enquiries were continuing. Anyone who has information about the above should contact the Police on Bristol 265655.

Emma re-read the cutting and looked at the photographs spread out on the table. She searched again through the pieces to see if there was anything further about the death of her uncle Ted, but there was nothing. What had happened that night, who was the mystery man? As so often it seemed to her, for every answer she found, more questions were posed.

+++++++++

Inspector Smurdon was just throwing his coat on and reaching for the door when Higton entered the CID office on the second floor of police headquarters in Maidstone. It was the next morning.

'I'm just on my way to court to give evidence on the Davis case, and I'm running late, so you'd better talk on the run.'

With that he shot past Higton and out into the corridor. Higton turned and caught up with him at the top of the stairs.

'News has just come through from Bristol on the Doreen Bertram business, and it's interesting! They say they have not had any investigation going concerning Doreen's sister Millie Lutterington and neither have they sent anyone to interview her,' Higton puffed.

'According to the Matron at the home, the policeman said he was from London. He flashed some sort of identification in front of her but it sounds like it was false. They've taken a description from her but its pretty vague. I've checked with Scotland Yard and they have also confirmed that they have no interest in Millie Lutterington. I've also drawn a blank with the Police National Computer.'

Smurdon and Higton passed through the doors to the car park at the back of the station. A car with driver was already waiting to whisk Smurdon off to the court.

Higton caught his arm, 'They have also interviewed Emma Bertram. It appears she went to her aunt's cottage and found it ransacked. The intruder was still there when she arrived, frightened the life out of her. Again not much of a description but probably the same man who called at the nursing home.'

Smurdon climbed in and shut the door, opening the window as he did so, 'Right, keep onto it and don't forget I want that woman interviewed ASAP. Go down to Bristol and drag her back yourself if necessary.'

+++++++++

In fact it wasn't necessary. Emma had returned the next afternoon by Intercity express train into Paddington, taken the Bakerloo underground line to Charing Cross and boarded a surburban service train to Westerham where Ray Brooks had collected her in his taxi. Constable Higton had already been on the telephone to *Tall Trees* several times by the time she had arrived home at 5.15pm.

'Could this not have waited until tomorrow,' Valerie Masterson said, glaring at the Constable now standing on the doorstep of *Tall Trees*. 'I have already told you on the telephone that Miss Bertram was travelling back from Bristol this afternoon, she only arrived home half an hour ago and she is very tired.'

'I presume she would prefer to answer my questions here rather than down at the station,' replied Higton unmoved.

'It's alright Valerie,' said Emma as she descended the stairs. She had overheard the end of the conversation. 'Let's go into the lounge, the Constable can ask his questions there.'

Emma sat in the high back chair by the window and offered Higton the settee but he said he preferred to stand. He turned and faced her. 'You said quite clearly Miss Bertram at a previous interview that your mother had no living relations. Now we understand from Miss Dennington that you have been in the Bristol area visiting your Aunt, your mother's sister. Can you tell me please why you lied to us?' He said brusquely, 'This is a very serious matter.'

'Now hold on a minute Constable,' said Valerie Marcheson loudly, 'I don't like your tone of voice.' She stood by the door defiantly, her arms folded across her chest, her eyes not leaving the constable.

Higton glanced in her direction for a moment but he was not intimidated. He looked back at Emma. 'Well Miss?'

'I didn't know Millie was my aunt,' Emma replied quietly. 'I thought she was just a friend of my mothers. She never spoke of her as a relation and I've not seen her for years. Not since I was about ten I think, and mother has not talked about her for years.' She paused, 'We found a few letters and old birthday cards in the attic that confirmed Mother and Millie were sisters and I recognised the address in Failand near Bristol. That's where I used to go with mother and why we went down there on Wednesday.' Emma replied.

'Did it not cross your mind to tell us what you had found out Miss?'

'No, I'm sorry. We didn't know if Millie still lived there or even if she was still alive.'

Emma's voice trailed off and her eyes began to fill with tears, she pictured again the moment when Grace Dowling had broken the news of Millie's death. 'Aunt Millie was alive on Wednesday but she died that night. I never got to see or speak to her.' Emma dabbed her cheeks with a handkerchief.

Constable Higton was taken aback by this news but tried not to show it. Why hadn't Jane Dennington told him when she had telephoned or perhaps she didn't know yet he thought. He moved closer to Emma and perched on the end of the settee, his voice was softer now. 'I'm very sorry Miss about your aunt; it can't be easy for you. But if we are going to find who killed your mother we need all the information you can give us,' he paused, 'Tell me Miss, did you find anything at your aunt's cottage or in her possessions that might help us?' Emma thought of the package and its contents. She avoided his gaze, 'No,' she replied simply.

Higton studied her for a moment. Was she telling the truth he wondered? He thought not but decided he was unlikely to extract any more information for the moment. 'Have you anything else to add to your previous statement Miss?' He asked watching her closely. 'Anything that might have come to mind since?'

Emma was a little more composed now; she dabbed her cheek again and looked at the constable. 'No, I don't think so,' she replied.

Higton leaned forward, he was just a few inches from her face and she could smell his stale breath on her face as he spoke.

'Why do you think someone visited your aunt pretending to be a policeman and then broke into her cottage?'

'Pretended?' Emma looked shocked. 'What do you mean?'

'Just this Miss, I've checked with the local force and with Regional Crime, there have been no enquiries relating to your aunt. Whoever called on her, it wasn't the police.'

He paused, 'Now why do you think someone did that?'

Emma stared across the room, she saw again the cottage with its contents ransacked and scattered with disdain across the floor. She remembered climbing the stairs and peering into the first bedroom. Her body physically jerked as she relived again the bathroom door being thrust open into her face. It made Higton move back a little but he kept his eyes on her waiting for a response.

Emma turned her head slightly and refocused her eyes on the detective. 'I'm sorry, I really don't know; I wish I did.' She replied.

Higton leaned forward again, 'Just a reminder Miss, we are dealing with a murder enquiry, if you should find or think of anything further, make sure you tell us first.' He tried to hold her eyes but the strain of the day began to tell on her again and Emma stifled a sob, her clenched hand pressing hard into her mouth.

'Right, that's enough. Police or not, you're harassing the poor girl.' said Valerie Marcheson sharply. Stepping towards him she said, 'I want you out of this house now or I will call Miss Bertram's solicitor.'

Higton stood up. 'That will be all Miss,' he paused, 'for the present.' He walked past the housekeeper, ignoring her, 'I'll see myself out.' He said.

++++++++

It was 10.30pm. Emma glanced at the bedside clock as she heard the muffled sounds of the grandfather clock downstairs in the hall strike its last note of the day before going into silent mode for the night. After Higton had left she had fallen asleep in the lounge for over an hour and Valerie had decided she was best left to ease the tiredness of the journey and stress of the day out of her body. A long soak in the bath followed by a choice meal from Valerie had revived her and for the moment all tiredness had gone. She had changed into her nightdress and now sat on the bed clasping the contents of the parcel she had found at Millie'. She went over the events of the last two days, sifting in her mind all that had happened and all that had been said. Why had mother kept the relationship with her sister secret? Why had they not been in touch more often? Had there been some event, some occasion when they fell out with each other? What had soured the relationship and when?

Emma leafed through each of the papers and photographs again in turn. The photographs, personal letters, marriage and death certificates were straightforward enough, but why keep an old hand drawn map and two receipts for fishing equipment? What was the significance of them? And why indeed keep them hidden inside the chimneybreast?

Still clutching the items, she laid her head back on the pillow and stared at the ceiling. Who had called on a defenceless old lady and ransacked her house? And was there a connection between that and mother's death?

A chill ran down her spine and she shivered. She laid the package down, climbed between the sheets and pulled the duvet tight around her neck. She looked around the room as chilling thoughts invaded her mind. She did not turn out the light.

Chapter 9

Aunt Millie's funeral was held the following Thursday week. She was to be buried in accordance with her wishes next to her husband Ted in the graveyard of St Andrews on the Hill. The cemetery and church were situated on a narrow strip of high ground at the western end of Clevedon. The coastal path that bordered one side of the ground and stood high above the Bristol Channel estuary was known locally as *Poets Walk*. Coleridge and others had trod this path above the swirling brown waters that separated North Somerset from the industrial coastline of South Wales. Was it here that he had penned *The Rime of the Ancient Mariner* as he watched the merchantmen sail up the channel to Bristol port before disgorging their cargoes of fine spices, cotton and other precious goods from far exotic places? What inspiration he and others had gained Emma could only guess.

She had travelled down on the West Country Intercity train from London to Bristol with Jane and they had taken a taxi to Clevedon. The mourners were few, Mrs Cuthbert, and her husband, the neighbours from the cottage next door to Millie, and her policemen brother, Grace Dowling and two of the nurses from *Rest Haven* plus two other ladies whom Emma didn't know.

They stood around the graveside as the Minister, a man in his early forties of slight build, began to intone the now familiar words of the funeral service. Emma found her mind wandering back to the crematorium in Chartwood and the emotions of that day began to weigh heavily upon her. Although she had hardly known Millie, and not at all in later life she was still moved to tears as the emotion of the moment took hold of her. She glanced at the other mourners. The two ladies were dabbing their faces with handkerchiefs. Mr and Mrs Cuthbert stood stony-faced and the policeman stood erect, his hat held across his chest. The breeze coming up the channel was whipping the few thin wisps of hair away from his scalp. Emma glanced to her left at Jane who stood there passively, no emotion reflecting in her face at all.

She thought about Jane. She had only known her a few months but in that time they had bonded well. Jane had been so supportive through her grieving and had given so much of her time that Emma was convinced that Jane's hairdressing business must be suffering, especially at a time when she should be concentrating on developing it. But Jane was adamant and insisted in accompanying her on these trips. No amount of persuading on Emma's part could change Jane's mind.

Another gust of wind rocked Emma and drew her out of her musings. She was glad she had worn the thick woollen calf length coat and knee length boots. The weather had turned colder again over the last few days and despite the bright blue near cloudless sky the wind was sharp and bit into her body and face making her eyes smart.

The cleric was coming to the end of the ritual. She looked at him and wondered what his feelings were on these occasions. She didn't think Millie had been a churchgoer from what Mrs Dowling had said. No doubt she was just a name to him, another £50 in the church coffers, an interrupted afternoon, an inconvenience? She stopped herself. She could well be doing the man an injustice, after all he did sound genuinely sincere and in fact when the short service had drawn to a close he immediately turned to Emma and spoke kindly to her.

'I know you live a good distance away Miss Bertram but here's my card, you can call me anytime if it would help to talk. And I really mean that, anytime, that's what I am here for.' Emma thanked him and blushed a little, remembering her thoughts about him only a moment ago.

Mrs Cuthbert had lain on a small spread at her cottage. The cleric had made his excuses; he had several parishioners on the sick list and he was behind with his visiting but he wished everyone a 'good time of fellowship in the circumstances,' as he put it.

Emma and Jane found the small talk difficult at they stood in the Cuthbert's dining room, cup of tea in hand. They felt more than a generation apart from this tightly knit community where talk of Millie's contribution to the local Women's Circle would be sorely missed.

'Another cake, dears,' encouraged Mrs Cuthbert, thrusting a plate of home made fancy cakes with bright icings of pink and yellow topped with an assortment of crystallised fruit, towards them. Emma and Jane both politely refused. 'But there's nothing to either of you, you both need building up. My husband Bob says he likes to get hold of something when he put an arm around a woman.' She laughed out loud at her own joke and the room went silent, all faces staring in her direction. She coloured, 'I'm sorry, that was inappropriate of me, I…'

'It's all right,' said Emma touching her arm, 'You're probably right and I'm sure Millie wouldn't want us to be all long faced.' There was a brief silence and then slowly the hubbub of conversation resumed amongst the other guests.

Emma tried to think of conversation, 'I was hoping I might learn that I had a cousin or two,' she said, 'But it looks as if I am the only one left in my family.'

'Millie told me once she couldn't have children; it's a hereditary thing apparently. She said it affected quite a few of her parents and grandparents generations so I should think there are very few of you altogether.'

'Oh I wish I knew more about my grand-parents and great grandparents,' said Emma, 'I know virtually nothing about the entire family, Mother never spoke of them,' she sighed.

'What will you do with the cottage?' It was Mr Cuthbert who had joined them from the kitchen.

'Well, it will have to be sold,' said Emma, 'I've really no use for it.'

'We ought to go and have another check round it before we return,' interrupted Jane, 'In fact we ought to go and do that now if we are going to catch our train.'

'I don't think we need to do that now,' said Emma, not feeling the moment was appropriate, 'I'm sure there's nothing there of immediate interest to us.'

'We ought to have a look round while we are here,' insisted Jane, 'You may not get another chance for weeks.'

'I've repaired the glass in the back door,' said Mr Cuthbert. 'And the door is bolted on the inside as well now,' he paused noticing Jane's puzzled look, 'Millie gave us a set of keys years ago, we've always kept our eye on the place for her. I'd better give them back to you.' He made to go back to the kitchen but Emma stopped him.

'That won't be necessary, please hang onto them, it will give me comfort to know that someone is keeping an eye on the place and has a set in case they are needed.'

'Oh right you are then,' he said. 'Well, I'll leave you two ladies to it.'

Emma reached forward and kissed Mrs Cuthbert on the cheek, 'Thanks for all you have done today; I couldn't have managed it myself. It was really kind of you.'

'Think nothing of it deary, it was my pleasure. We shall miss old Millie you know. Didn't see her every day, in fact she kept herself much to herself since her husband died in that road accident, poor chap, God rests his soul. But yes, we shall miss her.'

Emma waved a polite goodbye to the other mourners and thanked them for coming, and then she and Jane made their way round to the front path of the cottage next door.

Emma once again inserted the keys in the locks and pushed the door open, this time with no difficulty. The furniture had been righted and returned to its place and books and papers that had been scattered across the floor were now stacked in neat piles on the dining room table. The broken ornaments had also been cleared away.

Jane started immediately thumbing through any documents she could find while Emma went through into the kitchen. The Cuthbert's had tidied this room also and Emma knew she could rely on them to look after things when the time came to sell the property.

She climbed the stairs warily casting an eye into the bathroom first but the room was empty. The bookcase in the first bedroom and been righted and the books piled on the shelf. Emma sat on the edge of the bed and looked at the titles. There were some gardening books but Emma doubted they had been used much in recent years. Mrs Cuthbert had confided that Millie's garden looked a picture in years gone by but with the onset of Arthritis in the hands and knee joints, it had put a stop to her outdoor activities several years ago. By far the majority of books on the shelf were about the sea, ships and the merchant navy. The Hornblower series of the sea-faring exploits of Captain Horatio Hornblower by the well known author Cecil Scott Forester had been replaced on one of the shelves and stood erect in their beautifully bound bright red imitation leather covers like a row of grenadier guards on parade. Emma cast her eye around the room. The small dressing table had a crocheted runner across the top and on it stood a photograph of Millie's husband Ted in naval uniform. He smiled across the room and from the angle it was placed; Emma could see that it was one of the first things Millie would have seen when she sat up in bed each morning. A box of tissues and sundry bottles of scent and cleansing lotions sat at the other side.

Emma rose and pulled open a drawer. A few brooches and an imitation pearl necklace were in one corner; the rest was taken up with clothes and underwear. She made a mental note to ask Mrs Cuthbert to bag up what was worth saving and take it all to a charity shop. She doubted there was anything of value. She sat back on the bed again feeling little enthusiasm; she really didn't want to be doing this just now. It didn't seem right so close to Millie's death and on the day of the funeral.

She looked across at the fireplace and thought again of the package she had removed. She could still hear Jane downstairs opening and closing drawers and rummaging through their contents. On her return from Clevedon the previous week, Jane had wanted to know all about the circumstances of Millie's death and had insisted on seeing immediately the contents of the package found in the chimney. Emma was truly grateful for all the support Jane was giving her but at times felt it to be too intrusive. She wanted to find the answers to all her questions more than anyone but sometimes she felt as if Jane was taking over and that unnerved her. She needed to take control but just now she had no energy or inclination to say anything.

Jane came up the stairs and entered the bedroom where Emma sat and began to systematically work her way through the cupboards and drawers in this room. As she did so she caught Emma's eye.

'What?' said Jane.

'I really don't think we ought to be doing this, not now,' Said Emma.

'Nonsense!' replied Jane with determination, 'You want to find out about your mother don't you? Look you hardly knew the old girl, but she could provide some clues to your mother's background, so while we are here, we look. Okay?'

Emma was taken aback by Jane's vehemence and felt more than a little hurt by her attitude but was not in the mood to argue. 'I'll wait downstairs for you then.' She said, and with that she left the room.

+++++++++

Jane spent the next half an hour systematically working her way through the cottage until the taxi arrived to take them to the railway station in Bristol but she had discovered nothing new. She had been very thorough and had even reached up into the upstairs fireplace where Emma had found the original package but there was nothing to be found there either. Jane appeared to be quite irritated by it and was very sullen on the journey home. Although Emma was tired she tried to make conversation but Jane was not responsive and by the time the train had reached Bath they had sunk into an uneasy silence, a silence that remained for the rest of the journey home.

+++++++++

The next morning after a late breakfast Emma found herself wandering down the garden to her favourite spot beyond the laurel bushes. She sat on the familiar wooden seat and leaned back to drink in the morning sun. The wind had dropped from the day before and it was much warmer than had been expected. There were a few clouds but just now the sun shone out of a large patch of clear blue sky and Emma closed her eyes and savoured the moment. After a while she sighed deeply and looked down on the valley in front of her. Sheep and cattle grazed lazily in several of the fields. Over at Miles Farm two girls were exercising some horses, and a tractor trundled down the lane at the foot of the North Downs escarpment below her. Chaffinch and greenfinch fluttered to and fro around the nearby hedgerows looking for their morning feed and of course vehicle still chased vehicle in frenzied flight along the motorway below.

The chimney of a factory over at Broadhurst spouted a thick white smoke that looked so solid yet soon dissipated into a thin vapour and was then lost forever in the sky above. 'So like my life,' muttered Emma, 'Solid, dependable, then blown away by fate's cruel blow.'

She shuddered, sensing unease and automatically looked behind her but there was no one there. She looked across at the path on the North Downs Way but again it was devoid of people. Despite that a chill ran up her spine. 'What is all this about?' she wondered. She tried to turn over again in her mind all that had occurred since her mother's death. The recurring dreams of a sense of being followed, of seeing her mother's life ebb away, of Millie being interrogated by the bogus policeman and getting stressed as a result of it that probably caused her death. The funerals, the smashed ornaments and clock in the dining room and Millie's cottage being ransacked. What secrets did mother and Millie hold that suddenly had caused all this distress and why had it all surfaced now? What was the significance of that?

As much as she turned it all over in her mind, she could not unravel the mystery. There were still too many unknowns, still too many doors to open. If only she could find the keys to unlock them.

Her mind wandered back to the times before her mother's untimely death. When she used to sit in this corner of the garden and reflect on her life. Of the strange feeling of being incomplete, of feeling unfulfilled. Those thought used to depress her so much. At least that dream had faded into the background, though dream was not the right description in the accepted sense of the word. She would not picture images or see anything tangible. It was much more an inner feeling, one that touched her very soul. It would nag at her in the deep recesses of the night. She would wake before the first grey light of dawn appeared and it would be with her in an instant. Tearing at her soul like an unwelcome spirit that had come to torment her.

Many a time she had sat in this corner of the garden in the cool light of day and tried to analyse her feelings, but try as she might she could not find an answer to satisfy. Indeed the analysis would often depress her; she would sink into mood swings that mother found irritable, even annoying. She had tried once to discuss it with Mother but Doreen had been dismissive and told Emma she would grow out of it. But even then Emma knew it was something deeper, more profound. If only she could touch it.

She had confided once in Valerie who had been far more sympathetic and understanding in her own way, but understand she did not. No more could she provide the answer than to suggest that Emma would find it in love. 'The love of a good man will make you complete my girl' she had once replied.

But Emma did not believe her, although she had little experience of such. Mother had once introduced her to Gavin, the son of a local parish councillor. A little older than Emma, he was slightly on the short side and quite stocky but still impressed Emma. He had a small dimple on his chin that she found quite appealing. And there had been an attraction for a while. He was 'something in the city' and dealt with other people's money. He was clearly good at his job and earned a good salary from it.

Emma felt comfortably at ease in his presence and they dined and visited the theatre in both Maidstone and London for a while. Had she experienced love? Emma was never sure. It was pleasurable to be with Gavin but the intensity of feelings that people wrote about in magazines and books was never present. And the enjoyment of being with Gavin did nothing to assuage her feelings of loneliness and incompleteness. No, the answer if there was an answer was not to be found in the love between a man and a woman even if her relationship with Gavin had blossomed. Of that Emma was sure.

She could not help that she still had her times of depression, that she was often preoccupied with her own thoughts when she should have been giving Gavin her undivided attention. The friendship, relationship, whatever you could call it lasted for seven months but then the calls from Gavin became fewer and dried up completely during one particularly bad spell of depression. Emma could not blame him. She owed him more than she could give. It was not his fault.

The sudden noise of a helicopter as it broke across the ridge behind the house and swept on over the valley towards Broadhurst stirred her out of her musings. She was determined not to be beaten. Whatever the mystery was that surrounded her mother and Millie she would persevere until she knew the whole truth whatever it took.

+++++++++

That evening Ray telephoned. 'I've found your answer for you, well at least Kirsty in the office has, she looked it up on the Internet. The word *'nene'* means 'baby' in Spanish.

'In Spanish?' queried Emma.

'Yes – hope that helps' replied Ray.

'I'm not really sure.' answered Emma slowly, her mind already returning to the airmail envelope she had found in Mother's book. 'But thanks Ray, see you soon, goodbye.'

Emma sat for a while by the telephone table in the hall mulling over the information Ray had given her. Was there any connection with the airmail that had been sent to her from Spain all these years later and what had the envelope contained? Why had Millie written that note on the back of the photograph and what was the significance of the second phrase, *The bargain has been kept*? Once again she had only succeeded in raising more questions and found nothing in the way of answers.

Chapter 10

The relationship between Emma and Jane had remained strained since the return from Bristol. Emma had telephoned Jane and tried to rekindle the close relationship that had existed before Millie's funeral. Jane had enquired what Emma's intentions were now regarding the continued search for information but when Emma replied that she didn't know what if anything she would do, Jane remained distant. She made her excuses about coming round and said that she was very busy at present with hairdressing appointments and didn't know when she would be available.

It was true that at the time Emma was feeling quite low, partly because of all that had happened and partly because of the loss of Jane's companionship that she felt little enthusiasm for doing anything. She had come to rely so much on Jane and she missed her friendship more acutely than she cared to admit.

Now a new day had dawned, the brightest and warmest of the spring so far and Emma had risen early and walked the circuit of the garden savouring the sweet smells of hyacinth and forsythia that was now in full bloom. She had stopped briefly in her corner of the garden and surveyed the morning scene from her unique vantage point. The South Downs were just visible in the distance through the early haze and as she looked at them she realised that just beyond lay the towns of Hastings and Pevensey where perhaps, just perhaps she might find another clue to the mystery that surrounded her.

With determination she set off back to the house and announced to Valerie that she would be going out for the day. She had a quick breakfast and then gathered together a few things for the journey. Already, as before, having made a decision she felt so much better for it and there was a spring in her step as she made for the garage where mother's car was parked. Although she had used the car since mother's death she was still keenly aware of mother's presence within the car. She hadn't made any effort to clear out the tissues and make up that Doreen Bertram usually left in the glove compartment and as Emma opened the car door the feint smell of mother's perfume touched her nostrils. For a moment all the horrors of the last few weeks invaded her mind but she forced herself to push them away and purposefully started the car and headed out across the drive. Emma often drove but there had seemed little point in having a car of her own. More often than not they used to go out together and Doreen had always seen to things like insurance and servicing. Emma made a mental note to check when these were next due.

She headed down the lane and then slowed almost to a halt to take the sharp left-hand bend. Glad to be past it the road now widened a little and Emma was able to take in the view around her. The deciduous trees that lined the lane here were all breaking out into new leaf and the morning sun though still low in the sky was painting a bright dapple of colours across the lane in front of her as it shone through the trees. Emma took a deep breath and smiled to herself; she was glad to be out and doing something positive. As she approached the old brick-workers cottages she noticed a light blue car parked in the lay-by opposite. The driver, a young man, was looking intently at her and she was sure she had seen him before. Her heart skipped a beat and then began to race. It was the man she had seen through the window of the *Copper Kettle* in Westerham she was sure of it. Could he also be the one that had been watching her? She recalled that time in the garden, the day mother died, how she was sure she had seen someone looking across at her through binoculars. There had been other times all in the last few weeks when she felt sure she had been followed; though whenever she looked round there had been no one there. She accelerated the car slightly and looked in the rear-view mirror. The light blue car was turning round and following her.

She made her way down into Chartwood and headed for the traffic lights at the top of the high street. The blue car was still visible. On impulse at the last moment she turned left at the traffic lights and headed into the industrial estate. This was a maze of small roads, the site of the old clothing factory that a century ago had employed most of the townsfolk but which had closed down in the 1950's as cheaper imports from the far east flooded the country and made production here uneconomic. Now small factory and warehouse units had sprung up, their proximity to the motorway network ideal for both staff and transport links. Emma knew the area well and was able to turn first left then right through a number of manoeuvres in an endeavour to shake off her pursuer. She considered trying to get her mobile phone out of her handbag, which was on the passenger seat, and calling the police, but for the moment she needed all her concentration on keeping the car on the road and safely driving around the estate. The pale blue car was still behind her but at some distance. There was no doubt however that he was following her. She tried to read the licence number but dared not concentrate on the rear view mirror for too long. With one more turn to the left she realised she was beginning to leave the estate. Suddenly she saw her chance; a large articulated lorry was backing out of a factory gate. A workman in the road was signalling her to stop but she pressed her hand hard on the horn and swung the car out around the back of the truck. Thankfully she knew this was a one-way street and that no other vehicles would be coming towards her from the blind spot created by the lorry. She heard the workman swear at her as she passed and in her rear view mirror saw the shake of his fist. But she didn't care. The pale blue car was well and truly trapped the other side of the obstacle.

Turning onto the feeder road from the estate that led to the motorway, Emma let out a sigh of relief. She was shaking and perspiring and every muscle in her body was tense yet she allowed herself a smile. She had never done anything quite like that in her life before and in a strange way felt quite exhilarated by it. The feeder road took her over the M25 motorway and within a couple of minutes she had joined the main A21 road and was heading towards Hastings.

For the next ten minutes she constantly checked her mirror but there was no sign of her pursuer. She tried to think what possible connection he could have with the mystery that she was trying to solve. But as so often was the case, her thoughts only posed her more questions and she forced the thoughts to the back of her mind and tried to think what she would do once she got to Hastings. Questions she had plenty, it was answers that she needed.

As she drove on past Tonbridge and Pembury, and out into the leafy countryside of Lamberhurst and Flimwell she realised that she had no plan of action. It had been very much a spur of the moment decision and she was beginning to wonder just what she would do when she arrived there.

It was late morning by the time she pulled into the sea-front car park. The sun was warming the morning air though she was aware of a gentle but cool breeze coming off the sea. She realised that it was some time since she had visited the south coast of England and looking around couldn't remember ever having been to Hastings before. Feeling thirsty she made her way to a café across the road that thankfully was open at this time of year and ordered a coffee. She sat at a table by the window and looked out onto the seafront area.

Immediately across the road from where she sat were the usually seaside accompaniment of crazy golf, boating lake and various children's attractions and amusements based on a wide promenade. Further to the east she could just see the beginning of fishermen's huts scattered along the top of the beach. See reached for her handbag and extracted the picture of the fishing boat that had been in the package she had found at Millie's cottage. In the background of this picture there were similar looking huts but from this angle it was impossible to say if they were the same or if the picture had been taken here.

She finished her coffee and feeling refreshed set off across the road towards the huts. After she had passed the bright gaudy colours of the children's amusements the beach and seafront became more businesslike. Several fishing vessels were hauled up onto the beach, some being worked on by men doing repairs and others cleaning the hulls. Emma had to be careful here as she made her way across the beach. A number of winch wires ran down towards the sea from the machinery compartments at the top; and nets, tackle, boxes and pots were scattered and stacked seemingly at random between the many huts and vessels.

She spotted a short pontoon at the waters edge and made her way towards it. From here she turned around and looked back towards the beachhead and huts. Comparing the photograph with the scene in front of her she was in no doubt that this was the same place. The boat in the photograph must have been moored about a hundred yards out to sea but many of the huts were clearly the same ones and the contours of the cliff edge to the right that showed in the picture was undoubtedly the same.

So what next, Emma thought? She looked around. Most of the men working on the few fishing vessels that were there looked quite young so she doubted any would have been around to remember twenty-five or more years ago. One man perhaps in his late-thirties was working alone on a small boat nearer the waters edge. Emma took a deep breath and plucked up the courage to go and speak to him.

'Hello,' she said as she neared him.

He looked up, eyeing the young woman approaching him. She was of slim build, mid to late twenties he guessed and wearing beige slacks and cream roll-neck sweater under a three-quarter-length leather coat. Her face was also slim with a small nose and large dark eyes and she was smiling intently at him.

'Hello,' he responded, feeling a little uneasy at the approach of this not unattractive woman. He put down the scraper he had been holding and instinctively wiped his hands on the front of his overalls. He looked her up and down wondering what she would say next.

'I'm sorry to trouble you,' she said, 'I'm trying to find out some information about some relatives of mine. I think they may have been associated with a couple of men who fished here perhaps twenty years ago now. I'm sorry to sound vague but one of the fishermen may well have been named Joseph Hewetson.'

She looked at him but he pursed his lips and slowly shook his head. 'Sorry, name doesn't mean anything to me, but then I only moved here about fifteen years ago.'

'Would you look at this?' Emma proffered the photograph of the four men standing in the fishing vessel.

He studied it for a while and then said. 'That's a fine boat; a good-sized sea going trawler, and the picture was certainly taken here. Those huts are still standing, though they've had a lick of paint since by the look of it. And you can just see the edge of that antique shop there, see it? He said pointing. 'But sorry, no, I can't help you with the people. I don't recognise any of them and I've certainly never seen that boat around here. It's a fine vessel; I wouldn't have missed that one.'

He looked around, a frown of concentration on his face. After a moment he pursed his lips again. 'There's no one here that would have been around twenty years ago; they're all too young.' He was silent for a moment and then said, 'Old Bill Withers, he's the man you want. I think they built the town around him, what he doesn't know about Hastings and what goes on here isn't worth knowing. He was probably around when King Harold was shot in the eye with an arrow in 1066.' He laughed with a smile and Emma smiled back.

'Where can I find him?' asked Emma in anticipation.

'…Fraid I don't know where he lives,' the man replied, 'But he'll be down here later, always is. Was a fisherman himself before he retired. Comes down now of an evening to watch the boats come in and chat to the lads.' He paused, 'See that stack of boxes over there by that larger hut. No one dare move those, 'cause that's where he sits! His son fishes now, that's his hut.' Come about 6.30pm. If he can't help you, well, I doubt that anyone else will be able to.' He smiled, 'Hope you find the answers you are looking for.'

Emma thanked him and returned the smile. She walked back up to the pavement glad that she had worn stout shoes. The pebble beach had already made her ankles sore. She paused at the top and looked around wondering if she should approach anyone else. The man had seemed very positive about Bill Withers but if he didn't turn up this evening or was unable to help she would be back to square one. There were actually very few people around the huts and Emma guessed that most of them were out to sea taking advantage of the calm conditions. She searched the area but there appeared to be no one older than the man she had spoken to so she decided against approaching anyone else.

Emma took the package from her handbag and looked again at the contents. The other photographs were of no help, neither was the map - it could have been of anywhere. She had already followed up the receipt from the chandlery by telephone from home but the business had closed several years ago and the building pulled down for redevelopment. But several of the letters from Millie's husband were addressed to her at 427 Beach Road, Pevensey Bay, a small seaside village about twelve miles along the coast to the west. She looked at her watch; it was twelve-fifteen. She had plenty of time to get there and back before the evening when hopefully Bill Withers would at last be able to help unravel the mystery.

Emma headed back to her car and set off along the coast road towards Pevensey. Quite soon the road turned inland and she lost sight of the sea. The topography here was uninteresting. Most of the dwellings on the outskirts of Hastings were older style properties and the dust and dirt that swirled up from the busy road did nothing to lift their drab image. Emma was glad when she had left the last of the houses behind, but no sooner had she done so that she found herself on the outskirts of Bexhill. A town she remembered from a television programme that had the highest percentage of pensioners of all the towns in England. Exiting Bexhill the ground became very flat either side of the main road and she again remembered from the same programme a reference to the Pevensey Levels, an area of low marshland criss-crossed by streams and dykes that were a haven for many hundreds of water fowl including several rare species.

At last she could see the outline of Pevensey Castle in the distance and soon she turned off the main road, crossed the main coastal railway line and headed back towards the sea and Pevensey Bay. She parked the car in a space outside a café and realised that she was feeling quite hungry. Sitting at a table at the back of the café she was soon tucking into a bowl of hot chicken soup with a slice of granary bread. She looked around at the other patrons. Most she guessed were visitors to the area, drawn out by the warm spring day. But a couple of people, both sitting, like her, on their own were clearly regulars as they chatted frequently to the waitress each time she passed their tables. The waitress was an older lady in her fifties and Emma waited for an opportunity to show her the address on the envelopes in her handbag.

'Beach Road, Oh that's easy,' she said, 'it's just back there,' she said pointing the way Emma had come. 'But you'll have to go round the one way system now to get to it. Just follow it round and it will be right opposite you when you get to the end.' As the waitress had been giving the directions she had been drawing a great arc with her hand indicating where the road system would take Emma.

'You don't recognise the name by any chance do you?' enquired Emma.

The waitress squinted. 'What's that, Lufferton?' she said. 'You'd better read it for me; I haven't got my reading glasses on.'

'Lutterington,' said Emma, 'Mrs Millie Lutterington.'

'No, sorry, can't say I do. How long ago was that sent?'

'The postmark is a bit indistinct but it looks as if it is 1968, that's well over thirty years ago so I know it's a long shot.' Emma paused, 'They were my aunt and uncle, they are both dead now but I'm just trying to find out more about them, I know so little.'

'No but, how about you Edwin?' The waitress turned and shouted at the old man whom Emma had thought to be a regular. 'Lutterington, Millie Lutterington. Does the name mean anything to you?'

'Who?' Edwin replied cupping his hand to his left ear.

'Deaf as a post; poor old soul,' said the waitress. But before she had a chance to repeat the name again another voice spoke up.

'Millie Lutterington?' It was the other 'regular'; a woman probably in her late sixties who had sat stooped at a table all the time Emma had been there. She wiped a serviette across her mouth and looked up. Her jaw trembled slightly as she spoke. 'I remember Millie, she used to come into the Post Office regular when I worked there for John and Ivy, you remember Mavis.'

'Well I certainly remember you working for John and Ivy in the Post Office,' said Mavis, the waitress, 'But I don't recall no Millie whatever her name.'

A party of four had got up from their table and were waiting to pay at the till. The waitress excused herself and made her way towards them. 'Was everything all right with your meal?'

'Can you tell me anything about Millie or Ted Lutterington?' enquired Emma of the old lady. 'They were relatives and I would love to know more about them.'

'Mm... can't say much about them really,' said the old lady. 'She was a regular at the Post Office where I worked. We used to pass the time of day when she came in and of course I'd sometimes see her out in the street when I was shopping.' The old lady paused and Emma asked.

'What about her husband, did you see much of him?'

'No, he was away most of the time, in the navy. Merchant or Royal - I don't know which. So she spent most of the time on her own, didn't have any children as far as I know.' She paused again and then added. 'Strange about their going though.'

'What was that, what was strange?' asked Emma.

'Well they just upped and left. One day they were here, the next they were gone. I didn't know about it till afterwards. She had a savings account and would come in regular as clockwork on a Tuesday morning and take out enough for the weeks shopping. One Tuesday she didn't come in so I thought she must be ill, but she didn't come the next week or the week after. When I bumped into Mrs Stevens, that was their next-door neighbour, she told me that they had just left one morning. Removal van came and that was it. No goodbyes to anyone and no forwarding address.'

She shook her head, 'Very strange that, she always seemed so nice but to leave without saying farewell to your neighbour of many years, well that's just downright rude isn't it.' She paused again. 'Sorry my dear, I didn't mean to speak ill-mannered of your relatives especially now they have passed over to the other side.'

'That's all right,' Emma smiled, 'I'm very grateful for the information you've given me. Every little helps me to build a picture of what they were like.' She paused, 'Tell me, would you know when it was that they left?'

The old lady thought for a while, turning her head to one side and frowning with concentration. 'It would have been about the early seventies I should think, but it's a long time ago now so I may be wrong.' she said.

Emma thanked the old lady and paid the waitress who insisted on going over the simple directions to Beach Road once more. She returned to the car and set off. Negotiating the one way system she was soon entering Beach Road. It was an aptly named road for Emma could see that the row of houses on the right was built literally on the beach. Between each bungalow she had a glimpse of the sea and many of the gardens were little more than a mass of pebbles on which people had stood flowerpots and planters full of flowers. It was a long road and she must have driven over a mile before she reached the four hundreds. She pulled the car over and parked at the kerb-side. She checked her watch; it was just coming up to half-past two. Alighting from the car she walked up to the front of number 427 although in many ways it looked like the back of the house. A garage took up most of the width of the short garden and there was a dustbin alongside the door to the house. A couple of flowerpots had been strategically placed either side of the path but the small shrubs in them were well and truly dead. Blinds were drawn at all of the windows on this side of the property and Emma guessed that it must be used now as a holiday retreat rather than permanently lived in. From where she stood she could see that there was a pedestrian access to the beach two bungalows along and she made her way to it and up onto the pebbles. There was little sand along this stretch of the coastline although the receding tide was revealing a narrow band of soft sand well down the beach.

She made her way back to the seaward side of the house and surveyed the property from this side. Again all the windows were shut and had blinds drawn. In the garden area which consisted of just pebbles with a few tufts of grass growing between them, a yacht about twenty feet in length was propped up on heavy boards and had a large tarpaulin draped over it. Emma stood there for a while wondering what it would be like to live here right on the edge of the elements. She looked out to sea where it was still quite calm and could see the Sovereign Light Tower standing erect some twelve miles offshore. The reflection of the warm sun kissed the tops of the small waves as they danced their way inshore. Emma guessed it must be close to low tide just now but noticed the great gouge of stones near the top of the beach where the sheer edge of it dropped some seven feet at what must be the high water mark. She closed her eyes and tried to imagine the fury of the sea lashing at this edge, the winds whipping the water into a maelstrom of boiling froth just a few yards from the bungalow, the house where Millie lived for most of her life alone while Ted was at sea serving in the Navy. The thought made her spine tingle and she shook her shoulders and sucked air in through her mouth. It was something she preferred not to think about. She turned to look at the house again and realised that she was being watched from over the fence next door. A small elderly lady dressed in green anorak and with a scarf around her head was watching her intently.

'There's no one in; I don't think they are coming down this weekend. What do you want?'

'I'm sorry,' said Emma smiling and walking towards the old lady's garden, 'I didn't mean to alarm you. I was just looking at the bungalow. My aunt and uncle used to live here many years ago and I was just passing so I thought I would stop by and have a look at it.'

'Who was that then?' Said the elderly lady, still suspicious of Emma.

'Ted and Millie Lutterington,' Emma replied, 'Are you Mrs Stevens?'

'Yes I am, how do you know my name?'

'I've just come from the café, the one next to the greengrocers. I got chatting to the waitress and an elderly lady there, sorry I didn't get her name but she used to work in the Post Office, she told me about you.'

The old lady relaxed a little. 'Oh, I expect that was Edna.' she paused, 'Ted and Millie, my, that's a good long time ago. Did you come to visit them when they were here?' She asked, but then answered her own question. 'No, you would hardly have been born would you by the time they left.'

'When was it they left?' asked Emma, 'I gather they left unexpectedly.'

'You can say that again. We'd been neighbours for nigh on fifteen years, got on really well too. Then one day her husband came home from one of his trips and within a week they were gone! Not so much as a goodbye! No forwarding address; just vanished.' She paused, 'I ask you what sort of a person does that? Reckon he got himself into a spot of bother with the authorities; mind you I never read anything about him in the papers.'

'And when was that?' prompted Emma.

'September 25th 1972. I remember it well because my birthday is on the 26th and Millie always used to come in with a plant and a card and if the weather was kind to us we'd sit in the garden together and chat and I'd open a bottle of Brut and we'd toast my birthday.' Her voice trailed off and she fought back a tear. 'You know even now after all this time; I still miss her. She was a really good neighbour and what she did was so out of character. It must have been something to do with her husband.'

'Was her husband still in the navy when that happened?'

'No he'd left by then and was working the fishing boats over at Hastings. He didn't come home every night on account of them so often making an early start or fishing through the night, least that's what he said but you never know do you? Think he lodged with one of the fishermen,' she replied.

'Would you like a cup of tea, love? I'm just about to make a pot. Don't get too many visitors down here at this time of year and most of my neighbours are weekenders now.' She held the beach gate open and beckoned Emma in.

Emma smiled, thanked her and followed her into the sun lounge that stretched across the back of the bungalow. For the next three-quarters of an hour as they drank their tea Emma learn a lot about Millie and her husband Ted. How he had served as an officer in the merchant navy and was away for months on end. How Millie had coped with the long periods of loneliness and had forged a close friendship with Frances Stevens. But Frances could not recall Millie ever mentioning a sister or indeed, now she thought about it, ever speaking about her family at all. If there ever had been a mention, it was very vague and Frances could not recall any detail other than she believed they had moved to Pevensey from the east-end of London. Certainly the name of Doreen Bertram meant nothing to her.

Emma had to draw the conversation back several times as Frances would include all her previous neighbours in her responses. 'Twenty years ago this was a lovely little community,' she mused, 'Mary and Peter lived at number 438 across the road and Molly and John were next door to them. Then there was Ada and Edwin on this side,' she pointed, 'and Millie on the other. Then there were several others all permanent dwellers. We all used to look out for each other and help each other out Now they are nearly all owned by rich people from London and Surrey who come down and swank about at weekends in the summer. During the winter it's like a ghost town. The whole soul has gone out of the place.' She paused and stared at the little electric heater that intermittently would switch itself on and whirr away warming the area around their feet. Emma guessed she was not seeing the fire but scenes from the past that were gone forever. She took opportunity in the silence that followed to thank her host for the kind hospitality and said it was time for her to be going. Yes, she promised she would call on her again if she were ever in the area. It was not easy to get away from the old lady who wanted to continue the conversation but Emma eventually managed to extract herself and return to the car. She sat there for a while and mulled over all she had gained. She had learnt quite a lot but still seemed no nearer to the answers she was looking for. She turned the car around and headed back toward Hastings for her rendezvous with Bill Withers. Perhaps that would bring better results.

+++++++++

The journey back had been uneventful and she was now nearing the outskirts of Hastings once again. Watching for the signs to the sea front she glanced in her rear view mirror to check it was clear to change lanes. Two vehicles behind her a pale blue car pulled out. It was the same driver that had followed her through Chartwood earlier that day, of that she was sure. In a panic Emma pulled back into the inside lane and the pursuing car did the same. She shot across the next junction and the other car followed. The traffic was quite heavy and it was impossible to lose the other car. She thought it best to keep to the main roads and she turned with the vehicle in front of her. They were heading towards the town centre but she was unfamiliar with the road. She had not been this way before. Ahead the traffic was slowing and several cars were turning left. She followed them. The blue car did the same. She kept glancing in her rear view mirror. It was still there two cars behind but she could not see the driver any more clearly. She realised they were now heading out of town and away from the sea. The road became narrower now and the area more rural. There was only one car between them now and Emma could fee the cold sweat trickling down her back as she sat arched on the edge of the seat. She looked for an opportunity and saw ahead on the corner of the next right hand turning a country police house with the familiar blue sign above the door. At the last minute without indicating she went to turn right but her path was blocked by a tractor coming the other way. She was forced to wait in the centre of the road. The pale blue car slowed then turned to pass her on the inside; she steeled herself to look at the driver. It was not the same man who had followed her earlier after all. A great wave of relief flooded over her as she turned slowly across into the side road. The road soon narrowed and she was forced to drive for about a quarter of a mile before she could pull in by the gate to a field and stop. She switched off the engine and opened the window. She could feel the perspiration trickling down her face and between her shoulder blades; her whole body was tensed and shaking. She grasped the steering wheel at the top and laid her forehead on the back of her hands. As much as she steeled herself she was unable to stop her eyes from watering as the relief began to take effect.

Chapter 11

It was a full five minutes before Emma felt able to open the door and get out of the car. She forced herself to breathe in and fill her lungs with the fresh countryside air and to do it slowly in large gulps to help calm her. The shaking gradually stopped and she began to feel rather foolish over what had happened; she scolded herself for panicking so quickly. By the time she had finished mopping her face with a tissue and had adjusted her make-up she was even smiling to herself and laughing inwardly at how she would have looked to anyone who knew of the situation. She was very grateful to be quite alone just now on this country road.

But exactly where was this road. She had no idea. Emma took the road atlas off the back seat of the car and studied the page but the scale was too small to be certain. She stood up and looked around her. There were fields on either side of the road at this point, the one on her side of the road was fallow; the one opposite was occupied by a flock of sheep quietly grazing in the far corner. The most sensible move would be to return the way she had come. She was confident she could retrace her route until she saw a road sign that would point her back in the direction of Hastings sea front but she was far less certain about turning the car round in the narrow lane.

Ahead of her through the trees she could see the tower of a Norman church and the roof of another building next to it. They were no more than about a mile away and she decided to head in that direction and hope for a road sign or at least someone from whom she could seek directions.

Emma started the car and headed along the lane. Passing places were few and far between and she was glad not to have met any vehicles coming from the opposite direction. The lane eventually widened and she found herself at a crossroads where a small triangular patch of neatly mown grass bordered two sides of the junction. On the other side of the grass a short cul-de-sac led off the road she was on, past a public house, and up to the lychgate of the church she had seen earlier. Emma turned the car into the cul-de-sac and parked outside the pub. Locking the car she looked up at the Inn and took in its character. Stone built uneven walls with a slated roof and tiny leaded light windows with black painted frames, it wreaked history. The cobbled stone footpath gave way to a large flagstone that had worn to a smooth concave outside the great oak panelled door. Testimony to the many travellers and locals alike who had crossed the threshold in search of sustenance and liquor down through at least three centuries. Window boxes hanging below each ground and first floor window were full of winter pansies and primulas giving a bright splash of colour to the otherwise drab exterior.

As she approached Emma could hear the murmur of conversation coming through the open window. The heavy door swung easily on its well-oiled hinges revealing a small entrance hall. A door to the right was marked '*Private*', but to the left Emma could see across to the bar where a couple of regulars, she guessed, were deep in conversation with the Landlord. A low beam stretched across the opening into the bar area and Emma instinctively ducked as she made her way into the room. The ceiling, walls, bar, and furniture was all made of very dark wood but the deep red of the carpet, chair cushions and matching bar stool tops gave it a welcoming and homely look.

As Emma approached the conversation died and all three occupants turned to look at her. Emma smiled at the Landlord, 'I'm sorry to bother you but I seem to have taken a wrong turning. I want to get to the sea front at Hastings, can I carry on along this road?' she said pointing in the direction she had been travelling.

One of the regulars burst out laughing. He was in his sixties, Emma guessed, with a great shock of untidy white hair and bright red cheeks on a very rounded face. 'You carry on down that road young lady and you won't end up at the sea side, you'll end up at the mud side!' He said.

The Landlord seeing Emma's puzzlement broke in. 'Now don't you go confusing the poor girl Frank.' He turned to Emma. 'Take no notice of him, he just having a joke at Wilf Johnson's expense. He owns the farm down there and once you are past the farmhouse the road dips and it's always very muddy down there due to the water draining off the land.' He paused, 'No, take the road to the right here, past the back of the church, and in about a mile you'll come to the main road. Turn right there, it's sign-posted, and that will take you right down to the sea front.'

Emma thanked them and made for the door. As she did so the man called Frank spoke up again. 'That's a shame, you should have let her go down to Placketts Farm, I don't suppose old Wilf has seen anything so pretty in years.' And with that he laughed loudly again.

As Emma unlocked the car something was nagging at her brain but she could not think what it was. She sat in the car but it wouldn't go away. 'Think, girl, think!' she muttered to herself but to no avail. She turned the key in the ignition, put the gear into reverse and backed out of the parking space. Moving off she had almost reached the end of the turning when it came to her. 'Placketts Farm' was on the hand drawn map in the package from Millie's cottage. She stopped the car and rummaged through her handbag, which had been on the passenger seat, and found the envelope. Carefully she unfolded the map and compared it with where she was. She couldn't believe it but although neither the church nor the pub was named on the map there was no doubt this was the same place.

She turned the car towards the junction and could see now the confirmation she was looking for. A faded wooden sign, half hidden by undergrowth low down at the side of the road indicated that she was about to cross Fairlight Road. On another at right angles to the first, but now rotting and broken at one end, she could just make out the letters OR for Ore Lane. Fairlight Road was void of traffic so Emma crossed the junction and moved off along the lane. She had no way of telling the scale of the map or if indeed it was to any scale so she kept her speed down and watched out for any entrance on the left where according to the map, Placketts Farm was. The lane was bordered on either side about twenty feet deep by thick shrubs and trees but Emma could just see through the gaps to the open fields beyond. After about a mile and a half the road began to climb and Emma was beginning to wonder just how much further she had to go. Her car topped the rise and there just over the hill and edging the road was the wall of a large brick and corrugated iron barn. A wrought iron sign, rusting in places, and affixed to the wall of the barn announced that this was indeed 'Placketts Farm'. Emma slowed the car and turned through the narrow gateway that was attached to the far end wall of the barn. Immediately opposite the gate was another farm building and Emma had to turn the car sharply back the way she had come before she finally turned right into the courtyard, if you could call it that, where an old tractor and a battered land-rover were parked. Emma switched off the engine and got out of the car. She had made a point of parking at the one spot where the rough concrete was less muddy than the rest; though only marginally so.

The first thing that struck her was the silence. There was a slight breeze in the tops of the trees and a piece of loose metal hanging high up on the side of the barn banged occasionally against an iron bracket below it; but otherwise all was quiet. She took in the scene before her. Parts of rusting farm machinery lay scattered around the yard. Grass and weeds on clods and piles of earthy waste grew unhindered both against the buildings and across the middle of the rutted concrete. Parts of the corrugated facing on the barn had rusted away and there was little left of two of the wooden stable type doors on the other building whose windows also had lost their glass long ago. Emma didn't know what she had expected but there was such an air of dereliction about the place that she wondered if Placketts farm was in fact occupied any more and if the local knowledge from the inn along the road was up to date.

The farmhouse itself was in perhaps slightly better shape but only marginally. It was a modest uneven shaped building of stone with a tiled roof and from what she could see there were no curtains at any of the windows. Looking around she strained her ear to listen for any sound but there was none. She made her way carefully up to the front door of the farmhouse and rapped the large iron knocker against the plate on the door. The noise was louder than she had expected and it made her step back away from the door in surprise. She strained to listen if there was any sound from within but she could hear none. Plucking up a little more courage she stepped forward again to give it one last try. As she raised the knocker a second time a voice behind her suddenly said, 'What do you want then?'

The voice had so startled her that as she turned she let go of the knocker with a loud bang and that made her jump again. Peering out of one of the outhouse doors was a man. Emma strained her eyes to gain more detail but as she did so the man moved forward out of the shadow. He was about six feet tall and thin with what looked like a permanent stoop. He wore a check shirt with sleeves rolled up above the elbow, and faded denims tucked into calf length boots. His skin was well tanned and leathery and the thinning hair was wispy and untidy. Yet the eyes that never moved from Emma were sharp and focussed and suggested a younger man in an older body.

The man took another pace forward and as he did so a collie dog bounded past him and headed for Emma but the man shouted 'Stay!' and the dog immediately obeyed and settled in a crouched position by his feet. 'What do you want, I said?'

'Oh I'm sorry,' said Emma who smiled trying to hide her nervousness, 'You rather took me by surprise.' She hoped her smile would put the man at ease for she felt unnerved by his piercing eyes. 'My name's Emma Bertram and I was hoping you could help me, I…'

'How can I do that then, you lost or sommat?' He started to advance towards her and Emma began to feel frightened but she managed to hold her nerve and kept smiling.

'No, not at all, it's just that I found this,' she held the map out at arms length, 'It was in my aunts possessions. She died recently and, well, I didn't know very much about her and I'm just following up every lead I have.' Emma was still unsure of the man and decided not to tell him about the fact that it was hidden in a package and must therefore surely have some significance. The man took the paper from Emma and looked at it.

'Well its got my farm on it sure enough, but then its also got the King Harold Arms and St Peter's Church on it as well, so it could mean anything.'

'You've not seen it before?' enquired Emma.

'Why should I have done?' He responded, 'sides it looks pretty old to me. I've been here just on ten years now but that looks like it's a lot older than that.' He thrust the map back towards Emma.

'I'm sorry,' said Emma, 'I didn't mean to offend. It's probably at least twenty years old. Although it was in my aunt's things, I think it belonged to my uncle and he died in 1979. You see I know so little about them and my mother also died recently so I'm just trying to find out what I can. I've no idea what this map is about or why my aunt thought it important to have kept it so long.'

Emma paused and sniffed. She hadn't intended or wanted to show emotion but she found herself nevertheless blinking back the tears. The man studied Emma for a moment and looked again at the map she still held. Just then a cold breeze whipped across the courtyard picking up dust and debris that caused them both to shut their eyes momentarily. The dog whined and looked up at her master and Emma shivered.

His expression softened, 'You'd better come in.' he said, and stepping past Emma he opened the front door and disappeared inside. The dog padded past and Emma followed, closing the door behind her.

A narrow hallway led through to a large combined kitchen and sitting room at the back of the house. The dog had already settled on a blanket-covered chair and was eyeing Emma as she stepped into the room.

'You'll have to take me as you find me - I don't get too many visitors up here and that's the way I like it.' He was filling a kettle at the sink as he spoke but paused and turned towards Emma, 'No offence meant.' He said and for the first time a thin smile appeared on his face.

'None taken,' Emma smiled back.

He put the kettle on the large range where a fire was already crackling away. 'You'll have a cup of tea then?' he asked as he busied himself at the cupboards gathering a couple of mugs and the tea caddy.

'Thank you, if it's not too much trouble that would be very nice.'

Emma looked around the room and was pleasantly surprised how clean, organised and homely it looked; such a contrast to the outside. There were even curtains at the two windows, a bright pink floral pattern that suggested a woman's touch.

'I'm sorry, where's my manners, you'd best take a seat.'

He was carrying two steaming mugs of tea and indicated a chair behind where Emma stood. The fierceness in his face had been replaced with a softer look altogether and Emma felt more relaxed and less threatened.

'There's sugar on the table over there,' he said, pointing, 'but my guess is you don't take it, right?'

'Yes, I mean no I don't, thank you,' said Emma and they both laughed. Emma sat down and the man sat in the chair opposite, next to the dog, which received a pat on the head and a stroke along its back. He held the mug cupped between both his strong hands and stared into the brown liquid. They were both silent for a while, then he said, 'I'm sorry if I was a bit abrupt earlier, I've hardly seen a soul up here since my Doris died and they're usually people wanting something. DEFRA officials - that's government people, and people from the council, and tax officials and the like; always wanting to take your money for one reason or another.' He paused and looked up at a picture of a plump smiling lady that beamed back at him from above the fireplace. 'She's been gone nigh on five years now and I still miss her.' His eyes glazed for a moment and then he patted the dog again. 'Sally here is my companion now, aren't you Sal?' The dog gave a contented whine and licked his hand, her eyes staring longingly at him.

'Anyway,' he coughed and cleared his throat. 'You wanted to know about this farm. Let me have another look at that map.' Emma opened her bag and passed it to him. 'Hmm, well it would certainly suggest that this farm is the point of the map,' he said, studying it, 'Ore Lane is a dead end. There used to be another cottage about a quarter of a mile on from here but that fell into disrepair over fifty years ago I've been told, and it's impossible to get any vehicle past the gate to my top field now. It's not marked on the map anyway.' He paused. 'This makes it very interesting, could confirm the gossip.' He said looking intently at the drawing.

Emma leaned forward, 'Gossip, what gossip?'

'Well I don't want to cast any aspersions about your uncle but let me tell you about this place. Before my Doris and I purchased it, this place it had been unoccupied for several years. The fields had well and truly gone fallow and because of that we were able to get it at a knock down price. An old lady, a farmer's wife, had owned it. She couldn't cope with it after her husband died and then she had to go into a nursing home on account of her health. Now rumour has it, only rumour mind, that after she vacated it she rented the buildings out to a London man who used it for shady dealings. You know contraband cigarettes and booze from the continent; avoiding tax and the like. Used to come in on a boat at Hastings or Pevensey Bay where it was quieter so they say though I don't think anything was ever proved. The police raided the place once I'm told but nothing was ever found. Only evidence was from locals who said lorries and vans used to come up and down the lane at all times, especially at night.' He paused to take another sip of tea.

'Then it all stopped, just like that, nothing more was seen of the man from London, the old lady died without leaving a will - no children see - so the place laid empty till it was all sorted out. Then we came along and bought it. My Doris worked hard to make the place look nice.' He paused to look around the room.

'Why would my uncle have a map of this?' Emma said out loud, thinking to herself.

'Maybe your uncle had to drive a van, collect some goods, I dunno, I'm only guessing but he must have had the map for some reason, seems odd to hang onto it though.'

'Yes,' said Emma, slowly trying to make sense of what she had heard. But none of it made sense to her at all. Uncle Ted had been a seaman; he'd spent virtually all his life at sea as far as she knew. But then what did the neighbour, Frances Stevens at Pevensey Bay say? He had left the navy and was working with the fishing boats at Hastings, and he didn't always come home at night. These thoughts were beginning to trouble Emma, surely uncle Ted couldn't have been caught up is some sort of racketeering? She was shaken out of her thoughts by the clock on the dresser chiming six o'clock and she remembered she needed to be on the seafront by half-past to meet Bill Withers. And she still had to find her way back.

++++++++

Higton entered the CID office at Maidstone Police Headquarters with a bounce in his step and a beam on his face.

'What's up with you, looks like you've won the lottery or something,' asked Smurdon looking up.

'Almost as good as Guv,' replied Higton, 'Something very interesting on the Bertram case. Remember Donaldson over at forensics couldn't find any extraneous fingerprints at the house, well of course we had to print the victim and the family for elimination purposes.'

'Yes, yes, I know the procedures. What?' said Smurdon impatiently.

'Well, he got bored yesterday lunchtime and for something to do he fed the family and victims prints into the computer and got a match.'

'Who?'

'Doreen Bertram, the victim. Only she wasn't Doreen Bertram then; here's the details.' Said Higton holding up a file. Smurdon grabbed it, opened the cover and read. *"Doreen Patterson. Two offences for shop lifting at ages 15 and 17. First offence let off with caution, second offence fined £20 and put on probation for one year."*

'Well, well - and there's no doubt?'

Higton shook his head, 'None at all, perfect match apparently.'

'So our rather prim and proper middle class lady with wealth and housekeeper has a background to hide. That's interesting.'

'Ah but there's more.' Higton added excitedly, 'Turn over the page and see who she was known to regularly associate with.'

Smurdon turned the page, 'Now that *is* interesting. I read about that one, biggest robbery ever on the UK mainland at the time. It was one of the things that made me want to be a policeman. There was a lot of speculation as to what really happened. Everyone had their theories of course but nothing definite was ever proved as far as he was concerned,' he said pointing to a name on the file.

He paused and then made his decision. 'Right, go and pull all the files on this and we will look and see if we can make a connection.'

+++++++++

Emma's journey back to the seafront was straightforward apart from some difficulty in finding somewhere nearby to park. She now stood on the seafront pavement looking down on that part of the beach where the fishing huts were. There was a lot of activity now. Several small fishing boats were beached at the waters edge. Two larger ones were moored to buoys a short distance from the shore and men in waders were lifting crates of fish and equipment out of the boats and bringing them ashore.

A young man opened a doorway in a low wooden box near to where Emma stood, pressed a button and a winch sprang into life. The wire hawser lifted about six inches from the pebbles and began to slowly haul one of the boats up onto the beach.

The sun now low in the western sky brightly lit the white and cream fishermen's huts against the back drop of the darker cliff face behind and Emma recalled seeing a picture very similar to the scene before her on a calendar hanging in the tea rooms at Westerham.

Emma looked around. Sure enough there was an old man sitting on the boxes where she had been told earlier in the day that she would find Bill Withers. He wore dark blue trousers and jacket and sported a sailor's cap on his head at a jaunty angle. Poking out from underneath the cap a shock of white hair was visible at the back. Emma guessed he must be about sixty-five years old. He leaned his left elbow on a ledge attached to the side of the hut and was contentedly drawing on a pipe, the smoke curling away behind him on the slight on-shore breeze. He was watching intently the activity on one of the larger boats as Emma approached. She stood quietly behind him for a moment forming the words in her mind that she would speak. Without moving or turning his head he spoke. 'I suppose you are the young lass who was asking questions here this morning?'

'Oh hello, yes that's me, I'm Emma Bertram,' she said stepping forward. He took the pipe from his mouth and turning eyed her up and down. 'You've got a photograph I hear?'

'Yes,' said Emma reaching into her shoulder bag. 'This is the one. Do you recognise anyone or the boat even?'

He studied the picture for some time and then asked, 'Where did you get this?'

'It was in my aunt's possessions, she died recently and I'm just trying to find out more about her,' she paused, 'You see I only found out recently that I had an aunt,' she added quietly.

He looked up at her, a frown on his face and studied her eyes. He noticed there was a little moisture at the corner of each of them. 'You only just found out that you had an aunt?' he enquired.

Emma bit her lip and nodded.

He turned back to the photograph, 'Yes I know the boat and the men, or at least two of them. Not sure about this one,' he said pointing to Emma's uncle, 'Think I might have seen him around but it's a long time ago now. The two on the right,' he said pointing, 'are Jo and James Hewetson and the boat is the *Jenny Kathleen*. They named it after their mother, God rest her soul.'

'I think one of the other men is my uncle, the one you've just pointed to. He died some years ago so I never met him but my aunt has other pictures and I'm certain it's the same man.' She paused; 'Do the Hewetsons still live and fish around here?' said Emma surveying the beach as if she might even at that moment spot them. 'I'd love to talk to them.'

'That's something I'm afraid you'll not be able to do young lady. They're both six-foot under in St Peter's graveyard over there,' he said motioning vaguely behind him with his left hand. He paused to look at his pipe that had gone out. He turned it upside down and knocked it against the side of the hut until the burnt remains fell out onto the pebbled beach by his feet.

'You'd better sit down while I tell you a story. Here, put this on those boxes there and squat on that,' he said handing her a fleece lined jacket which Emma carefully folded before sitting on it. She clasped her knees up under her chin and looked up intently at him wondering what he was going to reveal.

The old man leant his elbow on the ledge again and sucked on his unlit pipe before turning towards Emma, 'Joseph and James were good lads when they were young. There was only about eighteen months between them. Joseph was the oldest but they got on extremely well together. Always helping their dad they were. He fished these waters for many years; always working long hours to see the boys had a good upbringing and schooling. Then one November a force nine suddenly blew up out in the channel. Edwin was out with the Foleys on their boat and he lost his footing as the boat hit a mountainous wave. He slipped poor bugger and cracked his head open on the forward hatch combing - dead in an instant.'

He pursed his lips and said quietly, 'I still remember the night they brought him ashore.' Emma watched as he relived in his mind the events of that night. He continued, 'Old ma Hewetson never really recovered from the shock and the boys went a bit wild after that. Word has it they got themselves into a shady deal or two, booze and cigarettes from the continent, that sort of thing. Perhaps something a bit more sinister - who knows? Anyway within a little over a year they had a new boat, would have cost a fair packet too and kitted out with all the latest sonar and radar equipment as well. Couldn't have afforded that on the strength of the fishing they did. Never worked as hard as did Edwin that's for sure.'

He paused and then asked, 'Was your uncle from London?'

'I don't think so,' replied Emma. 'He spent most of his life at sea in the Merchant Navy from what I can make out. My aunt lived over at

Pevensey, a navy widow by all accounts. Then shortly after uncle retired they moved to a place just south of Bristol. Why do you ask?'

'Well from time to time we would see the boys with a stranger or two. Word was they were from London. You know; not the sort you would want to bump into down a dark alley at night.'

'Oh,' said Emma.

'Still I don't suppose your uncle was mixed up in any of that,' he said to try and reassure her.

'No,' said Emma feeling less certain than her voice sounded. She recalled the gossip the farmer had related to her earlier in the day. Could uncle have been mixed up in something like this? Was that why mother had never mentioned she had a sister? Why she had kept a distance from them? It would certainly be in mother's nature to do that.

They both sat in silence for a while and the old man handed the photograph back to Emma while he took a new fill of tobacco from his pouch and re-lit the pipe.

Emma looked at the photograph that she held. Her uncle smiling, the forth man his face hidden in the shadow of his hand, the man she had first thought might be her father. No it can't be; I'm so confused she thought. Then the two brothers the fishermen, she studied them again.

'How, how did they die?' she asked quietly.

He drew on his pipe and exhaled slowly, 'In mysterious circumstances is the best way to answer that. It was, oh, about twenty-five year ago now. The brothers had gotten deeper into this thing with the London mob. Traffic was not just in contraband; it was in people too. The authorities never knew, but those of us who lived and worked here by the sea - we knew what was going on. Only the occasional passenger mind, sometimes one way, sometimes both. Don't know how they did it, whether they landed in a remote spot in France or if a transfer was made at sea; best not to know. You certainly didn't ask any questions.' He paused.

'I saw one or two of them, late at night when I was in the shed here and they thought everyone had gone home. Shady looking characters most of them. Anyway one night they went out with a passenger and the *Jenny Kathleen* never returned. They found James body first, in the water about eight miles out. Then Joseph's was washed up along the coast two day later. Boat was never found, nor any other body, but two of us saw them leave that night and there was certainly a third person with them.'

'What do you think happened?' Asked Emma listening intently.

'Well, that's a mystery too. They found the boat eventually, 'bout a mile from where they had picked up James. Divers from the Marine

Accident Department went down and found the sea cocks open, the boat sunk deliberately. Now why would they have done that? They had no money worries as far as anyone knew. The boat was all paid for. It all came out in the Coroner's Court. An open verdict was recorded on them both. I testified along with Bill Johnson that we had seen another person board the boat that night but nothing else and no other body was ever found to substantiate it.'

He stopped to draw on his pipe.

'How awful,' said Emma, 'And you're convinced there was a third man on that last trip?'

'I know there was but the local police weren't interested, it was all done and dusted as far as they were concerned. Funny thing was though, about three weeks later, we had a visit from a couple of London detectives, asked a lot of questions about this third man, what did he look like, how old was he, what was he wearing and so on. Well I couldn't tell them much - it was dark and raining, but they seemed very interested. Then off they went but I heard nothing more.'

He turned and looked at Emma. 'And that's about all I can tell you, young lady.'

Chapter 12

Emma drearily came to and focussed her eyes on the bedside clock. It was 8.45am. The sun was already streaming in through the gap in the curtains and painting a bright strip down the front of the pine wardrobe that stood against the far wall. She had had a fitful night. Images of her trip to the coast the previous day and more especially images of the events and happenings that had been described to her by the farmer, Wilf Johnson and fisherman Bill Withers had invaded her mind. Several times she had woken in a sweat, the bedclothes tangled around her. She had a vivid picture of the fishing boat tossing in tremendous seas, the look of pure fright on the faces of the two brothers as they battled against the elements - but then the sea was calm, there was a thick mist, but their fear remained. What were they afraid of? A shadow of a man appeared through the mist. He was turning a valve with his hands. Emma tried to see the man's face; it had a determined evil look. At first she thought it looked like her uncle, but then it changed. Now it looked like the young man in the car, the one that had been pursuing her. He was looking straight at her. Emma gasped; she heard a scream and looked round. There was mother lying on the ground, blood pumping from her chest. She turned, she wanted to run, but she ran straight into the man in the mist. He no longer turned a valve, but held a knife that dripped with blood. She forced herself to look at his face. This time it was the fisherman, then the farmer, her uncle, the young man, the man from the photograph - the man she believed may be her father. The face kept changing as she tossed and turned in the sweat soaked bed.

She lay there staring at the ceiling where a tree, just outside of her bedroom window, was casting strange shapes and images as it played with the sunlight while it danced on the morning breeze. Even these bright patterns seemed to have a sinister content and she shuddered. She was relieved when Valerie Marcheson tapped gently on the door and entered the room with a welcome cup of tea.

'My, you've been having quite a fight I see!' she said trying to make light of the scene in front of her and remembering that only recently had Emma begun again to sleep right through the night.

Emma pulled herself up while Valerie puffed up a pillow behind her. She took hold of the saucer with one hand and the cup with the other to stop it rattling, and took a sip. 'Yes, it wasn't a particularly pleasant one. All the events and happenings I heard about yesterday, they were all mixed up in a horrible dream. And that image of mother was there again…' Her voice trailed off in a sob.

Valerie gently sat on the edge of the bed and put an arm around her. 'O my poor love, you really ought to let things be. Just be content with the memories you have of your mother. You don't need to go delving into the past; you could bring up things that, well, are best left untouched.'

Emma turned to her, a questioning look spread across her face, 'You don't know anything about mother that you haven't told me do you? Please Valerie, I've got to know.'

'No my love, I don't. I often wondered, especially in the early days when I first came here why your mother never talked about her past, her family, upbringing and so on. I tried to raise things in conversation, casual like, but she always changed the subject as if it was best left untouched.' She paused for a moment and then continued, 'Your mother didn't show her emotions much did she, but I felt sometimes as if the reason she wouldn't talk about it was that the memory was too painful for her to bear.'

She sighed and then spoke again, 'That's why I said maybe it's best left untouched, whatever it is.'

'I know you mean well,' said Emma nestling her head against Valerie's shoulder, 'but I've got to know, I've just got to. And I can't rest or relax until I do.'

'I know my dear, I just don't want you to get hurt anymore,' she said with concern, 'You've suffered more than any girl of your age should.'

She gave Emma a hug with her arm and kissed the top of her head. Slipping off the bed she said, 'I'll leave you to drink your tea, why don't you have a lie in, there's no need to get up yet, I can get breakfast when you are ready.'

'Thanks.' Said Emma with half a smile.

'That's better.' Replied Valerie returning the smile, but as she turned and left the room there was concern written all over her face.

+++++++++

'All right Miss… No that's fine, you were right to call us. We'll have our patrols in the area keep a special lookout. Now try not to worry, we'll get to the bottom of this… All right, thanks for your call… Goodbye.' Higton replaced the receiver as Smurdon walked into the office.

'Anything important?'

'Just had Emma Bertram on the 'phone, seems she was followed for a while yesterday by a young man in a light blue car.'

'No doubt about it?'

'No, she took him on a tour of the Chartwood factory estate to try and shake him off, and succeeded but she says absolutely no doubt about it.'

'Description, registration?'

'She didn't get any registration and wasn't sure about the make of car. Thinks it may have been a Ford and quite a new one but that's all. She gave a good description of the driver though. Young, mid to late twenties, dark hair, tanned complexion, clean-shaven. Certainly sounds like the man we spotted at the funeral and Miss Bertram is pretty certain she saw him in Westerham a few days later.'

'He didn't make contact with her though?' Smurdon asked.

'No, seems he had every opportunity. She was sitting in a café alone when he walked past the window and as she put it, 'their eyes definitely met'.'

Smurdon slumped in the swivel chair behind his desk and leant back. Gazing at the ceiling and deep in thought he idly picked up a pen and ran it back and forth through his fingers. But his brain was far from idle. 'Now why would you want to follow someone, close up in full view rather than keeping your distance, if you didn't want to make contact with them?' He was quiet for a moment. 'And what connection is there between him and our two murderers in the black BMW?'

'There must be something,' said Higton pursing his lips and rubbing his chin.

'Hmm…' said the inspector. 'Right, make sure Uniform branch and Traffic as well as our boys keep a sharp look out for this chap and bring him in for questioning when he's found. He seems to be hanging around the area for some reason. Let's find out what it is.' He paused. 'Anything on the other business?'

'Files should be with us later today, the Met are sending them down on a courier.' Replied Higton.

+++++++++

After Emma had reported the incident to constable Higton, she telephoned Jane and tried to make conversation. At first Jane sounded a little icy but when Emma began to tell her of her trip to the south coast the day before Jane's attitude changed immediately and her tone became conciliatory. She had an appointment to do the hair of an elderly lady in Broadhurst just after lunch but she would call round to *Tall Trees* immediately after that. She wanted to hear everything that Emma had discovered.

+++++++++

As Emma shared with Jane all that had happened with the events of the day before Jane became her old self. The rapport between the two women grew and any frostiness had soon melted away as Jane eagerly took in all that Emma had to say. Jane was quick to ask questions and get clarification on various points as Emma unfolded the details of her trip. She showed especial concern when Emma related the incident of being followed and insisted that Emma should not do any more investigating on her own. Emma had found Jane's enquiring mind helpful and between them they tried to build up a clearer picture of all that had happened those twenty five or more years ago and what relevance if any there was to the mysterious and unknown early years of her mother, Doreen Bertram. At one stage Jane had asked, 'Have you told the police about any of this?'

'Only about being followed, I didn't think anything else was relevant.' replied Emma. 'Do you think I ought to tell the Inspector then?'

'No, I can't see that any of it is related to what has happened here and anyway much of it appears to be speculation.' Jane had replied.

Jane had stayed for tea and Emma sat back now sipping from her cup as she watched Jane looking again at the photographs and studying the notes that Emma had made the night before. As she bent forward strands of her long blond hair fell across her face and she flicked it back with a swift movement of her third finger. Emma smiled to herself as she watched. She was glad that their friendship was healed again and realised just how much Jane had come to mean to her over these past few weeks. She had really appreciated the strength and support that Jane had given her especially immediately after Mother's death and through the funeral and then with Millie's death coming so soon after.

She stifled a yawn and Jane looked up. 'It's getting late, I must go, and you look tired.'

'I'm sorry,' said Emma, 'I guess everything must be catching up on me.'

'Well you make sure you get plenty of rest and when you decide to do anymore detective work I want to come with you, okay?'

'Yes, I promise.' replied Emma.

After Jane had gone Emma checked the house was secure. Valerie Marcheson had gone to visit her sister who had been taken ill, and would not be back for a day or two. Emma had assured her she would be all right on her own and had made her promise not to rush back. She went from room to room on the ground floor checking that all the windows and doors were securely locked. She soon found herself in the day room; the room Mother liked to sit in most. Emma stood behind Mother's favourite chair and rested her hand gently on the back. She had not bothered to turn on the light and the nearly full moon shone brightly though the open curtains. Emma looked around the room at all the familiar things that were part of Mother's life. The books she liked to read, her favourite magazines, her embroidery frame and the box containing the silks and threads, her writing desk. She pictured Mother sitting there as she so often did, writing letters and dealing with the household bills. Emma walked across to the desk and sat down. It was a nineteenth century oak bureau, the type where the desk flap hinged down from the top. She touched the handle. Although she had had cause to open it several times since Mother's death she still felt an intruder. As if she was prying into what had been a very private life. She switched the desk light on and eased the lid down and sat there staring at the familiar things. Mother's reading glasses, the Parker fountain pen, ink bottle and blotter, paper clips and postage stamps. Emma sat there for a while her palms resting lightly on the leather inlaid desktop. She found herself thinking back to those times when her nanny would bring her in to say goodnight. If Mother were not busy she would be allowed to climb up onto her lap and play with the pencils and the relief stamp that impressed the *Tall Trees* address on the stationery when the large brass handle was pulled down. And Mother would let her open the secret drawer that did not look like a drawer at all until it was released by a catch hidden in one of the alcoves. The hidden drawer! Emma had forgotten about that. She reached in and found the catch and pulled it towards her. It was stiff but eventually she released it with a click and the drawer popped open. There were a few paper fasteners and a well-used rubber, no doubt put there by Emma herself when playing as a youngster, along with two little plastic people that Emma vaguely remembered getting out of a Christmas cracker one year. To one side a stiff tube of paper was tightly rolled with an elastic band around it. Emma picked it up, carefully pulled the band away, and unrolled the tube. She sat staring at the paper in her hand. It was another airmail envelope addressed to her in the same handwriting as the one she had discovered on the day of the funeral and like the first it was postmarked from Denia, Alicante in Spain. Again there was no letter inside, just the envelope. This one was dated about two months prior to the first.

Emma sat there for a while bewildered and then set about systematically working her way through every drawer and pigeon hole in the bureau, sifting through every piece of stationery and paperwork. There were bills and statements, old Christmas cards and holiday postcards from friends in the town, notepaper and envelopes. Estimates for repairs and notes about things that needed seeing to: insurance documents and bank statements, but no letters from Spain, nothing whatsoever to link with the mysterious envelopes. Why? Why would Mother have kept these envelopes and not the letters and what did the letters contain that was so important or secret that they could not be shown to her? And why open an envelope addressed to her daughter anyway unless she knew what it contained? And how did she know that - it must have been by the postmark or the handwriting. But Emma didn't know anyone in Spain and neither did Mother as far as she knew. 'Oh Mother!' sighed Emma, 'What am I to make of it all?'

+++++++++

It was late afternoon the next day when Smurdon returned to the office at police headquarters in Maidstone. He was fuming. 'I've been at court all day on the Bristow case and what did that little thug get? A slap on the wrist from that doddery old Judge Markham and a warning that he might go to prison if he did it again. My God, he's a psychopath that one. If someone doesn't lock him up soon they'll have a murder on their hands.' He slammed the door shut and threw his coat over the bench in the corner. Higton looked up wearily from the pile of files in front of him but remained silent. He knew better than to interrupt.

'The man had twenty-three stitches and was in hospital for four days and that bloody Bristow and his smooth counsel somehow convinces the Judge that he only responded in self-defence.' He shook his head, 'Makes you wonder if this job is worth doing sometimes.' He slumped hard in the chair and massaged the back of his neck with his palm. Tossing his head back he yawned and looked at Higton. 'You look like I feel, you got anything?'

'No, at least nothing to link Doreen Bertram, or Doreen Patterson as she was then, with this case.'

Smurdon shifted in his chair to get more comfortable, 'Go through the background of the case for me.'

'Well.' Said Higton, 'It started way back; there was the four of them. They were all teenagers when they first started to get into trouble. Doreen Patterson, Robbie Wilson, John Peters and Barry Masters, they were always together, couldn't be separated apparently. Got themselves into shoplifting, petty theft, and the boys for drunk and disorderly and so on. Then, in their early twenties, Wilson and Peters were put away for robbery on a sub-post office. Both got two years. It was generally believed according to the file that Masters was involved as well, quite probably the brains behind it but nothing could ever be proved.'

He paused to sip some cold tea. 'It was while these two were inside that Masters and Patterson became an item; kept out of trouble as far as we know. He was a bouncer in a nightclub just off the London docks; she worked behind the bar. The club was a well known haunt for gangsters of the day and according to the sheet was regularly raided by the local force.'

He shifted forward and picked up another file. 'Now we come to the big one. As you know the raid on the Sureguard security van near Heathrow Airport was one of the largest ever at the time. Around twelve million in gold bars, cash and securities went missing on an August Sunday afternoon in 1972. A Sureguard employee was shot dead. It was a well-executed raid with impeccable inside information. After extensive interviews it is still not known where the information came from. The file concludes it must have been the dead employee. There were no leads at first; then the Met had a tip off from a petty criminal named Hunter about Wilson and Peters. They raided a warehouse and found them in possession of some of the bonds and details of the robbery. At interview and at the trial they implicated Masters, they believed they had been set up, double-crossed and that it was Masters himself who had sent the tip off. They also denied the murder stating that they had no knowledge that Masters was going to produce a weapon.'

He sighed and looked up, 'An extensive search was conducted, one of the biggest manhunts in criminal history. There were reported sightings from Newquay to Newcastle, Hastings to Haverford West. There's still a warrant out for his arrest but what, twenty eight years on and he's never been found.'

'Not likely to either,' said Smurdon. 'If I remember right it's generally thought he ended up in the concrete foundations of one of those office blocks near St. Paul's Cathedral.'

'Yes, the file says they were unable to determine if Masters was the mastermind behind the robbery or if someone else was involved. In fact there was only the word of Peters and Wilson that Masters had anything to do with it. There was no other evidence. Word on the street at the time implicated the Harvan brothers who were believed to give concrete shoes to anyone who crossed their path but again nothing was proved. Masters never surfaced; his possessions and flat were left untouched, as was his bank account. There's a paragraph in the report that Patterson was interviewed at length but she was utterly distraught about his disappearance and convincing that she had no knowledge of the proposed robbery of Sureguard.'

'And no further monies or bullion were ever recovered,' said Smurdon.

'That's right.' Replied Higton. 'Nothing has ever come to light. Wilson and Peters maintained Masters drove the bulk away in a van but they didn't know where to.'

'Very trusting weren't they?' he said with sarcasm. 'Hmm...' he paused, thinking for a moment. 'So twenty-eight years later we discover Doreen Patterson is now Doreen Bertram and living the life of a well to do middle class lady that's not short of a penny or two. What about Wilson & Peters, they must have been released years ago. Anything on them since they got out.'

'Nothing on file on Peters, Wilson went down for another two years for handling stolen property within months of being released. Got out about eight years ago, nothing since.' Higton answered checking one of the files on the desk in front of him.

'Okay, so let's assume Masters got some or all of the money to Doreen Bertram before he was disposed of by the Harvan brothers, Wilson and Peters would be pretty anxious to speak to her wouldn't they.'

'So they eventually trace her, find her and kill her.'

'No, I don't think they meant to kill her, remember what I said at the time. It wasn't a robbery gone wrong, they wanted information, they wanted to know where the rest of the haul was but something went wrong and I don't think they got what they went for.'

He put both hands on the desk in front of him and stood up. 'Right, have we got addresses for Wilson and Peters? We'll go and pay them a visit first thing in the morning, and get a mug shot of them both down to that nursing home near Bristol and see if either of them was our bogus policeman that worried the life out of Doreen Bertram's sister.

Chapter 13

Emma was up early. She felt refreshed after relaxing at home the previous day. Valerie Marcheson had telephoned to say that she really needed to remain with her sister for another couple of days and Emma was happy for her to do so. She was quite enjoying the preparing and cooking of her own meals and even being alone in the house had not worried her as much as she thought it might. Jane had offered to stay but Emma would not hear of it and was insistent that Jane should get on with her hairdressing business.

It was another fine but crisp morning and Emma was just returning to the house after a circuit of the back garden when she heard the telephone ringing. She hurried through the back door and picked up the extension in the kitchen.

'Hello'

'Is that Miss Bertram?' It was a man's voice. It sounded young and nervous.

Emma was cautious, 'Who's that?'

'It's P...Peter Keywood, You may remember me, I w...work for C...Curtis Forsythe, the solicitors.' He stammered.

Emma relaxed a little, 'Are you the young man who fell over in the lobby when I opened the door that time?'

'Y...Yes, that's right. Um... I've met someone who knows about y...your mother, they want to meet you.'

'What do they know? Where, who?' Emma was puzzled.

'Th...they didn't say, just that it was important. C...can you come now; I'll meet you outside Woolworths in t...twenty minutes.'

'Twenty minutes? Why outside Woolworths?' Emma queried.

'Th...they said it was best, er; the office doesn't open until ten, and they ss...said it was important.' He stuttered again.

Emma thought for a moment, it sounded very odd but perhaps they had called at the solicitors' office and found it closed. She made up her mind, 'All right, I'll be there.'

She hung up and then dialled Jane remembering her promise to keep Jane informed. If Jane went with her she would feel better about the meeting. Jane's mobile was switched off and the answer phone cut in. Emma thought quickly and left a message, 'I'm going to meet someone who can tell me something about Mother. Can you meet me outside Woolworths at nine thirty this morning, hope you get this message, bye.'

Emma locked the back door, grabbed her coat and headed for the garage. At this time of the morning she should just make the rendezvous in time but it would be tight. She hoped the traffic would not be too heavy.

Emma was in luck; there were still a couple of parking spaces in the high street. They were limited to one hour but she reckoned that would be long enough for this mysterious meeting. She parked up with a minute to spare. There was no sign of Jane or the young man outside of Woolworths but she got out and walked the short distance to the shop front. She looked up and down the street to no avail but then out of the corner of her eye she saw Peter Keywood waving to her from across the street. He was standing at the entrance to an alleyway that led between two shops and then round the back of one of them to an overflow car park that was usually only used on market days. He beckoned her. She checked the road was clear and crossed. As she did so he began to walk up the alley.

'C...come on.' He called, 'This way.'

Emma felt a little unease creeping into her mind, an alarm bell was ringing caution in her ears but she needed to know everything she could find out about Mother and that drove her on, she so wished Jane were with her. She walked cautiously down the centre of the path, her eyes darting from left to right but the few recessed doorways that were there were empty. She turned the corner slowly and looked into the car park. There were just two cars parked near each other. One she could see was empty but the other had tinted glass that made it impossible to look in from a distance. The young man approached the tinted glass car, turned, and continued to wave her on. As she neared him she could see that he was very nervous.

'Are you all right?' Emma asked. But the young man did not respond, he opened the back door of the car and pointed.

'T...this is th...the man you want.'

Emma approached the car cautiously and ducked down to peer into the car. Before she could speak the occupant, a hooded man, grabbed hold of her arm and held her. A huge thick sack was thrown over her head from behind and pulled down quickly over her body to pinion her arms. She was bundled roughly into the back of the car and she heard the man say, 'Quickly Kev, let's get moving.'

The door banged shut behind her and she felt arms reach out and hold her down. She tried to scream but her head was pushed roughly down into the seat so that she could hardly breathe. She heard what sounded like the young man that had led her to the car, shout out, then the car jolted as if a struggle was going on outside. She heard the sound of a car door or boot closing somewhere and then the car rocked again as someone got in and started the engine. In an instant she felt a sudden motion and the noise of tyres squealing on the tarmac as the car sped out of the car park.

The man in the back eased his grip on her but as soon as she began to struggle he held he more tightly. He shouted harshly. 'Take it easy and you won't get hurt, struggle and it will be painful for you.'

Loud music blared from the speakers in the car as it wound its way through the traffic and Emma was conscious of the man tapping a beat on her back with his hand as he held her down. Emma fought to control her fear and breathing. It became very hot inside the sack and there was an unpleasant odour from it that made her feel nauseous. She closed her eyes and forced herself to breathe slowly. For a while the car travelled at speed but then Emma was aware of a slower motion with the car stopping regularly. Each time she could hear the noise of other traffic, the occasional honk of a horn and the sound of pedestrians as they walked past the car. It seemed to go on endlessly until the car stopped and this time the driver got out. Then she heard another sound. She guessed it was a metal shutter being raised by hand. It sounded just like the one at the greengrocers in Chartwood that she had often heard.

The driver returned, drove the car forward, then got out again and Emma heard the shutter being closed. Neither man spoke as she was bundled out. Her shoulder bag was pulled from her arm and a rope bound around her wrists as her arms were drawn behind her back.

Pushed forward she almost stumbled as her shin caught on a sharp hard object and she let out a yelp of pain. Someone took her arm roughly and led her down a passage; her heels echoing on the hard and dirty concrete floor that she could just discern from where the sack finished down by her knees. She was aware that the floor sloped and the further they went so the light dimmed that she could no longer see anything through the small opening.

'Stop here.' The same voice as the man in the car.

A door was unlocked and she was ushered through it.

'Don't waste your time calling and screaming, no one will ever hear you here.'

'What do you want with me, what is this all about?' Cried Emma.

'We'll be back.' Was all he said and with that the door clanged shut. Emma heard him turn a key and then his footsteps receded along the passageway.

For a moment Emma was frozen on the spot. Her face was hot from the confinement and wet from tears of fear. Again she had to force herself to stay calm, to control the shaking, if only she could get the sack from off her head. She knelt down slowly onto the floor and then gently rolled first onto her side and then onto her back. The floor was hard and cold but so far there was nothing to impede her movement. Holding the sack down with her hands she dug her heels in and pulled her bottom downwards, at the same time twisting her shoulders to lift it away from her face. It was working; she was slowly making progress out of the sack. After several attempts she was able to shake herself free. She rolled again on her side and brought her feet up tight in the foetal position and managed to force one leg and then the other through the loop of her tied wrists. She sat up. Her hands were now in front of her and she used them to brush the hair from her eyes. She looked around. The room was cold and dank, about three metres square with bare brick walls that had been whitewashed long ago and dirtied much since. The trappings of a disused office greeted her eyes. A broken and dust laden desk with a well-worn swivel chair occupied one wall, a cork display board above it held scraps of discoloured and curling paper with the printing and writing on them barely discernible. Against one wall a pile of cardboard storage boxes sagged under their own weight with some split open spilling their contents of old office documents across the floor. Wires poked from a tube on the ceiling where a lamp holder dangled a dirty bulb whose dim light barely reached the floor and walls. The only other light in the room came from a small narrow window high up on one wall. There were two doors in the room. Emma tried the first but it was locked, the second opened onto a narrow passageway with a door at the end of it. That also was locked but Emma could see from the strip of light around it and the cool breeze that she could feel at the edges of it that this door opened to the outside. Halfway along this short passage another door opened into a very dirty and smelly toilet that clearly had not been used and certainly not cleaned for a very long time. Emma returned to the main room, sank to the floor and stared at her prison cell, then resting both elbows on her knees she sunk her head into her hands and began to sob.

+++++++++

'What news?' asked Smurdon as he came through the door carrying two polystyrene cups of coffee from the machine on the landing. Smurdon had spent the morning interviewing Robbie Wilson at his dingy nightclub in the East End of London and at the same time Higton has called on Peters at his flat in Barking in the east London suburbs. Getting no reply, he called on a neighbour who said he had told her he was going into hospital for a few days but she didn't know what for.

Higton put the phone down, 'Checks out, he's in Ilford District Hospital. Had an operation yesterday to remove gall stones and is expected to be out in just under the week.' He paused. 'I'll make a note to follow him up as soon as he's out. How did you get on with Wilson?'

'Claimed not to know a Doreen Bertram. When I said she was also known as Doreen Patterson, he said he'd not see her in twenty years and had no wish to. But he volunteered that if it Barry Masters had still been alive he would certainly want to see him. He's still adamant that Masters was the brains behind the Sureguard robbery and that he was the one who shopped him.'

'Did you buy it?' asked Higton.

'No not really. He was pretty convincing but I'd never believe scum like that. They'd shop their own mother if it suited them.' sneered Smurdon. 'But we've got no evidence to link them to the killing of Doreen Bertram as yet so we'll just have to keep digging.' He sighed.

'We've also had a reply back from that nursing home near Bristol, they think the bogus policeman may have been Peters, at least they say he was the same build but that's about all. Not a lot of help really!'

+++++++++

Emma tried to rub her wrists against her face. The rope around them was quite tight making her wrists both sore and numb. Red blotches had already appeared on her skin where the rope had chaffed it. She looked at her watch; at least they hadn't taken that away, though she presumed they had her bag which contained her mobile phone. She had been bundled into the room just before 11am and it was now coming up to 2pm. Three hours. In that time she had heard very little. There was the distant rumble of traffic and she was able to distinguish the sound of railway trains quite frequently. Occasionally she could hear voices, mainly of children, but they were muffled and she was unable to detect what they were saying. By the fact that they had travelled for just over an hour and towards the end of the journey had slowed considerably in what must have been heavier traffic she thought that perhaps she was being held somewhere in a London suburb but it was no more than a guess. The tears had gone and she was calmer now although in the confines of this her prison cell a real fear remained. It clawed at her mind and she had to concentrate with all the mental strength she had left to push it into the background and focus her thoughts on her predicament.

Jane, she realised was the only one who would be aware of her trip into town. When would she get the message and would she follow it up? If she was busy she may not try to contact her until this evening and even then there was no certainty. Why had she been kidnapped? For that was surely what it was. Until now kidnapping and mysterious happenings like that with the Hewetson Brothers at Hastings were only found in novels or television dramas, although Emma cared for neither. She preferred natural world programmes and documentaries from far away places. She loved reading biographies and autobiographies. She had read with fascination the accounts of Christopher Columbus, Tasman and Magellan. Of David Livingstone, Scott and Hillary. Heroes of the real world, not some make believe James Bond type so distant from reality. It had to be something to do with Mother's death, and Aunt Millie and Uncle Ted, and the Hewetson brothers, but what? Emma scanned the room again with her eyes. The layout and drabness of it suggested it had sometime been an office of a store or warehouse but probably not been in use for a very long time.

She hauled herself up using the old chair as a lever and studied the notice board in detail. Fragments of paper still attached by rusting pins revealed little other than dates in the late 1970's and meaningless part numbers and references that meant nothing to Emma. There was a drawer to the desk that would not budge at Emma's first attempt but she braced herself and with all her strength managed to dislodge it with a further tug. For all her efforts the drawer contained little more than some rusty paper clips, a broken ruler, the stubs of two pencils and a couple of startled spiders.

Emma sat on the dusty chair and looked around again. She had long given up worrying about her trousers and coat which by now were marked and scuffed with dirt from the floor and furniture. She could still smell the nauseating odour on her clothes from the sack that had been thrust over her head and which now lay in the corner where Emma had kicked it. Her eyes settled on the cardboard boxes with their contents spilling out. She dragged the chair across the room and sitting there, searched the papers that had been scattered. They were all hand written carbon copies containing names and addresses of garages and motor spares shops. References and part numbers similar to those she had seen on the notice board filled the body of the form together with their prices. Other than that there was nothing printed on the forms. Emma reasoned they were copy invoices. If she could find a top sheet with the company's name and address it might just give a clue to where she was.

Although her hands were still tied and now getting very sore she ignored the pain and clawed at the next available box and toppled it from the stack. It fell to the floor with a thud but did not burst open, as she had expected the twenty-year-old tape holding firm. Emma kicked at the box in frustration and it soon broke open but the contents were more of the same. She grabbed a second box, then a third and a fourth, kicking each to spill the contents over the floor but was rewarded with the same. As she hurled maybe the twelfth or thirteenth box down her concentration was such that she did not hear the footsteps approaching in the passage outside. As the last box broke open revealing a different form with a printed heading the door threw open and a man entered.

Emma stepped back against the boxes and gasped in fear. He was the same man from the car, tall but slim and dressed in black from head to foot. His hands were gloved and he wore a balaclava over his head with slits just big enough for his eyes, nose and mouth. Emma could not look away from his eyes, they were green and piercing, it made her spine tingle just to look at them. There was something menacing and evil about them.

He spoke with a London accent, 'Well now, I see you've made yourself at home'. He looked around at the paper littered floor. 'Taking your frustrations out on that lot ain't going to help you none,' he laughed. Then his tone abruptly changed and he moved forward so his face was only a few inches from Emma's, 'Right, sit down Miss. You are going to answer some questions.'

Emma stood frozen to the spot, pressed against the boxes. She shook her head and tried to say 'No' but all that came out was a high-pitched squeal. The man stepped forward, grabbed her arm roughly and propelled her into the chair.

'I said sit down!' he yelled.

'Right now, you little stuck up Miss, I want some information. You are going to tell me where your father is.' He leant forward spitting the words out as he did so.

Emma was shaken. 'What do you mean,' she said, 'My father is dead.'

'Like hell he is, don't give me that one.'

'But he is.' cried Emma. 'I never knew him; he died before I was born. That was twenty-seven years ago. You must be mistaken.'

'No way girl. With twelve million in bullion and cash you may disappear, you may fake your death, but you don't die.' he sneered at her and Emma began to sob.

'You must believe me, I never knew my father, I wish I had, I don't know what you are talking about. Why have you brought me here? Why have you kidnapped me? I want to leave, you cannot keep me here. I want to go home!' Emma had become hysterical. She was standing now, shaking and shouting, tears streaming down her face. The man stepped forward again and slapped Emma hard across the face.

'Shut up you silly bitch and sit down!'

Emma slumped back in the chair and held her hands to her face. The shock of the slap now replaced with a searing sting. Her face hurt, her wrists and arms hurt, she felt dirty, confused and frightened. What little strength she had just seemed to ebb away as once again the tears came.

She was hardly aware that the man had returned to the door. He dragged a cardboard box in from outside and left it by the door.

'Here you are you little bitch, there's some food there and some interesting reading matter for you. Maybe after a night down here you'll be ready to talk.' With that he slammed the door shut and turned the key. Emma was too distraught to take any notice of his comment or hear his footsteps recede up the passageway.

++++++++++

It was just after 6pm and Smurdon was leaving the headquarters building at Maidstone. He had had a rough day. Statistics for the last quarter showed an increase in unsolved serious crime and he'd received a scolding from his divisional boss who in turn had received one from the Assistant Chief Constable. The mood in the CID office was not good and he was glad to be going home.

As he reached his car, Higton yelled at him from a second floor window and was beckoning him back. The noise of the commuter traffic on the roadway outside snatched his words away even though Smurdon had cupped his hand to his ear.

'This better be bloody good', he murmured to himself as he trudged the route back to the incident room.

'What's up?' he scowled.

'Just had that Jane Dennington on the phone, says Emma Bertram has disappeared.' Higton replied. 'Seems she switched on her mobile late morning and got an odd message from Miss Bertram asking to be met outside Woolworths. Said she was going there to meet someone who could tell her about her mother. Dennington went down there as soon as she could but of course was several hours late. She's also been up to the Bertram house but there's no sign of her. Says Miss Bertram promised to keep in touch and its right out of character for her. She can't raise her on her mobile either, it's switched off.

'H'mm' said Smurdon. 'More likely gone off on some wild goose chase like she did before. Did Dennington say if Miss Bertram was meeting a man or a woman?'

Higton shook his head, 'Bertram just told her 'someone'.'

Smurdon paused for a while thinking. 'Who's on late shift?'

'Kennedy is here,' Higton replied pointing to a thick-set man that had just entered the room.

'Right Kennedy did you hear that? Get over to Miss Dennington and take a statement. Get all the details you can. If Bertram has not shown or made contact by morning we'll alert Missing Persons and get her description circulated.' He paused and turned to the door, 'There's not much we can do now and we don't know for sure that she is missing.' he paused, 'This time I am definitely going home.'

+++++++++

Kennedy sat in his car outside Jane Dennington's house and looked at his notes. He had spent the best part of an hour taking her statement and she seemed clearly worried that this was out of character for Emma Bertram, especially in the light of recent events. He had questioned her at some length about Emma's state of mind. Could these recent events, the deaths of her mother and aunt have brought on a depression, was she under her doctor at present did she know? But Jane Dennington had been adamant that Emma was coping extremely well and that something must have happened as a result of the mysterious telephone call she had received.

Kennedy had helped Higton with a lot of the legwork on the Bertram case and he was quite familiar with it. Although Jane Dennington had been up to the Bertram house several times he decided he would take a look around himself. Anything was better than going back to the office and he was on 'till ten anyway. His route took him near the high street and instinct told him to look outside Woolworths, the place of the supposed meeting between Emma Bertram and the mystery person. Kennedy stopped the car outside Woolworths and got out. This end of the high street was quiet of an evening, the restaurants and pubs being at the other end by the town square. He eyed the road up and down. There were a couple of cars parked further up the road but there were no restrictions at this time of night so there was nothing unusual about that. He gathered his torch from the glove compartment and took a walk away from the square checking each shop front as he went. He had been in the force for nearly twenty years, fourteen of that in CID, and he loved it. He was not ambitious. He had been encouraged to take his sergeants exams more than once but he liked it on the ground. He liked being at the sharp end where the clues were often discovered and unravelled. He'd earn the unkindly nickname of 'sausage' by his colleagues after a combination of Kennedy's sausages, a well-known brand, and sausage dog, a very short-legged hound whose nose was very close to the ground. The unsociable hours of the job had taken its toll on his marriage and he'd been divorced for over ten years. One of his ex-wife's parting shots was that he was 'married to the job.' He in turn had replied that 'the job didn't nag so much.'

He reached the end of the street where it met County Road. Opposite was Heathfield Park, shrouded in darkness. There would be no point looking over there until first light if it was needed. He crossed the High Street and headed back the way he had come checking the shop fronts again and a couple of small yards that led to delivery bays at the back of the shops. In one yard he disturbed a couple of startled cats but had so far seen nothing out of place. He passed the alleyway that led up to the overflow car park and continued along the street towards the town square. As he approached the two parked cars he noticed the second one had a couple of parking tickets attached to the windscreen. He checked them. The first had been issued at 11.17am, the second at 2.40 in the afternoon so the car had been there all day. He looked inside and then tried the door but it was locked. Calling in on his mobile for a check on the registration number with the police national computer he continued along the street for some distance until he was about a hundred yards from Woolworths and then retraced his steps. The caller had said Woolworths so this had to be the starting point. Maybe Emma Bertram had got into a car outside the shop but that seems an odd place for a rendezvous. Parking was not permitted on this stretch of the high street and there would have been a lot of witnesses to such a pick up. He stood with his back to the shop, looked around and saw the alleyway again. Torch in hand he crossed the road and started up the passageway. As he did so his mobile rang.

'You've got a match there John', Phil Walker the duty sergeant said. 'The car is registered to Doreen Bertram so it looks like your young lady kept her appointment'.

'Thanks Phil, better let the Inspector know. I'm going to take another look round before I go up to the Bertram house.'

'Okay John, by the way it seems like it's the day for people going missing. We've had a report of a young man not returned home. Seems he left for work this morning but never showed up and he hasn't been seen since. Probably gone off with some bird eh?'

'Any connection with the Bertram case?'

'No, works for some solicitors in Westerham.' Walker replied.

'Right, well one missing person is enough for me thanks. I'll see you later.'

By now Kennedy had reached the top of the alleyway and looked across the deserted car park. Only one vehicle was parked there, which was not unusual but Kennedy decided to look at it anyway. It was an old Ford Escort, J registration and going rusty in places. He noticed that the driver's door was not completely shut and was beginning to think that perhaps it had been either stolen or simply dumped. He circled it cautiously shining his torch around and within it. He peered in the driver's window. There were no keys in the ignition and it didn't appear to have been hot-wired, a sure sign that it had been stolen. He pulled at the handle and opened the door. As he did so a noise came from the back of the car startling Kennedy. Instinctively he turned quickly thinking someone was approaching from behind. He raised the torch in defence but no one was there. He stepped back from the car and looked around him. There was just one central lighting pillar in the car park that only lit the middle part of the tarmac. The light barely touched where this car was parked and much was in near darkness. Kennedy was not easily fazed but as he looked around a cold shiver moved up his spine. The half-moon was veiled by a thin layer of cloud and the nearby trees cast dancing shadows across the tarmac as they moved with the wind.

He moved round so the light was behind him and cautiously knelt and checked under the car. There was nothing there but as he did so the car moved again slightly. He leant in the driver's door and punched the boot release button. Stepping round the car and pointing the torch he reached forward and lifted the boot lid. A very frightened looking Peter Keywood, hands bound behind him and mouth gagged with tape, stared back at him.

Chapter 14

Smurdon was not in a good mood. Dragged back to the office after the call it was now nearly midnight. All the necessary action had been taken and a full-scale alert sent out concerning the probable abduction of Emma Bertram. Peter Keywood had been thoroughly interviewed but he was so traumatized that his statement had been confusing and of little use. Smurdon only hoped that after a good night's sleep helped by the tablets the police doctor had given him, he would be more forthcoming with useful information and detail in the morning. He had at least remembered that the two men spoke with London accents and Higton had made sure the Metropolitan Police had been sent full details. The men had stopped him on his way to work and shown him a picture of his younger sister, told him that if he didn't cooperate and do exactly what they said, then some nasty things would happen to her. They were very menacing and Keywood was scared out of his wits.

Matters were made worse by the fact that Smurdon's two prime suspects had the best possible alibis. Smurdon himself was interviewing Wilson at the time of the kidnap and Higton had confirmed that Peters was in hospital in Ilford. The description Keywood had given of the men was pretty vague as they had both worn large baseball caps but said they appeared to be in their mid-twenties, much younger than either Peters or Wilson.

'Mid-twenties and with a London accent, that narrows it down to a couple of a million.' remarked Higton.

Smurdon ignored the comment and just glared at him. 'So Keywood worked at Curtis Forsythe.' he said reading through the statement. 'That's the Bertram's solicitor isn't it?'

Higton nodded.

'That's surely got to be the connection. Right I'll go and see him first thing in the morning, I'd like to go and wake him right now but without any direct evidence we'll be accused of police harassment and I don't

117

know what else.' Turning to Higton he said, 'I want you to pay another visit to Wilson first thing in the morning and see if you get any reaction from him. If the proceeds of the Sureguard robbery are still out there he'll be none too pleased that someone else is after it!'

'He looked round at the tired and drawn faces of his team. 'Right, let's go home and get some sleep, what's left of the night. I'll get the duty sergeant to call us if anything breaks.'

+++++++++

Emma sat perched on the edge of the office chair staring ahead at the blank dirt encrusted wall. It was dark outside now and the light from the dim bulb barely reached the extremities of her small cell. Each corner was in semi darkness and only heightened the tenseness she felt. The traffic continued to rumble past in the distance somewhere as did the occasional train but she no longer heard the voices of children playing. They were no doubt indoors with their families tucking into their tea or watching the television. Memories of her own childhood and many a happy teatime with nanny in the kitchen came flooding back but she could not even raise a smile at the thought, the desperation of her plight was overwhelming. She realized she was feeling hot. The coat she had chosen was ideal for an early spring morning trip to the shops but the atmosphere in the tiny room was stuffy and unpleasant and her head was beginning to thump. As she looked ahead she was seeing nothing but trying desperately to focus her mind. So many times over the last few weeks since her mother's death she had had to draw on every ounce of her inner strength and will. The simple, quiet and predictable lifestyle that she had enjoyed; enjoyed, was that the right word? She supposed it was. Many would call it dull and uninteresting but at least it had been secure and sane. How that seemed so distant now; like a long lost memory. What she was experiencing now was madness, a dream, a nightmare. Indeed she wished it were a nightmare for the reality was far more frightening. She wondered just how much more she could take.

The sobbing had subsided again and she had resorted to wiping her face on her sleeve. Something she had not done since a young child and the memory of her nanny scolding her for it came back to her. The thought that of all things she really missed just now was her handbag containing tissues only seemed to increase the insanity of it all.

She moved her neck in an arc to try and reduce the tension that was building in her head and for the first time saw the box her captor had placed by the door. Going over to it she found that it contained a bottle of water and two cellophane wrapped packs of sandwiches. The sight made her feel both hungry and thirsty, realizing that she had not eaten since breakfast time. She tried to undo the bottle but with her hands tied it was at first impossible to get a grip. She managed to clamp the bottle between her knees and twist the cap with her hands but the pressure of the rough rope on her wrists caused her to cry out in pain as she did so. Gripping the neck of the bottle between her teeth she tilted her head back and thankfully drank some of the thirst quenching liquid. Kneeling by the door, as she carefully returned the bottle to an upright position, she spotted a metal bracket sticking out of the wall about a foot from the floor. Although rusting, one side was quite sharp and she began carefully rubbing the bond around her wrists in a sawing motion against the bracket. The action was painful but she could see that it was having an effect on the rope. After some ten minutes her hands were free.

She gently eased her coat off and for a while she just sat there nursing her wrists and gently dabbing some of the water on them. When she felt a little better, out of instinct she tried both of the doors again now her hands were free but they were well and securely locked. The sight of the sandwich packets reminded her how hungry she felt and in stooping to pick the packet out of the box noticed that the newspaper in the bottom of the box was not a newspaper at all but a pile of newspaper cuttings.

Staring up at her from a large picture on the top cutting was a picture of a man. Head and shoulders he looked strong and forbidding, unsmiling and fierce. A shiver ran down Emma's spine, she had seen him before. He was the fourth man in the photograph of the men on the fishing vessel, the one from the package that she had found hidden in Aunt Millie's cottage.

+++++++++

Smurdon was in no better mood than he had been the previous evening. He had just returned to the CID room at police headquarters after visiting Felix Curtis at Curtis, Forsythe the solicitors. The meeting had not gone well. Again Curtis had refused to discuss the affairs of Doreen or Emma Bertram other than to confirm that the bulk of the estate of Doreen Bertram the deceased went to her daughter. Pushed for more information he just cited client confidentiality and said a court order would be required if Smurdon wanted more. Smurdon knew that he had no concrete evidence to link the killing to a financial motive and that he would be unlikely to obtain the necessary court warrant.

Smurdon now asked about his employee, Peter Keywood. Yes, he was a hard working quiet young man who kept his head down and got on with his work. His secretary had received a telephone call earlier from the boy's mother about his trauma of the previous day but he had not spoken to her himself. The mother had been asked not to mention the link to Emma Bertram and when Smurdon told him about the abduction he seemed for a moment to be visually shaken but quickly recovered. He had not heard, he said, from Miss Bertram for over three weeks and could think of no reason why this could have happened. 'A terrible business', he had repeated several times.

As Smurdon was leaving he turned suddenly and asked, 'Did you know Doreen Bertram when she was Doreen Patterson?' The Inspector was watching him closely and again there was that split second of recognition.

'Yes, er no, no, I've only known her since she came to Chartwood. Her husband is dead, I never knew him.' Then without a pause he said, 'Now Inspector I really must get on, I have clients to see.' And with that he ushered him to the door but Smurdon was not easily pressured. He stood his ground, turned for a second time, his face just inches from Curtis, and said, 'And I have a murder enquiry, and a probable abduction to investigate. I will no doubt be in touch again.'

Before Smurdon had descended the last flight of stairs of the drab stone stairwell, Curtis was already dialing an international telephone number, the same number he had dialed after Emma Bertram's last visit.

+++++++++

Just over an hour later Higton returned from his visit to Robbie Wilson.

'What news?' called Smurdon across the room as Higton hung his coat on the rack by the door.

'Says he had no idea that Doreen Bertram had a daughter and what was it to do with him anyway. He still claims he's not seen her for years and years and in those days she was Doreen Patterson. Threatened to complain about Police harassment etc, etc.'

'What was his reaction when you told him Emma Bertram had been abducted and that someone else might be after the supposed missing millions?'

'He was quite taken aback and asked exactly what time it had taken place and where. Seemed an odd question to ask, I'm sure he knows more than he's letting on, even if he's not involved himself.' He paused, 'I've had a word with Phil Johnson at the Met., and he's going to try and spare a couple of DC's to keep watch on Wilson's movements but he can't promise anything, they're overstretched as it is.'

Smurdon leant on his desk and rubbed his chin. 'Let's hope we get something more positive from young Keywood this morning.' he glanced at his watch, 'Kennedy should be with him now.'

'How long are you going to keep it under wraps?' asked Higton.

'We'll hold it until 4pm and see if anything comes from our present enquiries or informants, then we'll go public in time for the evening TV news.' replied Smurdon.

+++++++++

Emma had spent a fitful night dozing on a makeshift bed of the boxes and papers she had earlier disturbed and scattered. Initially she had lain awake for over two hours, the fear and tension denying her body the sleep it so desperately needed. Occasionally she heard a mouse or rat scurrying along the corridor outside and for that reason she did not dare or wish to turn off the feeble light that hung from the ceiling above her but thankfully none made any attempt to enter the room. She was conscious of the dank smell of the room mixed with her own body odour. How she longed for a bath. All kinds of images invaded her mind as she curled under her coat in the corner of her prison cell. She saw again her mother lying in a pool of blood on the dining room carpet, a fountain of red liquid spurting from her chest as the life ebbed out of her. Then it was the image of the man in the photograph his face threatening and evil as he slowly opened the sea cocks taking the *Jenny Kathleen* and her two brother occupants down to a watery grave. The hooded man, her abductor, was in the nightmare as well. She shivered as she recalled his hand holding her down in the car, pushing her face into the nauseating sack and seating so she could hardly breathe. The sting as he slapped her hard across the face. He was the one who had said her father had been a thief and if the newspaper cuttings were anything to go by - a murderer as well.

The cardboard box by the door had contained over a dozen press cuttings from several newspapers dated August, September and October 1972. They told the story of the largest and most audacious daylight robbery of gold bullion and cash that had ever taken place to date. A Sureguard security van had just left a bonded warehouse near Heathrow on its way to the airport when it was forced off the road by two vehicles. The driver and guard were forced out of the van at gunpoint and in a struggle that ensued the guard was shot and died later that day in hospital. There were at least three men involved possibly four as witnessed by a passing motorist who stopped at a phone box half a mile up the road and called the police. Although officers were on the scene within fifteen minutes and had cordoned off the area within twenty-five, the men, the security van and twelve million pounds worth of gold bullion, cash and securities had completely disappeared. The subsequent manhunt had been huge, all known villains capable of such a robbery were turned over and several arrests were made but without any evidence the police were forced to release them. The London crime scene had not seen such activity for years but no matter how hard the police tried there appeared to be no leads and no informants to offer any useful information. Questions were raised in the House of Commons about the lack of security around such a large amount of gold and several of the newspapers were very critical of Sureguard's handling of the operation. The company's shares plummeted in price and several large clients took their business elsewhere following the newspaper campaign. Then came a breakthrough. Following a telephone tip-off, two men by the name of Wilson and Peters were arrested at a warehouse in South-east London where plans and details of the robbery were discovered. In subsequent questioning they eventually admitted their part in the robbery and named a Barry Masters as the mastermind behind it. Masters was known to the police and believed to have been behind other robberies at a bank and two sub post offices but nothing had ever been proved. Wilson and Peters claimed that they knew nothing about a gun being used until Masters produced it on the day and that it was Masters who pulled the trigger.

According to Wilson and Peters it was Masters who planned the robbery from the beginning and they had no knowledge of where he had got the inside information he needed to carry out the daring plan. They had split up after the robbery and didn't know where Masters had driven the Sureguard van to or what arrangements he had made as to the disposal of the gold. At the time the police raided the warehouse and arrested Wilson and Peters, they said they had been waiting for Masters who had arranged to meet them there. They believed it was Masters who had double crossed them and shopped them to the police.

There were pictures in several of the cuttings of Wilson, Peters and Masters. The latter, there was no doubt in Emma's mind, was the man she believed could well be her father. Further cuttings reported a nationwide manhunt for the 'most wanted man in Britain' but although many sightings were reported from all over the country none proved to be positive. The last cutting carried an unconfirmed report of a feud in the criminal fraternity over the disposal of the gold that said Masters had been 'dealt with' by a notorious gang called the Harvan brothers. Someone had scribbled across this cutting, 'No Way!'

Of any further investigation or the subsequent trial to follow there were no further details and Emma could only speculate as to the outcome.

But none of this made any sense to her. Mother had always maintained that her husband, Emma's father, was dead. It was clearly a painful memory because she never wanted to talk about it. But what if the reason she didn't want to talk about it was because the truth was more frightening than death. That Emma's father had in fact been a villain, a robber and murderer. Emma had lain there with these terrifying thought tossing around in her mind for hours before she eventually dosed into that fitful sleep.

+++++++++

'You've done what!' screamed Robbie Wilson. 'You bloody idiot!' And with that he smashed his son across the face with the back of his hand propelling him against the door of the office where they now stood.

Darren glared back at him, 'Somebody had to do something,' he shouted, 'I'll get her to talk you'll see.'

'And what if she doesn't know anything, have you thought of that? This all happened before she was born. Do you think that her mother is going to tell her outright that she used to be a petty thief and that her father was a robber and murderer? I said we'd watch her, nothing else. I said she might lead us to someone, I said someone might try and make contact with her and then we would move. But then you go and bloody kidnap the girl! He shouted.

He turned suddenly on his son and grabbed him by the throat. Despite his obesity and forty-a-day habit he was remarkably strong and his large beefy hand pinioned the boy firmly against the door, the thumb pressing deeply into the flesh of his neck. His face was inches from Darren's, 'Right,' he said, 'this is what you will do...'

+++++++++

It was now just after 11am, twenty-four hours since she was first taken there. Emma had fully expected to have received another visit from the hooded man by now but she had heard nothing save the regular mooted sounds from outside. She wondered when Jane would have raised the alarm, had they found her car in the high street yet, how long might they have been searching for her? But searching where? She didn't know where herself. Then she remembered that she had found a box of stationery different to the rest and that it contained a printed heading. She got down on the floor and began to rummage through all the papers. Since finding the box yesterday she had moved the papers around to make a makeshift bed and now she couldn't find what she was looking for. She clawed desperately through the papers throwing them in all directions until she found one. She held it up; it was an address in Birmingham. Emma felt deflated; there was no way she could be in Birmingham. The boxes must have been transported here or this had been a southern distribution point.

As Emma sat there staring at the invoice she heard footsteps in the corridor outside. She quickly folded the paper and stuffed it in her trouser pocket. A key turned in the lock and the door was flung open. The hooded man stood there and although Emma could only see his eyes she sensed he was very angry.

'I see you've cut yourself loose you clever little bitch, right we've got no time for that now. Come on.' He grabbed her right wrist roughly just where the rope had bound her and she let out a scream in agonizing pain as he pulled her to her feet and towards the door. He led her back up the narrow corridor to a large near empty warehouse. Not entombed in the sack this time Emma was able to take in the surroundings. A number of empty metal racks were lined up equidistant across the floor, at the end of each rack a large letter A, B, C etc about 24 inches high was affixed to it. A car was parked facing the roll up shutter door and Emma assumed it was the entrance they had come in yesterday. The boot of the car was open so Emma was unable to see any license plate.

'Right, get in!' shouted the man.

Emma tried to back off but he pulled her towards him and twisted her arm behind her back, the pain in her wrist now excruciating. He forced her into the boot compartment body first then lifted her legs off the ground and pushed them in. Before Emma could move he had grabbed her arms again and bound them with new rope behind her back. Everything went dark as the boot lid was slammed shut.

+++++++++

Peter Keywood had not been able to add much to his statement from the night before. He had given a slightly better description of the young men but they had both been wearing large peaked baseball caps when they had at first stopped him. Later he had briefly seen the one in the car with a hood over his face. The car he believed had been a dark green Vauxhall. It was definitely not light blue and he could only remember the first digit of the number plate which was an R. A description had been put out but there was very little to go on. Johnson had phoned from the Met. Police to say he had been unable to spare any men to watch Wilson so far. Smurdon had growled something under his breath about 'next

time they want some bloody help!' and the mood in the crime room was
pretty depressed.

+++++++++

Emma had managed to shift slightly in the boot space to be less
uncomfortable and as her eyes had become adjusted to the dark so she
could discern narrow cracks of light around the opening. She could not
see her watch as her hands were still pinioned behind her back and her
wrists hurt like hell. Her head was hurting too. As the car bounced along
it was not being driven particularly gently and her head kept banging
against the floor of the boot as the car sped along and her cheek felt as if
it were being bruised to a pulp. The journey seemed a reverse of
yesterday's trip. At first they had traveled slowly, stopping frequently.
Sometimes she heard the familiar bleep of the pedestrian crossing as the
car idled but now the stops became less often and she could tell by the
whine of the transmission that it was traveling at some speed.

At last the car slowed and lurched over rough ground. Emma began
to panic. Was this young man about to kill her? She had told him she
believed her father to be dead, she had no information to give him. Was
she now of no further use to him? The fear engulfed her once again and
she fought back the tears.

The car continued to buck over the rough terrain for what seemed like
ages until it eventually came to a halt. She heard the car door open and
steps on the rough earth outside. As the boot was flung open sunlight
shone straight in her face so she was momentarily blinded. Before she
could adjust her eyes her head was roughly lifted and a scarf tied around
her head as a blindfold. The man manhandled her out of the car and led
her blindly along. She tripped several times on the uneven ground and
each time he hauled her up harshly by the arm.

When she fell the next time he let her go and she banged her head and
left shoulder against a tree. She thought her head was going to burst it
hurt so much and she began to sob again. She had tried to construct a
sentence to ask why she was being treated like this but all that came out
was an incomprehensible babble she was so traumatized.

'Right, shut up and be quiet or you are dead!' he screamed. 'Don't you
dare move.'

Emma rested her head against the tree. She knew she must be in some
forest for she could smell the fauna and flora around her. Her knees had
sunk into the soft moss at the base of the tree and she could feel the
dampness creeping along her leg. Her whole body was shaking with fear
and she tried desperately to keep quiet as instructed. 'What a place to die'

she thought, 'Why me?'

'P...please, why are you doing this to me?' She had managed to get the sentence out but he did not reply. Was he even now pointing a gun, about to pull the trigger? 'P...please, let me go, I'll try and help, but I really don't know about my father,' Emma cried.

She could not help it but the sobs began to get louder and grew into a crescendo. 'Please don't kill me,' she screamed.

Chapter 15

'The imminence of death focuses the mind.' Emma could not remember where she had heard the quotation or why in this surreal situation she should recall it or if indeed there was any truth in it. It had seemed like an age since she had pleaded for her life, in reality it was perhaps just a minute or two, but she dared not move. She could hear birds calling to one another in the trees above with happy cheerful sounds. She could hear animals scurrying in the undergrowth nearby, but of the man nothing, no response, no sound. What was he doing, why did he prolong the agony? And then another sound, a panting, close to her left ear, and something wet against her bruised cheek. What was he doing? Emma screamed again and rolled over on the ground away from the sound, but the panting was there again and she could feel warm breath on her face. A scurrying again very nearby and much heavier this time.

'Oh my dear, whatever has happened?' A woman's voice, elderly, calming. She felt hands tugging carefully at the blindfold and then it was off. A hand gently stroked her un-bruised cheek. Emma focused her eyes first on the kindly concerned face of the woman and then felt the wet lick again of the golden retriever who seemed to hold the same concern on its face as its master. Remembering suddenly the hooded man Emma turned and looked in all directions but there was no sign of him.

+++++++++

Higton was putting the final details for the press briefing together when the news came through. Emma Bertram had been found safe but badly traumatized, tied and blindfolded in a wood just outside of Wokingham near Bracknell. Berkshire police were at that moment transporting her back to Kent accompanied by a woman PC and a detective. She had refused hospital treatment, preferring to return home. Her own doctor had been advised and would meet her at *Tall Trees*, as would Smurdon. Knowing that Emma would be home by six p.m., they went ahead with the news conference and the kidnapping made headline news in London and the South East and took a prime slot on the national television news. Both the main TV channels dispatched reporters to the wood outside Wokingham, which was now cordoned off, and being searched by scenes of crime officers, and to the gates of *Tall Trees*, which were now being controlled by two uniformed police officer from Chartwood police station. The kidnapping was inevitably linked to the murder of Doreen Bertram and the usual press speculation ensued.

+++++++++

'Any good news to tell me?' called Smurdon as he entered the office. He had just returned from seeing Emma Bertram safely installed back in her house. Higton ignored the question and asked, 'How is she?'

'Considering all she's been through remarkably well, but very tired. Her doctor insists on no questions until tomorrow late morning at the earliest but I've left a WPC with her just in case she feels like talking. That Jane Dennington is with her as well and I've got a couple of PC's on the gate to keep the press away.' he paused, 'I'll call her tomorrow around 11am. Let's hope she can give us some leads.'

'Talking of leads, I've just had Berkshire on the phone. They've found a set of fresh tyre tracks and a couple of partial footprints but it's getting dark up there now so their Scenes of Crime boys won't have any answers until tomorrow.'

'Right, well we'll see what tomorrow brings. We've had some good press coverage too so hopefully we'll get something from that as well.' Smurdon paused then added, 'I wonder how long it will be before the press makes the connection between Doreen Patterson and Doreen Bertram and the Sureguard robbery. They're bound to start digging a lot more than they did the first time.'

'Does that bother you?' asked Higton.

'On the contrary, I'm hoping it might stir up a hornet's nest or two. If there really are some of the missing millions out there then the press coverage might cause a panic and then someone may slip up and lead us to it, and more importantly the murderers of Doreen Bertram.'

+++++++++

Emma opened her eyes, the sun was streaming in through a narrow gap in the curtains and she was conscious of a dark blur immediately in front of her. As she blinked her eyelids the uniform of a woman police constable came into focus.

'Hello, how are you feeling?' The WPC asked with a concerned smile. She was blond and younger than the one Emma remembered from the night before but the voice was just as soothing.

Emma tried to lift her head from the pillow but it felt like lead. 'Oh that hurts,' said Emma rubbing her brow and still trying to focus her eyes.

'That's only to be expected after all you've been through - would you like a cup of tea and some breakfast?'

'Tea and toast would be fine thanks. Where's Jane?' asked Emma.

'I sent her off to get some rest; she's been sitting here watching you most of the night.'

'Oh Jane, bless her.' Emma sighed, 'What time is it?'

'Just after 10am, I'll go and get that tea now. By the way we've already had a call from Mrs. Marcheson your housekeeper; she's on her way back from her sisters right now. She was very concerned about you. It gave her quite a shock to see you on the television news.' replied the policewoman.

'I've been on the news?' queried Emma.

'Yes, last night at six o'clock and again at 10pm, both the local and national TV. There's a bunch of reporters outside at the gate now but my colleague PC Murdoch is keeping them at bay. Now let's get that breakfast.' She turned towards the door, 'I'll be back in a moment, will you be okay?'

'I'll be fine thanks,' said Emma.

Left on her own Emma struggled out of bed and pulled back the heavy curtains. A blaze of sunlight entered the room and Emma felt the warmth caress her body. She stood there for a moment savouring the feeling and looked out at the familiar scene of well kept gardens, the trees now well in leaf, and the backdrop of the North Downs. She took a deep breath and stretched out her arms as best she could but her muscles still ached from the confinement and her wrists particularly were still very sore from where the bindings had chafed them. She was so pleased to be home where the familiar everyday surroundings helped to bring a sense of normality back into her life once more.

Making her way back to the bed she pumped up the pillows and climbed back in. Sitting there in the security of her own room the events of the last forty-eight hours seemed so far removed they could almost have been a script from a TV thriller yet the memory was far too intense for it to have been anything but reality.

Emma had slept well; no doubt helped by the tablets the doctor had given her the previous evening. She could remember little of the detail since she collapsed in the old lady's arms. She was a kindly soul and Emma made a mental note to get her address from the police and write and thank her. The cottage the old lady had guided her to, the arrival of police and ambulance and then the ride back home in the police car was all a blur to her. She had felt so tired and drained. In fact she had spent most of the return journey with her head resting on the shoulder of the WPC who accompanied her. Now after a night's sleep she felt more rested and awake but her head was still thumping hard.

'Hello, how are you now?'

It was Jane, followed by the WPC carrying a tray of tea and toast.

Emma smiled back, 'Much better now but I could do with a couple of Paracetamol, there's some in the bathroom cabinet, could you get them for me?'

'Of course.' replied Jane, leaning over the bed, taking Emma's hand in hers and giving her a kiss on the forehead. 'It's so good to have you back safe, I was really worried.' She held her eyes for a moment with real concern and then headed for the door.

'Here you are.' said the WPC as she lifted the tray across Emma and rested it on the bedclothes. 'Get some breakfast inside of you and you'll feel a lot better.'

'Thanks,' said Emma, 'I'm certainly getting a lot of attention.'

'I've had my boss on the phone, Inspector Smurdon; he wants to come and interview you as soon as possible. Would you feel up to it by 12 noon? I don't think I can fend him off beyond that.'

'Yes, that's fine,' said Emma, 'Best get it over with.'

'What's that?' said Jane re-entering the room with the tablets.

'It's Smurdon, he's coming at twelve.'

'Well I want to be there with you,' said Jane.

+++++++++

Smurdon's manner was considerably more cordial than when he had last interviewed Emma at *Tall Trees* just after her mother's death. He listened intently as Emma described in as much detail as possible all that had happened since she first received the telephone call from Peter Keywood two mornings ago till yesterday afternoon when the old lady found her in the woods.

As Emma described the hooded young man and mentioned his startling green eyes, Jane gasped loudly making Emma, Smurdon, and Higton, who had been in the corner taking notes, stop and turn towards her.

Jane apologized for the interruption. 'Sorry,' she said, 'He just sounds so frightening, that's all.'

'Do you think this was the same man that had been following you in the blue car recently?' asked Smurdon.

'I don't know,' replied Emma. 'He was about the same height and build but with only his eyes, nose and mouth visible it's impossible to tell.'

Emma suddenly remembered the invoice from the Motor Parts Company she had found in the office. 'It's in my trouser pocket.' Turning to Jane she asked, 'Where are the clothes I was wearing yesterday?'

'Oh my God,' said Jane I put them in the wash to soak last night. They're in the tumble dryer now.' Standing she said, 'I'll go and see.'

Higton and Smurdon looked at each other and Smurdon said, 'Did the WPC not ask you last night to keep the clothes for Forensic to have a look at?

'I'm sorry,' said Jane standing and heading towards the door, 'I'm not sure, I don't know. All I could think about last night was getting Emma safely to bed.'

'I'll come with you,' said Higton.

While they waited Emma turned to Smurdon and asked about the press cuttings. She had told him about them earlier and the implication by the young man that Barry Masters had been her father. Smurdon had not reacted then but now faced with the direct question studied Emma carefully. Was she genuine in her lack of knowledge of her mother's past or was she embarking on an elaborate cover up in an attempt to hide it? Smurdon wasn't sure.

'Your mother's finger prints,' he began guardedly, 'we had to take them for elimination purposes after she was killed. They match prints we have on file from the mid 1960's for a Doreen Patterson. We also know that Doreen Patterson was a known associate of Barry Masters.'

'The man implicated by Wilson and Peters as the mastermind behind the 1972 Sureguard robbery? asked Emma.

'Yes, that's right.' replied Smurdon.

Emma was quiet for a while then asked, 'Why did this Doreen Patterson have her finger prints taken?'

'Petty theft, that sort of thing. She was put on probation for a year. Didn't go to prison or anything.' He paused. 'You didn't know about any of this or about Barry Masters? He enquired.

'No Inspector I did not!' Emma was indignant at first but then the enormity of it all began to sink in. 'There's no doubt, about the fingerprints matching I mean?' asked Emma quietly, her eyes beginning to fill with tears.

'I'm afraid not. Look we can finish this tomorrow if you like; you've given us a good deal to be going on with. If we can locate the warehouse cum office where you were held we should be able to trace your kidnapper.'

'Yes...sorry,' said Emma, 'I think I'll go to my room now if you don't mind.' And with that she left.

A moment later Higton returned followed by Jane. As he entered the room Higton shook his head. 'It's been through the wash, I've got what remains.' he said, holding up a plastic bag. 'Forensic might be able to do something with it. Could Miss Bertram remember any part of the address?'

'Only that is was in Birmingham.' replied Smurdon.

'I'm really sorry,' said Jane again.

+ + + + + + + + +

'Well what do you make of that?' asked Higton as they headed the car back down Silver Lane away from *Tall Trees*. 'Do you think she's genuine?'

'I'm not sure, I'll give her the benefit of the doubt for the moment but what puzzles me most is this. Why go to all the dangerous and elaborate means of kidnapping the girl one day and treating her pretty brutally at that, only to let her go the next? Put yourself in the kidnapper's shoes for a moment. You ask the girl where her father is, she says he's dead so you believe her and let her go? I don't think so. And why ask where the father is? I could understand it better if he was asking her where the proceeds of the robbery were but Barry Masters...' he paused for a moment, 'so someone out there clearly thinks that he didn't end up in the foundations of an office block in London.'

Smurdon was silent for a while and Higton knew better than to interrupt him while he was thinking. 'What happened to the Harvan brothers, do we know?'

'Yes, I've checked up on that.' replied Higton. 'Josh Harvan was killed in a gangland shoot out in 1987 and Sam Harvan; his younger brother is doing life for the Harberson murders. There was a dispute over drugs territory. Eric Harberson was trying to muscle in on the Harvan's patch and Sam decided to teach him a lesson. He went round to Harberson's nightclub but things went wrong and Sam shot Eric and his minder at point blank range. Unfortunately for Sam he didn't see the CCTV camera that recorded the whole thing. He was sent down in 1991.'

'How strong was the rumour that the Harvan's had killed Masters?' asked Smurdon.

'Well reading the notes it was pretty strong. Seems that Masters and the Harvan's had crossed swords several times in the past, there was no love lost between them by all accounts. Sam Harvan has never confirmed that they did away with Masters of course. Mind you he's never denied it either.'

They had reached the dual carriageway and Higton steered the CID car out into the light afternoon traffic. Smurdon was thinking out loud. 'What if either of the Harvan's had admitted to someone that they had definitely not killed Masters, then that person would be very interested to trace just what did happen to him.'

'But who?' asked Higton.

'Find out if either of the Harvan's were inside the same prison at the same time as Wilson or Peters. My gut still tells me they are mixed up in this.'

'Right.' replied Higton, 'that's an interesting thought; I'll get onto it straight away.'

+++++++++

Jane entered Emma's bedroom and found her lying across the bed and sobbing quietly into a large white handkerchief. She sat on the edge of the bed and put her hand on Emma's shoulder. Neither spoke for a while, then Emma said. 'I feel totally numb, my mother a shoplifter and liar, my father a bullion robber and probably a murderer. How could she deceive me like this? I feel utterly betrayed. We were never that close in that we didn't hug and that, but she was my mother and I loved her as any child should. But now I don't think I could have really known her at all.' Emma blurted out between the sobs. 'What was true, what was false, who was the real Doreen Bertram. O God, I'm twenty-seven years of age and I've just learnt my whole life has been a charade.' The sobs continued and Jane could feel Emma's body shaking beneath her hand.

Jane tried to comfort her. 'Don't punish yourself; perhaps she did it to protect you. After your father's death with all the press coverage and everything perhaps she saw an opportunity to bring you up away from it all. To give you, and her, a fresh start, a decent upbringing.'

'She could still have told me when I was old enough to understand.' sniffed Emma.

'And you really didn't know about any of it? Enquired Jane.

'What?' Emma had turned to face Jane. 'What do you mean?' a questioning look on her face.

'Sorry…, I just meant…, surely, well you know, you must have known that all was not as it seemed?'

'No,' Emma shouted. 'And I resent the suggestion; I thought you knew me better!'

'Oh my dear, whatever is this?' It was Valerie Marcheson, the housekeeper standing in the bedroom doorway.

'Emma's upset' said Jane weakly.

'I can see that! Perhaps you'd better leave now.' Jane had not realized that Valerie Marcheson had overheard the last part of the conversation.

As Jane descended the stairs, the housekeeper went to the bedside and took Emma in her arms and held her tightly as once again the tears began to flow.

Chapter 16

The next morning Emma felt much better although the shock of all that had happened and all that she had learnt about in the last three days was still raw in her mind. Her world had been completely turned upside down since the death of her mother and although she could so easily have caved in she somehow found the traumas, the uncertainties and indeed the sheer hell of it all had hardened her resolve to get to the truth. She had surprised even herself by the determination she now exhibited and reflected that had someone suggested just a few weeks ago that such a scenario was about to break into her life she would never have accepted that she would be able to cope with it.

Nevertheless she felt very much alone and part of her longed that she had a brother or sister to share the burden with, someone who as kith and kin would be in the same position as her. Yet, she thought, how would a sibling cope? Would they be able to retain the resolve and sanity that somehow she had miraculously managed or would she find herself having to cope with the burden of comforting and carrying a sibling. Surviving the pain and hurt herself was one thing, to bear the load for two would be too much of that she was sure.

She was grateful for the ever constant care of Valerie Marcheson who was always there with comfort and love and treated Emma as if she were her own. In fact in many ways because of her own mother's remoteness at times there was a real sense in which she felt closer to Valerie. Certainly when a hug or a woman to woman heart to heart was needed, Valerie would always take her in her arms or sit her down and lend a listening ear. Valerie was practical too and Emma appreciated her down to earth advice and guidance, although on this subject Valerie had of course encouraged her to leave things alone for fear of further distress, but Emma did not agree and was determined not to leave a stone unturned until she discovered the truth; whatever that would be.

And then there was Jane. Jane had become such a good friend to her over the past weeks. Emma realized that in recent years she had become quite reclusive, living at home with mother, only going out with mother and leading a very routine and predictable lifestyle. The circumstances had changed all that of course and Jane's friendship had made it all the more bearable. She had resolved that when it was all over she would change, she would go out more, she wanted to meet new people, go to new places, do new things, and make a new life for herself. But that was in the future; the now had to be dealt with first, and Jane her good friend had left last night without saying goodbye following Emma's outburst.

The last thing Emma wanted just now was to destroy the friendship she valued so dearly and she determined that immediately after breakfast she would telephone Jane and apologize for her reaction to Jane's question.

'Oh, I didn't expect you down for at least another hour.' said a surprised Valerie Marcheson as Emma entered the kitchen. 'I was just about to bring you up a cup of tea.'

'I'm feeling a lot better today and I *was* in bed a lot earlier than usual yesterday.' replied Emma. 'I couldn't stay up there any longer.'

'Well even so, you need to take it easy for a quite a few days young woman. You've had more than enough to cope with lately.' said Valerie seriously.

'Is the policewoman still here?' Emma enquired.

'No, I told them I was quite capable of looking after you and that you were quite sensible enough to telephone them if you thought of anything else to add to your statement. There's still a Bobby on the gate although I think all the reporters have left now. It still gets a bit chilly at night so I don't blame them for not staying. I took the liberty last night of telling them all you had no intention of speaking to them and that they were wasting their time being here.'

Emma thanked her and smiled to herself. She could just picture Valerie Marcheson standing at the gate in her ample frame, hands on hips, and telling the news reporters to go away.

Emma walked through to the front of the house and sneaked a peep out of the window from behind a curtain of the dining room. She could see the policeman standing at the gate, hands behind his back, while two newspaper men stood nearby chatting animatedly. One was stamping his feet to keep warm and had his hands in the pockets of his anorak; the other kept looking towards the house and fiddled with two cameras that were strung around his neck. Just then one of them pointed in the direction of the road and Emma moved the curtain further to see what had caught his attention. She could just see John English, their regular paperboy pedaling furiously up the hill. The policeman stopped him for a moment, looked in his sack, and then waved him through and up the drive. Emma wanted to open the door to him as she so often did but resisted the temptation and waited for the paper to drop through the letterbox.

She scooped it up quickly and ran back to the kitchen scanning the paper as she did so. There, two-thirds of the way down the front page was the headline: *DAUGHTER'S KIDNAP LINKED TO MOTHER'S MURDER. Kent Police revealed last night that the kidnap by knifepoint of 27-year-old Emma Bertram from Chartwood near Westerham in Kent is almost certainly linked to the murder of her mother, Doreen Bertram, six weeks ago. Police originally believed the murder was the result of a burglary that went tragically wrong, however they are now considering other possibilities but a spokesman at police headquarters in Maidstone refused to elaborate. 'We are following up several lines of enquiry', was all he was prepared to say. Miss Bertram was found yesterday afternoon in woods near Wokingham, Berkshire, by a woman out walking her dog. She was said to be disheveled and dazed and somewhat confused but otherwise unharmed. For full story and pictures turn to page five.*

'Knifepoint! You said nothing about knifepoint!' exclaimed Valerie with alarm looking over her shoulder.

'There was no knife Valerie, that's just the media getting it wrong as usual. You know what they are like.'

Emma turned the newspaper to page five and there was the picture again of Mother that had appeared in all the papers at the time of her killing. There was also a picture of Emma herself taken by a local newspaper at a craft fair a couple of years ago when she had won a prize for some quilting work she had done, along with a picture of Peter Keywood posing in the car park where it had all begun. The account of the abduction, where it had taken place together with details of the car used and of the wood where Emma had been found were accurate enough along with the description Emma and Peter Keywood had given the police of the two men who had taken her captive. The newspaper then went on to speculate about the link between the murder of Doreen Bertram and the abduction of Emma. There were wild suggestions that this could have been connected with money laundering or a drugs syndicate but it was all vague speculation and not detailed enough to be libelous. They had not had time overnight to make the connections between Mother and her past life as Doreen Patterson, but no doubt it would not be long before it all came out. The report concluded with the usual police plea for anyone who saw the incident or who could offer any information to come forward or call the incident room at Maidstone in confidence.

Emma sat back and stared at the newspaper, both hands clasped around a mug of near cold tea, which she sipped absently. 'Life will never be the same again for me will it?' she said looking up at Valerie.

Valerie stood behind Emma, held her shoulders and stroked her hair. 'I guess not my dear, I guess not.'

+++++++++

'No I'm sorry Emma, I heard her earlier on her mobile. She was canceling appointments for today and tomorrow and then said to me that she had to go up to London and may not be back until tomorrow. She left about an hour ago. I thought it was something to do with your situation, you know.' It was Jane's landlady on the other end of the telephone.

'Okay, thanks,' said Emma replacing the receiver. She had already tried Jane's mobile but it was either switched off or out of a service area.

'No luck dear?' enquired Valerie from the kitchen doorway, 'Don't worry, I'm sure she'll call you as soon as she gets your message.'

'I do hope so.' said Emma.

+++++++++

Higton was already in the office sifting through the information that had come in overnight following the news broadcast the previous evening when Smurdon arrived. He threw his coat over the nearest chair and went straight to Higton's desk.

'Anything interesting?'

'A postman returning from his round remembers Keywood beckoning Miss Bertram from across the road outside Woolworths and the time tallies but he didn't go in the direction of the car park so saw nothing else. We've also had a call from a motorist who regularly uses the cut through by that wood where Miss Bertram was found. Says he saw a white van coming out of the track where the tyre print was found about half an hour before she was discovered.'

'I thought Emma Bertram said she was stuffed in the boot of a dark coloured car?'

'She did,' replied Higton.

'Right, well you'd better get the local boys to check his story anyway and get a statement.' He paused. 'Anything else, and what about forensics?'

'A couple of calls suggesting who the abductors might be. I've got

Kennedy checking but there doesn't appear to be any connection. They're almost certainly crank calls. The Photo-fits from Keywood's descriptions are on their way over now and forensics in Berkshire hope to have some answers later today regarding the tyre print and partial footprints. Our own boys tell me they are up to their necks and are unlikely to give us an answer on the Invoice fragments until tomorrow.'

'Great,' said Smurdon with disdain, 'another twenty-four hours and they could be the other side of the moon by then.' He went round to the other side of his desk, sat heavily in the chair and rubbed his face with his hands as he let out a big yawn.

'Right, let's concentrate on the abductors. It's not the same car but could either of them have been the young man we saw at the funeral or who was following Miss Bertram?'

'Could well have been.' replied Higton.

Smurdon thought for a moment, 'Go and see that Major Whatshisname, the neighbour of the Bertram's.'

'Cowdrey.' interrupted Higton.

'What? Oh yes, Major Cowdrey, go and get him to look at the descriptions and the Photo-fits and see if he can tie the two together for us. And go and show the Photo-fits to that Jane Dennington and see what reaction you get. I still don't think she's told us everything she knows. Remember that Major reckons he saw her talking to the young man in the blue car.'

+++++++++

Emma had promised Valerie Marcheson that she would take it easy today and was glad to do just that. She sat on the wooden seat in her corner of the garden. It was early afternoon and the sun was well up in the sky with only a wisp of occasional high cloud to break the near perfect expanse of rich blue sky that Emma could see from this high vantage point. Below, travellers continued to speed frantically along the motorway from one appointment to the next while horses and sheep grazed lazily in the fields nearby. For a while she watched three new born lambs prancing around on the grass, enjoying the new life that nature had given to them. She noticed that while they seemed to play happily together, none of them strayed very far from its mother.

Mother. That dragged her thoughts back to reality. She thought again of all that had happened and particularly of all that she had learnt since Mother's death. Of the contents of the package at Aunt Millie's cottage, of the tale of secretive boat trips under the cover of darkness, of the old farm being used to store contraband, of Uncle Ted's hit and run killing in

Somerset and so much more. She realized as she dwelt on it that she had told so little of this to the Police and that only she and Jane knew the entire account of everything.

But would the police be interested. It was all hearsay and talk, just gossip really. There was no concrete evidence to substantiate any of it and what did it all mean anyway. As hard as she tried to make sense of it all there were still too many pieces of the jigsaw missing and if she was somehow to complete the puzzle would she be able to understand the picture it presented, she wondered?

'Hello, I'm not disturbing you am I?' The voice came from behind and it startled Emma who turned at the sound of it. It was Ray Brooks, the taxi driver.

'Sorry, I didn't mean to frighten you.' he smiled, 'your housekeeper said it would be okay to come down and see you. Bit like Fort Knox at the gate though.' he grinned.

Emma had stood and smiled back, 'No, of course not Ray, it's good of you to come.'

'Well, after I heard the news I just had to come and make sure you were all right. I did try to phone Jane but I can't raise her. Apparently she's gone to London.' he said.

'Yes, I know I've tried as well; she seems to have left her mobile off. I hope she is okay.' she paused, 'Here, come and sit for a while and enjoy the view, it's beautiful isn't it?' asked Emma spreading her hand out across the vista in front of them.

They sat in silence for a while enjoying the warmth of the sun and watching the scene below them. Emma turned and looked at Ray. He was not unhandsome and she liked the way he always had a smile and was often a little cheeky with anyone in authority. She thought for a moment about Gavin and wondered if she would ever find true love. But Ray, he had been very kind to her and she was pleased that Jane had found in him a good boyfriend.

Ray turned and smiled that smile again but then looked serious. 'Do you think this is all tied up with what happened to your aunt down near Bristol?' He enquired, then quickly added, 'Stop me if it's none of my business.'

'No, that's okay Ray, it's nice to have someone to talk about it really. I guess it must be. The man who kidnapped me was convinced my father is still alive and that it was he who planned the Sureguard robbery in 1972. I just can't believe it Ray, Mother always told me that my father had died in a car crash and that she didn't want to talk about it. I just assumed that it must have been too painful for her to speak about it. Now it appears that my mother is not who I thought her to be.'

'How, what do you mean?' queried Ray.

And so Emma told Ray about Doreen Patterson and the shoplifting charge and her supposed relationship with the notorious bullion robber Barry Masters and all that she had learnt over recent weeks.

'You know Ray, amongst my mother's things I found an old jewellers receipt for a ring. It was made out to a B Masters. I wondered whatever Mother was keeping this for, I had never heard of a B Masters. Now I know its significance.' Emma stopped and held her hand to her mouth a small tear droplet forming at the corner of each eye.

Ray sensed the emotion and remained silent for a while keeping his eyes on the view below then he said. 'If there's anything I can do to help, well you know you only have to ask.'

Emma turned towards him, reached out and squeezed his arm, 'Thank you Ray, you and Jane have been good friends to me, I'm really grateful.'

+++++++++

Higton found Smurdon in the police canteen having lunch and chatting to the Inspector in charge of traffic. 'Sorry to interrupt but we've got some answers back from Forensics and I thought you'd like to hear them.'

'Yes, great, what have you got?' asked Smurdon putting his knife and fork down and looking up.

'The tyre prints from Berkshire are from a cheap import tyre. Suggests the car was probably old and there are a couple of distinctive cuts showing up as well so they reckon they could confirm an exact match if we found the car for them.'

'What about outlets for the tyres?' asked Smurdon.

'Unfortunately quite a few, it's carried by two of the big tyre and exhaust repair chains, so it could have come from virtually anywhere in the country.' Higton paused. 'The trainer print is also pretty common, size eight *Nike* sports. You can get them almost anywhere, but again this one has got a couple of distinguishing marks that may enable Forensic to make a match.'

'Okay, any news on the warehouse?'

'Yes, the Birmingham Company went out of business in the recession of the early 90's. I've got Kennedy trying to track down the owner so we can find out about their distribution depots.'

'Good, anything else?'

'Yes, Sam Harvan was in Pentonville in 1993 at the same time as

Robbie Wilson. They overlapped for about seven months and were on the same wing together.'

'Now that is interesting.' said Smurdon. 'Good work; I have a feeling we are getting somewhere at last. I'll be up in the CID room in about twenty minutes.'

+++++++++

Emma had spent the best part of the afternoon chatting to Ray Brooks and then when he had left to return to work she had taken to walking circuits around the pathways of the garden. Despite being out in the open and enjoying the freshness and warmth of the glorious spring day she felt trapped. She was of course grateful that she no longer endured the dreadful stifling room that had been her prison and bodily she felt so much better. But mentally there were still so many unanswered questions and she so desperately wanted to get out there and find some answers. But where to look she pondered? As she mulled it over in her mind it occurred to her that there must have been a lot more recorded in the press at the time of the robbery and subsequent trial. The Sureguard robbery seemed to be the key to all that had happened and she decided that tomorrow despite any protests that were certain to come from Valerie Marcheson, she would drive into Tonbridge to the reference library and scour the newspapers of the time for any information she may have missed and to read up on the trial.

+++++++++

As expected Valerie did kick up a fuss the following morning about the fact that Emma ought to be resting but Emma could not be moved and Valerie reluctantly agreed to inform the PC on the gate that Emma would be coming out and she did not wish to be followed by any of the press. Five minutes later as Emma sped down the lane she saw in her rear-view mirror that the Constable was restraining one of the pressmen from getting into his car.

As Emma drove through the streets she thought again about Jane. She had tried to telephone her several times the previous evening and again this morning but always her mobile was switch off and all Emma could do was leave a message. She had telephone Jane's landlady and also Ray but neither of them had heard from her.

'Oh Jane, where are you? Said Emma out loud as she turned through the morning traffic.

+++++++++

Emma sat in a quiet corner of the reference library working her way through copies of *The Times* newspaper for most of 1972 from August onwards. The accounts of the robbery were more factual and dispassionate than the tabloid cuttings she had seen in the warehouse office but nonetheless the details of what happened and the cold-blooded killing of the security guard made for uncomfortable reading. It was a blatantly daring daylight attack that also left one of the other two guards, the driver, seriously injured as he had been beaten repeatedly for refusing to hand over the keys of the vehicle. However there was nothing in these columns that Emma did not already know.

The trial was eight and a half months later at the Old Bailey Central Criminal Court in London. Wilson and Peters in the light of overwhelming evidence had pleaded guilty to the robbery but were adamant that they had nothing to do with the killing of the guard, or the attack on the driver and implicated Barry Masters, a known criminal. A warrant had been issued for Masters arrest but despite an extensive search by the police for Masters there had been no trace found of him. There was also no other evidence to support Wilson and Peter's claim that Masters was involved other than the passing motorist who saw at least three people taking part in the attack. He was however unable to give any clear descriptions as he was some distance from the ambush and could only simply say that he had seen three people, possibly a fourth at the scene who were not dressed in the uniform of security guards.

The background of Masters past criminal activities was catalogued in the newspaper including mention of his long time girlfriend Doreen Patterson who it said had been interviewed by police but had denied any knowledge of the robbery. The report added that she appeared to be genuinely worried about his disappearance and could offer no explanation for it.

In a further article a week later it was reported that there had been signs of a power struggle in the criminal fraternity and that Masters had been the victim of a gangland dispute. Rumours were circulating that Masters had been killed and the fact that he could not be found seemed to give weight to the report. The only police response was that their enquiries were continuing.

At the end of the trial Wilson and Peters were both given life sentences and sent to the maximum security prison on Dartmoor in Devon. Police reported that so far none of the bullion had been recovered and admitted that the trail had gone cold.

Emma sat back and sighed. She had learnt a lot about the robbery and the trial and received confirmation that Doreen Patterson was Barry Masters girlfriend, which she supposed, meant that she had been born out of wedlock. If she had been told that at any other time it might have destroyed her but coming after so many other revelations about her past and that of her parents it just made her feel numb. She looked up and was conscious that an elderly man a few tables away was watching her. There were only half a dozen people in the reference section of the library and this man she remembered had entered shortly after she had arrived. He had a book in front of him but she could not recall ever seeing him turn a page. It unnerved her and she tried to ignore him and concentrate on searching through the remaining issues that the librarian had brought. A moment later as she turned another page she suddenly became aware of someone standing over her.

'Good afternoon, Miss Bertram?'

Emma looked up, startled.

'Please don't be alarmed, I mean you no harm. My name is Frank Cowton, I was…'

But Emma finished the sentence for him. 'The investigating officer for the Metropolitan Police on the Sureguard robbery. There's a picture of you in one of these earlier editions.' said Emma pointing to the pile of newspapers on the table. 'And your name is mentioned several times.'

He smiled, 'I'm surprised you're able to recognize me after all these years.'

A look of concern came over Emma's face. 'How did you know to find me her?' she asked.

He smiled again and laughed. 'I've still got the detective in me even though I retired several years ago. I followed you from the bottom of Silver Lane. I knew it would be no good coming up to the house and I didn't want to let the press know I had made contact with you anyway.'

He had been trying to whisper but with his deep gravely voice he was struggling and two people sitting nearby were now glaring at him and one coughed loudly to attract his attention. 'Look,' he said looking round. 'Do you think we could go somewhere for a coffee? It will be easier to talk than here.'

+++++++++

That same morning as Emma left for the library, Jane Dennington was walking unfamiliar streets of London. She had been to the office and the club, but of the people she wished to confront, none were to be seen and no one was able to say where she would find them. She knew they rarely let anyone know of their whereabouts believing that way that they 'stayed one step ahead of the crowd' as they put it. She had stopped off earlier at a pavement café and ordered a coffee and Danish pastry, though immediately wished she hadn't as both items were barely drinkable or edible. As she sat there she racked her brain. The most likely place she would find them would be the warehouse she decided. But could she remember where it was? She had been there with them once before and knew it was in Bermondsey, just south of the River Thames but if only she could remember the name of the street. She had closed her eyes trying to picture the drive through the Rotherhithe tunnel and the short ride after that that took them there. It was no good, she couldn't remember the street name but decided to head in that direction anyway. There was little else she could do. She had hailed a taxi and got the driver to drop her off on the corner of Southwark Park Road and Dunton Road. She was certain it was somewhere in this area.

Walking slowly up Dunton Road now she was less certain as nothing seemed familiar, ahead she could see that the road rose to form a bridge and she remembered there being a railway yard near the warehouse. Perhaps she was heading in the right direction after all. She quickened her pace and turning into the street just before the bridge saw the building she was looking for, a drab and dirty two-storey brick built warehouse that backed on to the now nearly defunct railway yard. Opposite, a row of terraced houses with small front enclosures looked similarly bleak. The constant dust and grime of this inner London suburb meant that the inhabitants had long ago given up on any attempt to tend them as gardens. Old bikes and prams, brick, plaster waste and old wood from attempted house conversions littered these dismal pockets that bordered the roadside.

She waited for a lorry to pass, the driver hooted his horn as he did so and his mate leered out of the window but Jane ignored them. Being attractive had its downside as well sometimes. Crossing the road she went up to the heavy shutters through which vehicles could pass into the building but they were tightly secured. Following the frontage she then turned into the small yard to the right of the building where she remembered there was a pedestrian door towards the back of the warehouse. There were no cars parked in the yard and she was beginning to think that her journey had been wasted but as she approached the door she could see that it was slightly open, the almost bare wood newly splintered around the lock.

Pushing the door gently she stepped gingerly into the dim interior, the filth encrusted windows letting scant light into the cavernous space. She caught the edge of a yard broom with her toe and sent the handle crashing to the ground which echoed loudly through the near empty building and made her start. She paused but there was no response to the noisy entrance she had made. Across to her left she could see a corridor leading down into a brick built area inside the main shell, a faint sign above it announcing the way to offices. From this corridor glowed a dim electric light, perhaps there was someone here after all. She made her way across to it calling the names as she went but there was still no response. At the end of the corridor she turned into the office and saw piles of old stationary scattered across the floor and in one corner the remains of a partially eaten sandwich. Just then she saw a movement out of the corner of her eye but before she could react a rough hand clasped tightly across her mouth and she felt her legs being kicked from under her.

+++++++++

Although they had only just met there was something in Frank Cowton's manner that was reassuring and Emma agreed to join him in the cafeteria attached to the leisure centre next door.

Emma sat at a table in the corner and watched him as he ordered the drinks from the counter. She guessed he was in his late sixties. He was smartly dressed in grey suit, lighter grey shirt and dark grey tie. The colours complemented his neatly groomed silver grey hair which topped a round and youthful looking face and he walked with a lightness in his step that suggested he exercised regularly. He noticed Emma looking at him and smiled again as he brought the tray of drinks over to the table.

'I must apologize once again. I do hope I didn't frighten you, I should think you've had more than enough frights for quite sometime, but I did want to talk to you.'

He sat down, the smile disappeared and age crept into his features. He stared into the brown liquid in front of him as if he were struggling to find the words to say. Without looking up he said. 'I was at the peak of my career when that robbery and murder broke. I'd investigated and solved several major serious crimes and was really chuffed when I was given that one.' he paused. 'It was a tough one to crack, very carefully and secretively planned. There was not a word on the street, that's a police term for informants etc. No one anywhere seemed to have had any inkling that this was going to take place.'

'Is that unusual?' Queried Emma, not knowing anything about the criminal underworld.

'Yes it is, there's nearly always someone somewhere who's heard a whisper or been asked to provide equipment or been recruited as a driver and so on and we had plenty of informants in those days who kept their eyes and ears open in the pubs and clubs, anything to earn a backhander from the police. But here there was just nothing and it upset quite a few of the criminal fraternity that something so big had gone down without them knowing about it.' he paused, 'Barry Masters certainly made a few enemies that day.'

'What do you think happened to him? The newspapers seem to suggest that he was killed by a notorious gang.'

'The Harvan brothers.' Cowton responded. 'Well that's one possibility but somehow I'm not so sure. His body has never been found and you can buy an awful lot when you have money of that magnitude.'

'That's what the young man who kidnapped me said, he was certain that Barry Masters was still alive,' she paused, 'He said Barry Masters was my father.'

Emma leant forward, 'Was Barry Masters my father Mr. Cowton?'

He looked up and studied her for a moment and could see the hurt in her eyes, the longing to know the truth yet also the fear and pain that the truth might bring.

'My honest answer is that I don't know. We do know that your mother and Barry had a relationship for quite some time and for at least part of that time they lived together. But did your mother have a relationship with anyone else? All I can answer is that we weren't aware of anyone at the time. Mind you if your mother did have an affair with anyone else she would have wanted to keep it quiet from Masters that's for sure, not a very pleasant character at all. We interviewed your mother twice, possibly three times if I recall, shortly after the robbery and I don't remember her being pregnant or any sign of a baby.' he paused, 'When were you born Miss Bertram?'

'4th June 1973, ten months after the robbery took place.' replied Emma.

'That would have made your conception one month after the robbery.' he said as if thinking out loud. 'Well your mother was certainly around then but the whereabouts of Barry Masters is anyone's guess. If I remember right we put a stake out on Doreen Patterson's flat for a while in case Masters tried to make contact.' he paused, 'Sorry but that's all I can offer.'

'So I'm still no nearer to the truth,' sighed Emma staring at her now luke warm cup of coffee.

They were both silent for a while then Emma asked, 'did you know Barry Masters before?

'Yes I'd interviewed him on two previous occasions relating to post office robberies where people got hurt badly. I think he carried them out but we didn't have enough evidence to charge him, they were the only other two serious crime cases that I was unable to solve. Masters was like a thorn in my side and when Wilson and Peters shopped him I thought I had him. I was looking forward to putting the 'cuffs on him personally.' He paused to drain the rest of his coffee. 'Then he just disappeared into thin air, every trail went cold, every sighting proved to be false, and nothing of any use from our informants. It was if the man and the gold just didn't exist.'

Clearing his throat he looked down at the table and spoke more quietly, 'Two months after the robbery there was a senior review meeting at Scotland Yard and I was taken off the case. A month after that I was moved off the Serious Crimes Squad. 'Organisational restructuring' or some such bull they called it. All I dealt with after that was petty shoplifting and household burglaries; my career was finished.'

Emma watched him as he spoke. She could almost tangibly feel the pain with which he spoke and something made her reach out and gently touch his arm.

Emma was silent for a while; trying to decide whether she should reveal some of the things she had learnt over recent weeks. Then she made up her mind, 'Among the many sightings of Barry Masters, do you recall one of him boarding a fishing boat at Hastings?'

'Yes, that was sometime after the robbery if I remember.' he paused, 'What do you know about it?' he queried.

So Emma told him all she had found out since her mother's death, about the package in the attic and the one from her aunt's near Bristol. The photographs and the map, the circumstances of her uncle's death and what she knew of the out of the way farm for storing contraband and the fishing boat incident and the loss of the two brothers. She didn't leave anything out and as she spoke she saw the old detective come alive again as he drank in every word and sorted the information into the compartments of his mind.

When she had finished he spoke. 'Thank you for sharing all that with me. Perhaps I can help you find the answer to your question. I still have friends in the force, I'll see if I can look through the files again from that perspective, there may just be something there.' he paused and stood up offering her his hand. As they shook he said, 'If I can at least help you there I will feel that I have gone some way to redeeming myself.'

With that he turned and left.

Chapter 17

While Emma had been drinking coffee with Frank Cowton, Smurdon and Higton were doing the same. Kennedy and two other detectives were with them and they had been brainstorming the evidence and trying to piece everything together. 'If Masters really is alive, he's managed to keep it quiet for nearly thirty years? I don't think so…no I don't buy it!' said one of the others.

'I'm not so sure,' replied Kathy Smart, a newly appointed woman constable to the CID department, 'That's an awful lot of money for buying silence.'

Just then the telephone rang and Higton who had been sitting at his desk snatched it up and answered. It was his colleague from the Met in London.

'Yes… right… Oh my God!'

Smurdon turned and looked at Higton whose face had now gone pale.

'There's no doubt? Asked Higton, 'No… right… yes okay I'll wait to hear from you… thanks.'

He put the phone down slowly. 'What?' said Smurdon with concern.

'Phil Johnson and his team have just raided the warehouse where Emma Bertram was held; I got hold of the address for him earlier.'

'And?'

'They found Jane Dennington there'

'Jane Dennington?'

'Yes, stabbed several times, she's dead!'

The room was silent for a while; Smurdon rose from his chair and walked slowly to the window his mind whirring. 'How the hell… first the Bertram girl and now Dennington… and why was the Bertram girl released but Dennington killed?'

'Did they say how long ago?' asked Kennedy.

'Only a few hours by all accounts,' replied Higton, 'the body was still warm.'

'Did they say if she was killed there or killed somewhere else and taken there?' It was the new DC, Kathy Smart.

'What are you getting at?' asked Smurdon turning.

'Well, I just wondered if she was taken there or if she knew where to look. You said yesterday that she was a bit funny about having put the address of the Motor Parts Company in the wash.'

'My God!' exclaimed Smurdon. 'Are we missing something here? Could Dennington have known where to look?

'What do you mean?' asked Higton.

'Well the bullion that went missing was H M Treasury, British Government owned wasn't it, and it's never been recovered, so when the police can't find it what do they do? They put their own government agents onto it. Right from the start there has always been something about that woman. Always asking how our investigation was going, always wanting to be in on the interviews we had with Miss Bertram, and remember she was seen talking to that young chap in the blue car but always denied it.' Smurdon paused, 'Kennedy I want you to check on her background, find out what you can about her before she came to Chartwood and have a word with your contact in Whitehall and see if there's any hint that she might have been a government agent. But do it discreetly, if she was an agent all hell will break loose when her masters discover she's been murdered.'

'What about Emma Bertram?' asked Higton. 'Are you going to tell her?'

'Yes, I'd better do that myself, you'd better come along too Kathy.' replied Smurdon.

+++++++++

Emma sat alone in the day room stunned by the news that Smurdon had broken to her half an hour ago. 'First Mother, then Aunt Millie, then the kidnap and now Jane.' she thought. When would the nightmare end? She tried to make some sense of it all but she was too distraught for her mind to settle into any coherent thought. Valerie had brought her a cup of tea and put it on the table. She had squeezed Emma's shoulder and lightly touched her head and was going to say something but instead had fled the room in a gush of tears.

The unusually warm weather continued to enliven the garden and bright colours were bursting out all over the flower borders but Emma didn't notice any of it as she stared out across the lawns. As the sun settled towards the west turning into a deep ball of fire, its final warmth of the day still penetrated through the patio windows and into the room but again Emma did not feel it and shivered as if the tentacles of death were touching her every bone.

A gentle tap on the door interrupted her muddled thoughts and Ray Brooks put his head round. His eyes were red and his face full of despair and sadness. Emma stood and they just looked at each other for a moment and then slowly they met and just held each other in silence.

+++++++++

Smurdon had returned to the office to tidy his desk before going home for the evening. Higton had already left but Kennedy was still there. He looked up as Smurdon entered. 'Looks like we could be right about our Miss Dennington.'

'What's that?' asked Smurdon.

'Initial investigation suggests that Dennington didn't exist before she came to Chartwood. There's no record of her under that name elsewhere.'

'What about fingerprints?'

'I've got the Met checking, they're running it through their computers now.'

'And the suggestion she may be undercover?'

'Again nothing yet but we're still digging. If she was working for a government department they're not going to come straight out and say so without clearance from their top brass.'

'No, that's right, okay keep digging, I'll see you in the morning.'

+++++++++

Ray and Emma had sat opposite each other lost in their own thoughts for some while, and then Ray broke the silence.

'What do you make of it all Em?'

'I don't know, I'm so confused, I keep turning it all over in my mind and it just doesn't seem to make any sense. Mother and I and Aunt Millie were all related and there is a connection between us and Father, but Jane, she was outside the family. She was Mother's hairdresser and had only been doing it for what, about four months. How can she be connected?'

'The police didn't tell me very much,' Ray said, and then added quietly, 'Other than to say that it would have been very quick.' He swallowed and looked down at the floor. 'I suppose she was kidnapped like you and taken to the same place.' he added. A statement rather than a question.

'Smurdon was a bit vague.' replied Emma, 'He said details were still coming through from the London police but he asked me a strange question. He wanted to know if I thought Jane knew where to look for the warehouse where I was held. What was he suggesting? How could she have possibly known where to go! I don't like that man, his mind is warped.' said Emma angrily.

'What I don't understand,' said Ray, 'is that these people, whoever they are, have killed your mother and Jane and probably had a hand in progressing your aunt's death yet they kidnap you with every opportunity to kill you, but release you unharmed.'

'That's what really frightens me,' said Emma. 'I really thought I was going to be killed. That man was so terrifying I really believed I was going to die, and then he just disappeared. The way he did that, leaving me there kneeling in the woods, expecting a bullet any moment....' Her voice trailed off and Emma began to cry.

Ray moved across the room, sat on the sofa next to Emma and put his arm around her shoulders. Through the sobs Emma continued. 'Jane and I didn't part the best of friends when she left that evening and now I will never be able to put that right.'

'She knew you were distraught and didn't mean it.' said Ray trying to comfort her.

They were silent for a while then Emma blew her nose and said, 'Smurdon thinks they were after information from Mother and killed her by accident. He thinks they think I know where either my father Barry Masters, if he is my father, and the missing money or gold is and that I can lead them to it. But I can't, I just don't know where it is. I didn't know they even existed before a few days ago.'

Emma began to get distraught again and Ray tightened his arm around her shoulder. 'Try not to let this beat you. You've been so strong up till now.' he said comfortingly.

'Oh Ray, I'm sorry, you've just lost your dearest friend and here you are comforting me.'

'She was your friend too Em.' Ray said quietly and then looking at his watch stood up. 'I'm sorry but I've got to go, I've got another two bookings this evening, my boss said I could take some time off but I prefer to keep working, I can cope better that way. Will you be alright Em?'

'I'll be fine, don't worry about me, you take care of yourself now.'

They stood awkwardly facing each other then Emma reached up and lightly kissed him on the cheek. 'Thanks for coming Ray.'

+++++++++

The morning brought nothing but bad news for the murder squad at

Kent police headquarters. The Met had reported that there were no fingerprints on file to match Jane Dennington's and an interview with her landlady had also revealed no leads. Dennington had responded to an advertisement for a room to let placed by the Carters and had paid cash for three months rent in advance. She had seemed a nice enough young woman and they didn't bother to ask for any references. All enquiries to various government agencies and to Sureguard security and their insurance company had also drawn a blank. All denied they had any agents employed in trying to trace the missing millions after all these years. Emma Bertram, Valerie Marcheson and Ray Brooks had all been contacted by telephone and asked if Jane had ever spoken of family or relatives. They all replied in the negative. Major Cowdrey had just returned from a holiday in the Bahamas and had reported that the description of the two men who had abducted Emma Bertram was nothing like the young man in the light blue car he had seen talking to Jane Dennington and also in the lane leading up to *Tall Trees*.

'Where do we go from here?' It was Higton who asked the question.

'Someone clearly thinks that the money and possibly also Masters is still out there, either they have inside knowledge or it's just guess work. Whichever it is they are very determined and will clearly stop at nothing to get it.' said Smurdon. 'We have two murders and a kidnap to demonstrate that. The only reason I believe they let Miss Bertram go free is because they think she will lead them to it.'

'Does she know where the money is?' asked Kennedy.

'I'm not sure, maybe, maybe not. I suspect she may know but not realize it herself yet.'

'What do you mean by that?' asked Kathy Smart.

'Well, maybe she knows something, a place, a bank account, maybe there is something in the house, a contact person or telephone number, anything. Since her mother's death she's gone chasing after various leads herself, we know that. The Dennington woman may well have instigated it but I don't think she will stop now. She has told me several times that she wants to get to the truth.'

'So we stake her out?' Higton again.

'Yes, I've got the old man's permission, round the clock surveillance for as long as it takes.

+++++++++

That same morning was miserable for Emma also. She hadn't slept at all well and the weather echoed her mood. It was raining heavily with wind gusting from the southwest causing the rain to wash against the patio doors in great waves. Unable to get out of the house Emma wandered from room to room just wishing there was something she could do to take her mind off it all. She had picked up a quilt she had been making. One that she had last touched the day before Mother died but her heart was not in it and she could not concentrate and began to make mistakes. She threw the work down and stood at the window looking blankly out. In the watery whiteness she could see Jane walking out of the room upset at her outburst and her eyes began to water again. 'O Mother!' she mouthed again, 'When will it all end?'

Her thoughts were interrupted by the sound of the telephone and she heard Valerie answering it. She came to the door with the phone in her hand. 'It's a mister Cowton; he says you're expecting his call. If he's a reporter just trying to get past me I'll get rid of him.'

'No, it all right thanks Valerie.' said Emma taking the handset from her. 'Hello, yes, this afternoon at 2.30, same place, that will be fine. Thank you, goodbye.'

Valerie had wanted to know who Cowton was and Emma explained about the meeting at the library. She hadn't told her before because she didn't want her to be worrying and Valerie, as expected, was not keen for Emma to meet Cowton again, mumbling as before that in her view, things were best left alone.

Emma gave her a kiss and told her not to worry. 'Anything is better than just moping around here and I owe it to both Mother and Jane to get to the bottom of this and I'm determined to do just that.' she declared, feeling far less confident than she hoped her voice sounded.

After lunch Valerie made the same arrangement with the constable on the gate in case there were any reporters about and Emma slipped out to make her meeting with Frank Cowton at the leisure centre café.

Cowton was waiting for her at the same table as before, this time smartly dressed in a matching dark blue suit, shirt and tie. He stood as she walked over to him and pointed to a coffee already waiting on the table. 'It's fresh; I purchased it less than a minute ago.'

Emma sat down opposite him. 'What information have you been able to find out, Mr. Cowton?'

'Not as much as you would like I'm sure but here goes. My friends at Scotland Yard have enabled me to sift through the files again, unofficially of course.' he added. 'Even before Wilson and Peters were caught Masters was considered to be a likely candidate to have pulled off the robbery and his place was watched. He and your Mother were living together at the time as far as we know so surveillance was in place virtually from day one but there was no sign of Masters at the rented house. When Wilson and Peters implicated your father the watch was stepped up. It was thought that your Mother was bound to be contacted by Masters but he never showed. That certainly made us suspicious that he was involved but your mother just said that Masters didn't live there all the time and she had no idea where else he lived. There's a note on the file by one of the interviewing detectives that she seemed genuinely worried as to his whereabouts and probably wouldn't know if he had been involved in the robbery. Either she was telling the truth or she was a good actress. Her house was searched twice without warning in case he had slipped in but nothing was found, neither was there any evidence of someone else living there. There's also no record of any other male visiting the house while we had it under observation which was for about three months after the robbery. So if your birth date is correct I'm afraid the identity of your father remains a mystery.'

He paused and sipped his coffee. 'When three months was up, after I had been taken off the case, the watch was lifted. Two months after that the new detective leading the investigation decided he would have a chat with Doreen Patterson. When they got to the house they found she had gone, no forwarding address, nothing. She had a Building Society account for around £6,000 that had been cleared out two weeks previously and like Barry Masters she had simply disappeared.

We now know that she turned up just over a year later as Doreen Bertram and purchased *Tall Trees*, with her was a two and a half month old baby called Emma. Where she had been in the meantime and where the money came from to purchase the house remains a mystery.'

'So we still don't know if Barry Masters was my father?'

'Sorry.' was all Cowton could say.

'Did you look into the fishing boat incident?' asked Emma.

'Yes, it was just one of many possible sightings and reports that the police had to deal with then. Of course at the time there was no connection made between your uncle and Masters, it just wasn't known. Then the rumour that the Harvan brothers had taken care of him was pretty strong and no further action was taken. It's possible that there was some involvement with the boat but if the two fishermen were found why was Masters body, if it was him, not found?'

He paused again and looked at his cup, 'These people must think that you have some knowledge either about the gold or your father and what happened to him, that must be why they released you.'

'That's what the police think, but I don't, I just don't!' Emma sighed.

'I know, I believe you, but maybe there is something in the house, something in your Mother's possessions that's a clue but you just haven't found it yet.'

'Mother kept virtually nothing of interest from the past, 'Emma replied, 'I've been through all her things, there was nothing to connect her with her old life of Doreen Patterson or Barry Masters apart from that photograph and the jewellery receipt. You know I still can't fully grasp that, that my Mother was someone totally different in character and lifestyle before she had me. I just feel so numb when I think about it.'

'Well all I can suggest is that you have another look, there must be something somewhere.' suggested Cowton.

++++++++++

Emma returned home determined to do as Frank Cowton had suggested but she felt unable to face it that evening. The events of the last few days and the lack of sleep the night before were catching up on her and she felt very tired. She remembered sitting down to watch a wildlife programme on the television to take her mind off of things but she was asleep in the chair within seconds and Valerie didn't wake her until the news at ten. Despite three hours of sleep during the evening she still managed to sleep right through until after eight the next morning and felt much better for it. The rain of the previous day had passed and the cloud was breaking up to allow a weak sun through into the day room. Emma had spent the best part of the morning up in the attic rooms again looking to see if there was anything she and Jane had missed that first day they found the photographs. She hadn't like being there on her own as it brought back too many memories of Jane. Emma then turned her attention to Mother's bedroom but couldn't face going in there. She had not been in there since her death and was thankful for Valerie's offer of help to check through all of the clothes and personal effects for anything of significance. Both rooms drew a blank and Emma now stood in the day room looking at the desk and bookshelves. She had been through the desk thoroughly before and was certain she had not missed anything.

She reached up and took down a book of poetry by Tennyson and leafed through it turning the well-thumbed pages. Her eyes fell on the following lines:

Tears, idle tears, I know not what they mean,
Tears from the depth of some divine despair
Rise in the heart, and gather to the eyes,
In looking on the happy autumn-fields,
And thinking of the days that are no more.

A teardrop fell on the page just where the passage from *The Princess* ended and Emma sniffed hard. As she replaced the book she ran her hand along the spines of a dozen books of poetry that Mother had loved. They were all there, Milton, Keats, Wordsworth, Vaughan, Shelley, Pope, and Gray. She stopped and looked back at the one by Shelley, Mother always used proper book marks but this one had a thin piece of folded paper just poking out from between the pages. She took down the book and extracted the paper. It was airmail paper and on opening it, saw that it was the same handwriting as the two envelopes that had been addressed to her from Spain. Perching on the edge of Mother's chair she read:

Dear Miss Emma, Did you get my last letter? Please I hope you are able to help us. It is urgent; I hope you will come please. Thank you, I am Juan Delgardo. That was all, no address and no date but Emma was sure that this must have been the letter from the second envelope she had discovered that had been sent from Spain.

Emma stared at the letter and read it over and over again. What did it mean? Was this connected with the deaths of her Mother or Father? It was just another mystery. Why was it that every time she discovered something new it only raised more questions rather than providing the answers she so desperately craved?

She had been so taken up with the discovery of the letter that she hadn't heard the doorbell. Valerie Marcheson stood in the doorway with Constable Higton hovering behind her.

'Just a few more questions please Miss.' Higton called.

Emma quickly stuffed the letter into her pocket and invited him into the room.

++++++++

'What?' shouted Emma, 'Are you having me followed?'

Higton had told her that she had been seen having a meeting with Frank Cowton. He wanted to know what the conversation had been about and reminded her that Cowton was retired and had no right in discussing anything about the case in hand. 'So my Mother and Jane are just a case now are they?' Emma had stormed.

'I am just reminding you who is in charge of this investigation and that failure to cooperate with the police is a serious matter.' He had replied. 'Perhaps if you had been doing your job properly instead of following me around, Jane would still be alive now.' she had screamed surprised by her angry response to his questioning.

'Just making sure you understand Miss, that's all, I'll go now.'

As soon as she heard the front door close she took the letter from her pocket and read it again, and then systematically she took every book off the shelves and one by one search through every page for any sign of the first letter, which she knew from the envelope must exist. An hour later and there was not one nook, cranny or book that had not been searched thoroughly in the day room, but of the letter there was no sign.

She sat in Mother's chair again and thought long and hard and then made a decision. Picking up her mobile she dialed Ray's number. He answered.

'Hello Ray, is it convenient to talk?'

'Yes, no problem, I'm parked up outside Tesco's in Chartwood waiting for my fare, they'll be at least another ten minutes yet. What can I do for you?'

'Can you come to the house tonight after dark, but don't park out the front as usual, bring the car round the side to the garages, okay?'

'Yes of course, sounds mysterious!'

'I'll explain when you get here.'

+++++++++

Kathy Smart stifled a yawn and looked at her watch; it was just coming up to nine in the morning. She had taken over watch on the lane from *Tall Trees* at six am. and had another five hours to go yet. She picked up a flask of hot coffee and poured herself a cup just as her mobile rang. It was Smurdon.

'Got anything to report?' he asked.

No, nothing at all this morning, doubt if they are up yet. There's one report from Connor on last night's watch, the taxi driver Brooks called up at the house at 9.34pm and left at 9.52pm. That's all.'

'Okay, keep me posted if anything breaks.' and with that he cut the line.

Kathy Smart was just about to take a drink from the cup when she heard a car. Instinctively she ducked as Emma drove by though she knew of the words between Higton and her the previous day and was aware that Emma knew about the watch.

The morning traffic was light and it was no difficulty keeping Emma in her sights. She was heading for the town centre and soon pulled into the multi-story car park at the back of the high street. Despite being early the first level was already full and much of the second level also but Emma found a parking space near the walkway through to the shops and parked her car. She got out and lifted a large shopping bag off the back seat, put it over her shoulder and headed for the shops. Kathy parked the unmarked police car across the other side of the same level where she had a good view of Emma's car and debated whether to follow her but decided it would be too obvious at this time of morning and in any case Emma would have to return to her car. She settled down with her cup of luke-warm coffee and began to flick through the pages of the latest *Hello* magazine.

As she did so Ray Brooks eased his taxi out from the level below and headed through the one way system and onto the dual carriageway towards the motorway. As he did so he checked his rear-view mirror several times.

'No, definitely, no, we are not being followed.' he smiled and turned to face his passenger.

Emma smiled back. 'Thanks Ray, and thanks for picking my bag up last night.'

'No problem,' he said, 'Gatwick Airport here we come!'

Chapter 18

Emma felt not only frustrated but was beginning to feel foolish too. In the last three days since she had arrived in Spain she had gone over in her mind the events of the last three months. So little if anything made any sense. Every direction she had taken, every avenue she had explored had led to a dead end or confused her even further. What had it all meant? The kidnap, the questionable deaths of Uncle Edward and the fishermen, and most of all, the murders of her mother and Jane and the mysteries surrounding her father. Could he still be alive? She didn't think so. If he was why had he never contacted her or her mother? Nothing made any sense and yet it must mean something. If only she could discover what.

She had arrived by scheduled airline at Valencia on Monday and hired a car at the airport. There had been a holiday atmosphere at the busy terminal, schools across Europe had finished for the summer and the excited chatter of hundreds of families lifted her spirits as she pushed her way through the crowd to the car hire desk. The warmth of the sun, the bright colours of the bougainvillaea in the gardens and adorning the roadside, and glimpses of the deep blue Mediterranean Sea away to the left as she drove down the A7 motorway continued to give her that feeling of well being, the purpose of her visit temporarily forgotten as she concentrated on driving on the right hand side of the road.

The journey to Denia was about 100 kilometres and had taken her just over an hour and a half. She had been content to let other motorists speed past her as she took in the new vista. The hillsides of neatly terraced stone walls to give level steps of soil on which were planted rows of vines and fruit trees, the upper barren slopes of brown rock standing sharp against the azure blue sky of this summer afternoon. And the pretty *fincas* dotted seemingly at random across the landscape and painted stark white against their drab backcloth. Even those buildings that stood derelict, Emma mused, had a magical quality about them in what to her was an almost alien landscape.

She left the motorway at junction 62 and headed down the main road into the town. The orange and lemon groves soon gave way to industrial buildings, a timber store, and several large motor car showrooms that now bordered the roadside. She successfully negotiated the hire car past several roundabouts at the end of the main road and gingerly steered it in the direction of the port as the travel agent had instructed her. The town was packed with cars; cars double parked, parked across street corners, parked across pedestrian crossings, and parked seemingly everywhere. Emma had seen nothing like it. She began to feel nervous now and despite the air conditioning in the car could feel droplets of perspiration running down her back. Regardless of the fact it was siesta time there were many people ambling along the dusty streets, perhaps tourists, unable to accept the Spanish way of a respite from the heat of the afternoon sun. Arriving at the sea front road by the port she turned right and made her way past the yacht club to the *Port Denia Hotel* and booked in.

For the next two days she had walked the streets searching for some clue, some identity, something that she could link with all the event of the last few weeks back home since her mother's untimely death. From the narrow, almost dingy back streets to the wide palm lined *Ave del Denia* and the main street *Marco de Campo* with its fine and expensive shops. The fish market, the fresh produce market, the cafes, the wine bars, the port, and the harbour. Whenever she had opportunity she asked if anyone knew the name of Juan Delgardo, she even showed people the old photographs of Ted, Millie and Barry and spoke their names. But she knew nothing of the Spanish language and it was impossible to communicate with most of the locals although even if she had the result she was sure would have been the same. People just shook their head or shrugged. Some spoke words she did not understand but the look on their faces gave the answer. After all, she reasoned, the photographs had been taken years ago and she had no idea if the name Delgardo was common or not.

The town was much bigger than she had expected. It sprawled way back some three miles onto the lower slopes of the *Montgo* Mountain to the south west and north up the coast for several miles, let alone the little clusters of houses that stretched back into the hills for miles behind the town. And all these places probably used Denia for posting a letter. And post letters someone did. From Denia, and they both arrived just a few weeks before Doreen Bertram was killed. Who was it, and why address them to her? And what was the content of the first letter? She had asked the question a thousand times over. Before she flew out, Emma had been certain there must be a connection with all that had happened over the last few months; and yet now sitting at a pavement café looking out over the marina she was not so sure.

She had been here now three days and felt tired after another long day in the hot sun. A delicious meal of *melutha* cooked in garlic oil with rice and local vegetables and a glass of *Rioja* had done little to lift her spirits and she now sipped her coffee contemplating her folly at being there.

The honk and a shout from a passing car made her look up. Some Spanish lads in a car were calling across to three sun tanned girls on the other side of the road who burst into giggles and waved back. Emma smiled and wished she could be as carefree and happy as they appeared to be. And then her heart took a beat. Walking beyond the girls with head turned also to look in their direction was the young man whose eyes she had met as he passed the window of the tea rooms in Westerham and who had tried to pursue her through the streets of Chartwood. She could not forget his face. There was no doubt that it was him.

She hurriedly dug into her purse for enough *euros* for the meal, signalled to the waiter and left it on the table. She ran across the road causing a car to brake sharply and the driver to curse her in Spanish. Reaching the edge of the marina her eyes scanned the direction in which he had gone. She was standing near where she had parked her hire car and was debating whether to hurry along on foot or take the car. He was nowhere to be seen. A car slowed in the road by her but it was a young woman waiting to occupy a parking space that was just being vacated further up the road. It was her man, she could only see a back view but the distinctive yellow tee shirt was the give away; he was pulling out and heading into the traffic. She ran back to her car and jumped in. A gap in the traffic enabled her to pull straight out. She sat forward on the seat clutching the wheel until her knuckles were white. The young man was three cars ahead of her, driving a red Citroen estate and indicating to the left, she pulled out and now there was only one car between them. He turned and wound his way through the back streets passing the ramparts of the old Moorish Castle on their left. The roads were unfamiliar to Emma but he was driving at a gentle pace and she was easily able to keep up.

After further turns they emerged onto the main road out of town. Emma checked the petrol gauge. It suddenly occurred to her that they could go miles and that she could get completely lost. She had no maps of the area and her mobile phone had been left in England, as it was not compatible with the Spanish networks.

About a mile up the road he took the slip road sign posted *La Hara* and turned under the main road. The other car had continued towards the motorway so there was nothing between them now. Emma held back and fortunately his speed was still steady as they drove through the village. The road opened out across a flat plain with groves of lush orange, lemon and grapefruit trees touching the roadside. As they turned a bend the evening sun, a deep orange, was low in the sky and now shone directly in her face. She pulled the visor down quickly and hoped she was far enough back for the young man not to notice her.

They continued like this for some ten minutes, every so often he would disappear around a bend but he was always there about a hundred yards ahead. As she emerged from one bend however he was not so distant but pulling up at traffic lights which had just turned red. She slowed to a crawl hoping that the lights would change before she reached his car. But it was not to be. Other cars were now behind her and she had no option but to stop just a couple of feet behind his bumper. Emma watched him carefully from under the edge of the visor; he seemed preoccupied with the music that she could just hear above the noise of the engine. He was tapping away with his right hand on the steering wheel.

'Come on lights, come on', Emma said out loud. She realised she was feeling very nervous again and the palms of her hands were sticky on the steering wheel. The lights changed and as they did so the young man glanced in his mirror. A frown came across his face and he seemed to look more intently and then he was off across the junction and continuing along the road.

Emma's heart was racing. Had he spotted her; what might he do? They went on under a wide road bridge that Emma could see from the signs carried the A7 motorway, and then on into a small town where he slowed momentarily to fork right. They had been travelling for over half an hour now and Emma began to be scared. The town was behind them and here the sparsely covered scrubland, which opened out on either side of them as they climbed deeper into the hills, gave an air of desolation to the place. Only one other vehicle was on the same road and that was some distance behind. Where were they? How much farther? Emma was seriously worried now. Would she be able to remember her way back to Denia? She really ought to turn around now. This was madness. Her heart raced, her breath quickened. She was sure he had recognised her in that brief moment at the traffic lights. Was he even now luring her out to her fate? They had not passed a house or farm for over five minutes. The sun had dropped behind the distant mountains and together with the darkening sky cast rocks and scrub into shadows that only served to heighten the fearful imaginings that were invading Emma's mind.

The young man had switched his lights on and Emma reluctantly did the same. She decided now it was too dangerous to go on and began to look for a pull in where she could turn the car round safely. Just then, the brake lights of the car ahead came on and he indicated to the left. Emma slowed and saw the car pull through a stone archway into a tree-lined drive. She drove on no more than seventy yards and saw what she was looking for. Here there were the remains of a thin pine forest with a track leading off the road into it. She nosed the hire car into the trees and parked. She got out and stood listening. Silence. All she could hear was the cooling of the car engine.

She grabbed her coat off the back seat and set off towards the direction of where she had last seen his car. There was just enough light to see where she was placing her feet but she cursed that fact that she had entirely the wrong shoes for such a venture.

After a couple of minutes she reached the drive and could see the stone archway to her left, the drive to her right arced round further to the left and she could see nothing from here. She decided it was easier to walk on the drive and reckoned she could dive quickly into the trees if she heard anyone or anything approaching. A feint cooking smell reached her nostrils as the small *finca* came into view. She cut through the trees to get a closer view from the side of the building. It was a typical whitewashed stone built house of the region, the large central chimney reaching proudly to the now cobalt sky above. Single storey; not large but probably with two or three bedrooms as well as a living room and kitchen. A covered veranda with gentle arches ran the full length of one side and across the back of the house. Flowers and vines climbed around and across the arches and several wicker chairs and a table were scattered along its length. A shaft of warm light illuminated the veranda immediately outside the open doors at the rear. Emma could hear guitar music softly coming from the radio within. Just then the young man appeared at the door a glass of wine in his hand. He sat on one of the chairs and relaxed in it. If he had seen Emma it appeared not to have disturbed him. He was holding a conversation with someone inside the house but she could not hear the reply to tell whether it was male or female. After a while he stood up and went back into the house.

Emma waited for ten minutes but the man did not reappear, she contemplated what to do next. She realised now that when she had left

Tall Trees she had given no real thought as to what she would do in any situation that confronted her. She wished Jane could have been with her, she would have known what to do. There was no point in going to the police, what did she have to report, that she saw this man in England? Should she wait? It seemed unlikely that the man was going out again tonight but if she left and came back in the morning, she took the risk of losing him. It was certainly too dangerous to confront him now on her own.

The decision was taken from her. She half sensed; half heard a movement behind her but before she could properly turn two arms had roughly grabbed her. Before the scream could leave her throat a cloth was held over her nose and mouth. She choked as the pungent smell took its effect, her eyes glazed over, she felt her legs go limp, and then all was blackness.

++++++++++

Sitting in his car at the traffic lights Juan Delgardo had spotted Emma in the car behind him. It came as a shock to find her in Spain even though that was all he had ever wanted. Was she following him or had she found out about Edwardo he puzzled. He continued driving at a steady pace wondering what to do. It was too dangerous and risky to stop and confront her now on the open road and in any case it was getting dark and he knew that it would scare her badly if he did. He eventually arrived at his home and turned off watching her car as he did so. She drove straight past heading towards Edwardo's place. Perhaps she now knew her true identity and was going to confront him.

He stood now on the veranda listening to the quiet, trying to think what, if anything he should do. Just then there was the noise of doors slamming and the distinctive sound of a VW truck or camper van revving nearby. It was coming from the direction of a track in the wood just a short distance away. Something about the revving sounded urgent and he decided to investigate. He jumped the low stone wall and headed through the trees. It was the car he saw first, the same one that had followed him earlier, and then as he reached it he saw the back of a pale blue camper van disappearing down the track at speed to the main road. He turned back to the car. Inside was a woman's handbag on the seat. He picked it up and opened it. It contained makeup, keys and other personal items and a purse with credit cards in the name of Miss Emma Bertram.

He debated what to do. She must have pulled up the track and been watching him from the woods but unbeknown to her someone must have either followed her or been here first. He tried to recall if he had seen a blue camper around the area in the last few days but he was not aware of it. The keys to Emma's hire car were in the ignition and he decided to move it back to his house and secure it first and then make his way to Edwardo's place. He drove it back quickly and ran into the house to tell his cousin what had happened. He had made sure she had all she needed for the night and then left, taking with him the rifle that Edwardo had given him. Two years earlier Edwardo had taught Juan to shoot and he had become an excellent marksman. Though he had only ever shot at targets and refused to shoot at birds when Edwardo had tried to get him to do so. Driving through the dark towards the *finca* he did not know why he had picked up the rifle. He hoped it would not be needed and he wasn't sure he could fire it in anger against another living being anyway.

On instinct instead of driving up the track to the front of the house he took the turning to the left before Edwardo's and then turned up a disused old farm track on the right. Arriving at a small clearing he again on instinct turned the vehicle around so it was facing back the way he had come. It was completely dark now but there was enough moon for him to find his way to the path that led across the ridge to Edwardo's. He had played in these woods as a youngster. He knew every part of this land better than Edwardo did. Topping the ridge he looked down on the house. Lights were on in a couple of the rooms and the sound of a radio or television could be heard but otherwise all was quiet. Only Edwardo's four-wheel drive was parked outside, there were no other vehicles. He decided to cut across to the other side of the narrow valley to the only other path that led out of it. This was little used and quite overgrown in places and he doubted anyone could find it but he knew it had to be checked. He skirted the house without making a sound and worked his way up the steep side opposite to where he had entered. Once over the ridge he followed the path through the trees. It was darker here because the canopy above had blotted out the moon and he had to tread carefully. He followed the narrow path down the gentle slope until the trees thinned out and the path joined a wider track that came up from the metalled road. Brighter here he could see fresh tyre marks in the dust. He had last come this way about a week ago so a vehicle had been here very recently and there were several cigarette butts on the ground which had not been there before. He had checked further down the track but there was no sign of any vehicle.

He considered what he should do. He wondered about calling on Edwardo and telling him what he had discovered but he was unsure how Edwardo would react and he was not supposed to know anything about

Emma anyway. No, Edwardo was best left alone. He was sure that Emma had not gone voluntarily in the van otherwise her keys and handbag would not have been left in her hire car. But where had they taken her and who were they? It would be impossible to search the area at night besides she could be anywhere. No, as frustrating as it was, the key was here at Edwardo's, they had to come here, they just had to. He decided to retrace his steps back along the path to the ridge and then across the valley floor to the track on the other side of the bowl where he had first entered Edwardo's. At the top of the ridge on this side, about fifty metres from the track stood an old stone built hut. He often used it when taking a break from his chores on the farm. From this vantage point he could watch both of the pathways and the main entrance from the road should anyone approach. The track from the road was clearly visible in the moonlight but at this distance he was unsure of the point on the ridge opposite where the other path emerged from the wood. He strained his eyes until they began to smart but it made no difference. He prayed that he would hear or see something before it was too late. The hut had a deep window so he was able to prop himself in the corner on the bench seat and look out across the farm buildings to the ridge beyond. He found an old cushion and wedged it behind his head. He propped the rifle against the wall close to his hand and settled until he was comfortable. It could be a long night.

He looked out through the window and saw the white rock of the stone boulders on the rise opposite begin to move in his vision as he tried to distinguish between the shapes and the greys of the night. Thin wisps of cloud fetched across the moon from time to time causing patterns to dance on the backdrop. He felt his eyes go heavy and he strained to keep awake.

++++++++

Back in England Smurdon was fuming. Kathy Smart had just received the dressing down of her life and had been threatened with school crossing patrol for the rest of her life. Both Valerie Marcheson and Ray Brooks had been interviewed but denied all knowledge of knowing where Emma might have gone. They both knew the police would find out eventually but had promised Emma they would give her as much time as possible.

The police had also gone to interview Frank Cowton but his wife said he was on holiday in Scotland 'travelling around' so he couldn't be contacted. They would have to wait until he telephoned home.

++++++++

Emma slowly came round, her eyes stung and she felt groggy. She went to stretch her legs and found that they were tied together as were her hands behind her back. She ached all over and her head was spinning. A cloth saturated with her own saliva was stuffed in her mouth. She closed her eyes again and then gently opened them. This time she was able to focus them more clearly. She was lying on her side on a small bed. The room was tiny with a low slightly curved ceiling and she quickly realised she was in a room within a caravan or camper van of some kind. The furniture was simple and fixed to the walls. It consisted of the bed she was on, a bedside cabinet, and a chest of drawers on the wall at the foot of the bed. To the left a curtain was drawn tightly across a window and on the opposite wall a narrow door was shut tight, the butt of a key protruding through the back of the lock. The cabin had a stuffy, musty smell about it, the bed she lay on smelt of unwashed bodies. It was all Emma could do not to heave. A grey light crept in around the edges of the curtains but the sun was not yet up as far as she could tell. The van was stationary but she could hear distant traffic and subdued voices nearby.

She considered whether to try and make a noise by swivelling round and banging her feet on the wall by the window. If there was someone nearby perhaps she could raise help. She arched her back and turning drew her knees up under her chin. Then with all the effort she could muster slammed her feet against the side of the van. At the same time she tried to shout help but nothing came out through the rag. She heard a man's voice swear and the sound of a door opening in the van. She brought her feet up a second time but the door to her prison burst open, a man rushed in, slapped her face hard and spun her feet round roughly.

'Do that again and you are dead meat!' he threatened.

But it wasn't the young Spaniard as she had expected; it was the evil looking green-eyed man. She was his captive once more.

'Well, well, quite the little detective aren't we coming all the way out here to Spain?' he sneered, 'But you were looking in the wrong place my darling.'

He put his hand on her leg just above the knee and leered at her. Emma cringed and tried to shrink back against the head of the bed but he just kept it there. He saw the fear in her eyes and just laughed. He bent his head close to her face and puckered his lips; she could smell a mixture of stale sweat and tobacco. He moved his hand up across her stomach and followed the contour of her breast.

'I wonder what your lips are like, how about a nice kiss for Darren?'

he played.

Just then the door burst open and Robbie Wilson came in. He took in the scene in an instant and roughly grabbed the boy throwing him back against the wall by the dresser with a mighty thud. Darren looked daggers at the older man, he thrust a finger inches from his face.

'One day you'll regret doing that', he snarled.

'Get out of here you little worm, go and find John and tell him it's time to go', replied the older man fixing the boy's stare with his own.

For a moment neither man moved, then the younger one swore and crashed out of the door. The older man turned to Emma.

'Sorry about the discomfort my dear, and the manners of my son. We try to bring them up decent, but they pick up such bad manners at school these days don't they?' He smiled. 'Now I'll take that rag from your mouth if you promise to be quiet, otherwise I can make it quite uncomfortable, what's it to be?'

Emma nodded her head and as he took out the cloth he said, 'It was rather fortunate of you turning up like you did yesterday. It will make our... what shall we say... confrontation with... well I'll leave that as a little surprise for you too.'

He paused, 'I rather like mysteries, don't you.' And then he became serious; 'I've waited over twenty years to solve this one!'

With that he was gone. Emma lay there; she didn't understand what was going on or what it was all about only that it must be connected with her mother and father. What she did realise was that she was totally at their mercy and although she tried to be brave her eyes began to water once more as the van started and began to move off.

Chapter 19

They had been travelling for about twenty minutes. Emma had managed to lean back and kick at the curtain covering the back window and opened it partially but she was too low to see anything other than the sky, a few trees and electricity poles as they sped by. She had no idea where they were. She was aware of traffic passing occasionally in the opposite direction but it seemed to be quite light. Then the vehicle slowed, turned to the left and rocked violently as it dropped off the surfaced road onto a rough track of some sort. Emma banged her head heavily on the wall as the van lurched on the uneven surface and she tried to push herself more upright but it was not easy with her hands tied behind her back. There were more trees here Emma could see through the gap in the curtains. They were beginning to form a complete canopy over the van and the interior darkened noticeably. It was now climbing slowly, the engine labouring at the incline and unevenness of the track. The vehicle was at a crawl now; it lurched twice and then came to a halt. The engine was switched off. Silence.

The men got out of the van. 'Get her,' said the older man to the one who had called himself Darren, 'And keep your dirty little fingers off. I want this one in pristine condition, for the moment.'

'I'll get the guns,' said another voice as he unlocked a compartment on the side of the van.

The young man, Darren pulled Emma roughly from the bed; he undid the rope from around her feet and pushed her out through the door into the open. Emma blinked and waited for her eyes to adjust to the brightness. They were on the edge of a spent almond grove, the trees old and decaying through lack of water. Emma looked around. The ground dropped away to the right down the track that the vehicle had come but the line of it was soon swallowed up by further trees lower down. There were more fruit groves across the wide valley to the left but of a road or any sign of habitation she could see none.

Her ankles stung where the rope had been and she wanted to rub them but her hands were still tied tightly behind her.

'Come on,' said the older man, 'Let's pay a visit.'

They moved off along a narrow path that led at right angles to the track and followed just inside the edge of the trees. The older man led the way, then Emma being pushed along by Darren who followed next and behind him was another older man whom Emma now saw for the first time. All three men carried rifles.

The path continued between the trees and here on the edge of the once cultivated land there were spruce trees and gorse bushes as well which gave it good camouflage. Emma could see that it was quite overgrow in places but also thought she saw a footprint in the dry dust that pointed in the direction from which they had come.

After about five minutes of climbing the track turned gently to the left and the ground dropped away. Looking ahead from the ridge where they now stood she could see a narrow valley which was more in the shape of a bowl with the hillside climbing quite steeply in all directions. Below in the centre of the bowl stood a *finca* in traditional Spanish style with several outbuildings to one side of it nestling on the valley floor. The place would be completely hidden from all but the air and judging by the distance they had travelled, she estimated that the main road must be at least a mile and a half away. She could see a four-wheel drive vehicle parked by the side of the house but could not see where the track led out of the valley. The land adjacent to the *Finca* had been cultivated in times past. Emma could see almond and pear trees planted in neat rows some five metres apart. Now many were dying or already dead through lack of attention. Their branches, twisted and gnarled, hung lifeless. The base of many of the trunks split open for lack of water. To the left a row of fig trees marked the boundary, their long tendril branches scuffing the ground. The remnants of last years crop shrivelled and dead on the branches where they once knew life. Between the trees the long grasses, bleached a pale gold by the sun, swayed back and forth in the gentle breeze.

The old man motioned for them to be quiet and squat down behind the large rocks that mounted the ridge. He lifted a pair of binoculars that he had slung round his neck earlier and focussed them on the house. He stayed motionless for some time then lowered the glasses.

'Looks quiet enough, right you know what to do,' he said.

Darren slung the rifle over his shoulder and pulled out a handgun. He pulled Emma roughly towards him and pressed the gun to the side of her head.

'Now you do exactly as you are told,' he snarled, 'Cos I'll have no hesitation in using this.'

Emma struggled to compose herself, she was so frightened, every limb in her body ached and she didn't know how much more she could take of all that was happening.

'Are you going to kill me like you killed Jane?' She asked in a trembling voice.

'Like I killed Jane?' he spat at her, his menacing green eyes almost popping out of their sockets. 'Like I killed Jane?' he repeated. 'You still don't get it do you girl? I didn't kill Jane, your father did. Jane was my sister!'

++++++++

Emma could remember little of the trek down from the ridge. Whether she had been carried or whether she had walked as it were by remote control, she did not know. She felt as if she were in a trance following the news of this latest revelation. Jane, her friend and companion, who had been so kind to her and helped through Mother's death, who had been so encouraging and helpful in the quest to find the truth. Jane? This evil man Darren's sister, she couldn't be. And yet there had been things about Jane that didn't seem to add up at the time. But her mind was a muddle, she couldn't think straight; tears were coursing down her cheeks, smudging what little makeup was left. Her legs felt so weak and she was shaking uncontrollably and close to being hysterical.

A sharp slap across the face from Darren brought her out of her confusion.

'Stop babbling and keep very still and quiet,' he whispered through clenched teeth. She was being held against the wall of one of the outhouses, out of sight of the house. Darren pressed his left hand against her neck and held the gun in his right hand, still menacingly close to her face. She could see the older man across the yard crouched behind an old farm vehicle. He was looking away from her up into the trees, to the right of where she thought the house must be. A glint of metal reflected the sun back from that direction and she guessed that must be where the other man was.

It looked as if the older man was about to motion something to Darren when a voice called out from the direction of the house.

'So you've come then, Wilson…, Peters…, what took you so long?' The voice was deep and measured with a feint accent.

'Why are you hiding? Do you think I don't know you are there? Carlos saw you park the camper and I've been watching you ever since you came over the ridge.' The voice went on.

Emma saw the older man whom she assumed to be Wilson straighten, his rifle raised to chest height and pointing in the direction of the voice, but he remained behind the old tractor.

'Yes, I'm here Barry, or do I call you Edwardo now?' Wilson said with a sneer. 'Did you think you could hide from me for ever?' He paused but Masters remained silent while Emma gasped at the name. Was this really her father, alive, she wanted to see him and without thinking she struggled against Darren's hold so she could peer round the corner of the building but he was too strong for her and held her back.

'Why did you do it Barry? You planned to double cross us right from the beginning, didn't you? For fifteen years we nearly rotted in that hell hole of a prison, but you know what kept me going? The knowledge that whatever the newspapers said about you being killed by the Harvan brothers or lost at sea, I just knew that you were still alive and that one day I would face you, have my revenge, and collect our share.' He paused, 'Today Barry, today is that day!' He spat those last words out with venom; his face and fat neck colouring a bright red as he spoke. Emma could see the side of his face glistening with great droplets of sweat as the morning sun, now clear of the ridge on the eastern side, bore down on his balding head.

There was silence again for a time then Masters spoke slowly and deliberately. 'You shouldn't have bragged about our little venture Robbie. You told that little snitch Hunter what we had done didn't you? Couldn't keep you mouth shut could you; that was always your problem Robbie. And what did Hunter do? Went straight to Cowton and grassed you up 'cause you were screwing his bird behind his back and you thought he didn't know.'

Masters paused and then continued, 'You gave me no choice Robbie, Cowton followed you to the meet and arrested you and Peters. I watched it all from the tenement block overlooking the railway sidings. Did you hear that John?' he called out raising his voice. 'I know you are up there somewhere Peters. It's not me you've got to blame for your incarceration; it's your old buddy Wilson here. He can't keep his mouth shut or his trousers zipped!'

'Shut up!' cried Wilson, 'You set us up and now you are going to pay.'

'I don't think so, I have you covered from every angle, as I said we have watched your arrival since you parked the camper van back on the old track,' Masters bluffed.

Wilson was silent for a moment, he had no idea how many men Masters had in hiding; he had seen none but now he was less certain, was Masters bluffing?

Masters continued, 'You shouldn't have killed Doreen Robbie, there was no need for that, she was a good woman, she had nothing to do with my coming here.'

'Is that why you killed my daughter?'

'I came looking for you, to teach you a lesson for killing Doreen, she just happened to get in the way.'

'You bastard!' shouted Wilson.

'A life for a life,' replied Masters evenly.

'A life for a life, Masters is it,' shouted Darren dragging Emma out from behind the stone building, 'Then how about your daughter next,' he yelled.

Masters stared at Emma and for a moment there appeared to be a flicker in his eye but then he simply said, 'I have no daughter.'

Emma looked at him bewildered and confused. Was this the man whom they claimed to be her father? He had spoken of Doreen her mother and admitted killing Jane but now he was denying her. She tried to call out; she wanted to ask, 'Are you my Father?' But nothing came; her throat dry with fear.

Darren held Emma more tightly with his left arm and pressed the gun to her right temple. Emma froze with fear and looked pleadingly at Masters. Masters stood motionless; the gun still clasped at his side. Without taking his eyes off Darren he assessed his chances; he knew he could never raise it quickly enough. Besides the girl was shielding the boy and he would not be able to get a clean shot without the risk of killing her. It was two against three. The odds were not good. Carlos was behind the rocks to his left and would be able to take out Peters and probably Wilson but it was unlikely he could get any better shot at the boy than he could. He cursed that Juan had not shown at the house that morning, he could do with another gun. He had trained him well, he was a good shot, but Juan had never fired a gun in anger and he doubted the boy would have the guts to shoot if it came to it. He must play for time; it was his only chance.

'There's been enough killing boy, kill the girl and you are dead, you must know that!'

'You betrayed my father and Peters here, and then if that wasn't enough you murdered my sister,' Darren screamed.

Emma could feel his spittle on the side of her face, the foul odour of his breath as he spat the words out.

'You have destroyed our lives, now you will die. But first you will see your daughter die before your eyes,' he yelled.

Wilson said, 'Darren...'

'Shut up, shut up,' he was almost dancing with rage. 'All my life I've had to put up with you screaming at me, abusing me, and treating me like dirt. Well not any more, no more are you going to tell me what to do.' For a moment he pointed the gun at his father but his hand shook so much with rage that he quickly brought it back to the side of Emma's temple.

'Don't do it boy,' Masters yelled.

'One... two...'

+++++++++

The sound of someone shouting woke Juan with a start. He looked out through the window. Dawn had broken and the early sun was just clipping the trees at the back of the ridge opposite. 'It must be about eight o'clock,' he thought, and cursed himself for falling asleep. There was more shouting now. 'Why are you hiding?' he heard. He recognised it as Edwardo's voice but he could see no one from where he sat. He carefully picked up the rifle and crept slowly out of the hut. Keeping his body low he edged along the ridge until he could see the yard below.

Edwardo was outside the front of the house standing behind the old water pump, a rifle held loosely by his side. Facing him less than ten metres away but sheltered behind the tractor was a man of similar age to Edwardo. He also held a rifle. To his left and nearer to where Juan lay hidden a younger man stood behind one of the outhouses. His left arm was tightly holding the upper body of the young girl Emma, his right hand held a gun to her head.

Juan tried to stay calm. He brought the rifle slowly round and pointed it in the direction of the young man. He bent and looked through the scope trying to line the cross hairs on the man's back but he was shaking too much. His palms were sticky and he felt the cold sweat trickling from under his arms. His heart was thumping and his breathing became shallow. He began to panic but then he caught sight through the scope of the utter fear in the girl's eyes. He steeled himself to be calm and steadied the rifle in his grip. He watched as the young man dragged Emma out into the open and was screaming at both Edwardo and the older man. He waved the gun in his direction and then brought it up to the young girl's temple again. Juan tensed and steadied himself. He heard Edwardo shout, 'Don't do it boy!' and then the young man was counting, 'One... two...'

Juan knew it had to be now or never. He took final aim and gently squeezed the trigger and then watched as both Emma and the young man fell, almost slow motion like, to the ground. Then all hell broke loose as

175

several guns opened up at once. Juan took little of that in as he raced down the steep track and across the orange grove to where Emma and the man lay by the outbuildings. His heart was pounding; there had been no room for error. The young man had been holding Emma so close to him and he now panicked that he had hit Emma instead.

+++++++++

A shot rang out and Emma felt a jolt. Warm liquid splashed down the side of her face and neck and she began to fall. As she did so a fuselage of shots filled her ears, someone screamed, someone else shouted. She fell awkwardly, her left leg twisted under her and she was on the soft earth. Suddenly her whole vision was filled with Darren's face, as his body lay prone across her. His eyes wide in the incomprehension of death; a trickle of blood fell from the corner of his mouth onto her neck and Emma screamed. She tried to push the lifeless body off of her but it was heavier than she thought. The air was silent now but the acrid smell of gunpowder filled her nostrils.

Just then she was aware of a movement behind her. A hand touched her shoulder but before she could cry out a soothing voice said, 'It is alright Senorita, I will help you, you are safe with me now, but we must hurry.'

Emma turned her head. It was the young man she had followed the night before, the one she had seen those many weeks ago in Westerham just after her mother's death. He had a rifle in his hand, which he laid on the ground as he crouched down. He pushed Darren's lifeless body away, pulled a knife from his pocket and cut the ties that held her wrists then took her hand and helped Emma to her feet. Emma hesitated and looked round. The body of Wilson lay on the ground face down by the tractor. Of Peters there was no sign. She looked to find the man they had called her father. A pair of feet stuck out from behind a bush about twenty yards away but there was no movement. The shooting had finished. She wanted to go and look at the man they called her father but the young man pulled her away.

'Quickly, we must hurry. It is not good to stay here,' He said.

He took her arm and set off behind the outbuilding and onto a winding path across an area of scrub that rested on the valley floor. They climbed a low wall and entered an orange grove. The sweet smell of orange blossom touched Emma's nostrils though she barely noticed it. She stumbled on an irrigation hose and fell forward but the young man caught her. He paused and held both of her shoulders gently as he looked into her eyes.

'It is okay now... you are okay with me... you not worry... be safe soon.' He gave her a reassuring smile and then set off again climbing now up the opposite side of the valley from which they had descended. They reached the top of the ridge and began the descent on the other side. Here it was much steeper and the going was tough. Loose stones slipped under their feet as they half ran half fell through the trees to a gentler path. They crossed a dried up gully and then clambered up onto a dirt track. Emma was exhausted. 'I can't go any further,' she panted, 'I must rest.'

'Look there,' said the young man pointing. Emma followed the line of his hand with her eyes and could just see amongst the trees the outline of the red car she had followed the previous evening.

They reached it and he smiled at her again. 'Please you get in now. This is not a good place to be I don't think.'

Emma was too traumatised to object; she sank into the front seat and closed her eyes. She was aware that he had started the engine and set off along the track but she was totally fatigued and numb and on the verge of passing out, the events of the last few minutes a maelstrom heaving and tossing in her mind.

++++++++

Further along the ridge overlooking the *finca* Frank Cowton lowered his binoculars and nodded to himself. He had seen it all and was content. He had watched the young man and girl run from the scene and though he was sure no one else was alive he waited twenty minutes all the same to be sure there was no one else around that might come to see what all the gunfire had been about. He was a patient man. He was used to waiting. It had been part of his job for so many years, ever since he had moved from traffic division to the Criminal Investigation Department of the Metropolitan Police some thirty-five years ago.

Satisfied that all was quiet, Frank climbed slowly down to the garden below. He knew there were a couple of last things left to do. He reached the fallen body of Darren Wilson first and extracted a pair of thin rubber gloves and a rag from his pocket. He picked up the rifle the young man had left there and began to carefully wipe it clean of fingerprints. At the same time he scoured the ground for any sign of anything the young girl or man might have dropped or been torn off their clothing but he could see nothing.

He had heard Masters call out about there having been too much killing, that was certainly true, and there was no point in implicating the young man. He walked on to where Robbie Wilson lay. He had taken at least three bullets and would have died almost instantly. Frank paused for an instant and then climbed to where Peters had been hiding. He found his body behind a large boulder and then moved on to find Masters accomplice. He also was dead. Climbing still further he followed the track back to where they had parked the camper and carefully cleaned all traces of Emma's imprisonment from the rear compartment of the camper van. Finally he retraced his steps, went back to the front of the house and stood over Masters lifeless body.

'Well Barry, we meet again at last,' he said out loud. But there was nothing but the breeze to snatch up his words. He bent down and laid the young man's rifle across the body, took the still warm hand and folded the finger round the trigger.

He surveyed the scene. Satisfied that everything was in order he looked down again at Barry Masters. 'Case closed, justice done,' he murmured. And with that he climbed back up the way he had come, past where he had watched events unfold and onto his waiting car. He did not look back.

Chapter 20

The car jolted over a rut in the road and Emma came to and became aware again of her surroundings. 'Where are we, where are you taking me?' she asked with alarm.

They were on a tarmac road now but there was no other traffic.

'It is not far now and you must not worry,' he smiled.

His smile was disarming but Emma was still apprehensive. 'Where are you taking me?' she asked again.

'Please you must not worry, trust me, I am taking you to meet someone who very much wants to meet you.' He paused, 'my name is Juan Delgardo, please you call me Juan. You are Emma I know, I am very sorry I frightened you in England, I did not mean to.'

Emma felt weary. 'You wrote a letter to me in England, what is all this about?' She pleaded.

'It is not long now, then you will see. Please relax, you are safe now.'

Safe? Emma thought, safe from what? People had just been violently killed. Where was she being taken? Who was this man? She sat back her mind still reeling with all that had happened. She looked out of the window. The sun was well up now in the bright azure sky. Back in Denia people would be going about their normal routine; the tourists would be making their way to the beaches or just strolling along the harbour side soaking up the warmth of the sun. Sitting at the pavement cafes, engaged in happy conversation. She wondered if she had been missed at the hotel. Would they have been worried that she had not shown last night? Would they have telephoned the police? Perhaps they may not have even noticed. But if they had where would they start looking? She had no idea where she was herself, so how could the police, if they were looking, find her?

Her thoughts were interrupted, 'Please, you will see now.' He pointed along the road and there ahead was the entrance she had followed him to the previous evening. As they pulled into the front of the house she saw her hire car parked outside. Had she left the keys in the ignition? She did not remember or care. Juan or someone had found it and moved it from where she had parked it among the trees. He drew up along side it and switched off the engine.

'Please you must come with me,' he smiled again but Emma hesitated. 'Please,' he beckoned, 'There is someone you must meet.'

Emma followed him across the veranda and in through the main door. The door led straight into a large square room that was simply furnished in pine. A long dresser stretched against the far wall and a small cabinet and two upright chairs were to her right. The floor was laid with large blue veined quarry tiles that helped to make the room feel cool. A row of hooks on the wall to her left caught her eye and she noticed the distinctive blue anorak hanging there that she had seen him wearing in England. They continued through a door opposite that led into a hallway with several doorways off from it. There was a well-laid out kitchen to the left and a small bathroom to the right. The young man paused at a doorway further along the passageway and spoke something in Spanish but she did not understand it.

'Si,' a woman's voice replied softly from within the room.

He looked at Emma and gestured to the open doorway. 'Please, you must meet I think.'

Emma slowly turned the corner of the door and stood shock still. She gasped, raising her hand to her mouth as she did so. There propped up on pillows in a bed against the opposite wall was a young woman. Of similar height but thinner, darker skinned yet somehow pallid. The hairstyle was different, but the colour identical. The facial features in every respect the same as hers. Emma could have been looking in a mirror.

'Hello,' the woman said quietly with a soft accent. 'I am Juanita, I am your twin sister yes?'

Emma felt her knees buckle, her eyes lost their focus, hands came out to hold her and then everything went black.

+++++++

Emma slowly opened her eyes and tried to focus them, her head felt light and dizzy. She had slept fitfully. The events of the last few hours spinning and tormenting in a whirling confusion of her mind. She saw again the look in the eyes of the man they called her father, heard his words of estrangement - 'I have no daughter,' smelt the bad odour of Darren's breath, heard the crack shot of the rifle, felt the hot blood splatter across her face. And in the midst of all that saw again the gaping wound in her mother's chest, the wide staring eyes that would focus no more. She shuddered. Something above her was moving. She squeezed her eyes shut then opened them again. It was a large fan quietly turning on the ceiling above her. She gently turned her head and looked around. She lay on a single bed under a thin pink coloured duvet. The room was neatly furnished in the same pinewood she had seen in the first room. The ceiling and walls were white and several watercolour pictures of flowers hung around them. She felt the sheet against her and lifted the duvet. Only her underwear remained; her outer clothes had been removed.

Just then the young man looked around the door. 'Ah, you are awake now, that is good. You feel better now?' He saw Emma looking beneath the sheet and smiled.

'Don't worry, it was Anna,' he paused, 'She is, how do you say, my Auntie. She comes in every day to see to Juanita. It was she who undressed you and put you to bed. She has cleaned and pressed your clothes. I was bringing them to you now.' He held up a small pile of neatly pressed clothes sandwiched between his hands.

Emma sat up holding the duvet to her. 'What is happening please, who are you, who is Juanita? I am confused. Please, I want to go back to my hotel.'

He smiled again. 'This has been very bad and difficult for you I know. I will explain all I know to you in a moment over some food yes. You must be hungry and thirsty? I will leave your clothes here; there is a bathroom across the hall where you can freshen up. Please, you will come to the kitchen when you are ready?' With that he left; leaving Emma on her own. She clasped her knees to her chest and looked around the room again although her eyes did not focus on anything particular.

The thought of food had been far from her mind but the mention of it made her realise that she had not eaten since the night before at the pavement restaurant before all this had happened. And that seemed an age ago. As she became more awake she felt very vulnerable, there alone with little chance of escape, yet the sound of his voice was somehow soothing. Who was this man? Who was Juanita? How could she be her sister? Mother had never spoken of a twin sister; surely she could not keep such a matter from her, and why was she here in Spain and not in England? The idea was preposterous, and yet the striking resemblance was uncanny. She knew that here for certain must lie answers to some if not all of her questions. She steeled herself to be brave yet again. Slipping out of bed she put on a robe that had been left for her, picked up her clothes, and went to the bathroom.

++++++++

Ray Brooks paced up and down the foyer of the hotel and despite the air-conditioning was sweating profusely. Emma had promised to telephone him every evening at 9pm and when she didn't call he headed straight for Gatwick and caught the overnight flight. He had lost Jane and feared now for Emma.

Thankful that she had told him where she was going, he was still somewhat confused by all that was happening. Whether he liked it or not he had been sucked into the mystery of Doreen Bertram and had found that he had taken up a kind of big brother role with Emma. She often seemed so vulnerable and yet had a strength of character and determination that made him admire her. He had been very fond of Jane of course and was beginning to feel a real love for her but whenever he had tried to take the relationship further, Jane had resisted and stepped back from it. He had found this very confusing and now she was dead.

The manager eventually appeared and made his apologies. There had been a staffing problem in the hotel kitchens that needed dealing with. How could he help? Ray explained that the receptionist had confirmed that Emma had not returned to the hotel the previous evening and that she had not been seen since.

'Ah is that all,' the manager said with a smile, 'Oh that is nothing to worry about, it happens all the time. A pretty young girl on holiday alone, she meets with a Spanish boy yes, and they go off and enjoy the evening together and one thing leads to another and...' he began to say with a smirk.

'No!' shouted Ray. 'Emma is not like that; she may be in danger. I must find her. We must go to the police.'

'And they will say exactly the same,' said the manager shrugging his shoulders.

Ray grasped the forelock of his hair until it hurt and sighed deeply in frustration. He knew the manager was right. He banged his fist on the reception desk and stormed out.

++++++++

Emma sat at the kitchen table picking at the dish of rice and fish that Juan had prepared. She was quite hungry but her thoughts were preoccupied listening as she now was to the incredible story that he was unfolding. He sat opposite sipping a mug of coffee, watching her as he spoke. He told her what he had pieced together from papers he had discovered and telephone conversations he had overheard when he had worked up at Masters *Finca* in the hills. He had of course only known him as Edwardo Marcos and not Barry Masters. Masters had often sent him on errands to England and when he had opportunity he tried to discover more details about the incredible deception he was uncovering but he was afraid of Masters and had to be very discreet lest he should find out what he was doing.

He told the story with great sensitivity knowing how the revelation of it all, particularly about her mother would hit her hard. He paused and looked across the table at Emma. Her eyes now staring into the distance not seeing anything but the deception of it all and he could see the torment in those eyes as she struggled to come to terms with the sham and deceit. The strain of the last twenty-four hours stretched across her face, her shoulders sagged, and tears welled in her eyes. She so looked liked Juanita, the facial features, the ears, the eyes and nose, the gently curve of the lips; he so wanted there and then to go to her, put his arm around her and comfort her. But she was like thin porcelain; he could see that, on the verge of breaking into a thousand tiny fragments.

Instead he sat very still and watched as she dropped her fork on the plate and large teardrops rolled down her pale cheeks onto the barely touched meal below. He could see that she was fighting the emotion. Now perhaps was not the time. Here in a foreign country, away from friends and close ones to release such personal and intensely intimate feelings.

Emma looked up slowly and spoke quietly, her voice cracking with the strain and yet somehow devoid of the emotion she surely must be feeling. 'Thank you for telling me. I don't want to believe you. What you have just said destroys all I have known and believed about my family, my mother, me.' She paused, 'yet in my heart I know that what you have told me must be true. It answers so many questions, questions that have been building in my mind ever since mother was murdered, confirms the many things that the police and that evil Darren told me when he held me prisoner. I didn't want to believe them. I prayed that it was all a sick joke, a crazy dream. Yet deep down I think I believed them even then.' She lapsed into silence and they both sat there quiet and still, Emma with her own painful thoughts; Juan patiently waiting until she was ready.

Emma spoke softly, 'You wrote to me didn't you, about Juanita, but Mother intercepted the letter and I never saw it. She did the same with the second letter you wrote, I only found it five days ago. How could she have been so callous, she was prepared to gamble with Juanita's life to protect her own.' she paused, 'Why did you not come and speak to me when you came to England?'

'At first I wanted to be sure that what I had discovered in Edwardo's papers was really true. I followed you at a distance; I needed to be sure.

Then I saw you through my binoculars and I was certain but I didn't know why you had not replied to my letters and so I didn't know how you would respond if I approached you. Then before I had decided what to do the Police were everywhere and I read in the newspapers that your mother had been killed. Then I had to return to Spain or Edwardo would wonder where I had got to. Then Edwardo sent me to England a second time and I made up my mind that I would confront you but you drove away from me, I had scared you and again the police were always there so I returned here to Spain. I had failed Juanita again and I was very sad.' He paused and then brightened, 'But there is a God in heaven because he has brought you to us now.'

The sun had lowered in the sky and dipped behind the two large date palms in the courtyard that now spread their shadow across the kitchen window. The room had darkened and a light breeze began to ruffle the curtains.

Emma stirred, 'It is all so much to take in, but you have not failed Juanita, I can see you have been good to her and looked after her and now that I am here I will not fail her either.' she paused, 'I think I would like to go back to my hotel now I am very tired but I will come again I promise. I don't think I could drive; would you take me please?'

'Yes of course, don't worry about your car, I have a friend who will help me get it back to you first thing in the morning, and...' he paused, 'Emma, may I call you Emma, I think it is best you do not say anything to anyone, especially the police about what has happened. There is no reason why they should connect you with Edwardo or his farm. They will no doubt interview me because I work there but I will say nothing. It will be all right, you will trust me?'

'Yes,' she smiled faintly, 'I will not say anything but will you be all right?'

'Don't worry about me, I will be okay.'

'Can I see Juanita again before I go?'

He looked at the clock. It was half past four. 'She usually wakes about now.' Standing he took her arm and gently steered her towards Juanita's room.

++++++++

Ray Brooks was returning back in the direction of the hotel. He had had a fruitless afternoon walking the streets of the town and waterfront. While most of the population of Denia had snoozed their way through the afternoon siesta, Ray had worked up a sweat searching in vain hope of finding Emma. He knew that it was almost certainly futile but he had to do something. The manager had at least consulted the hotel register and provided him with the make and licence number of the car Emma had hired and Ray had searched every street he could find within a mile or more of the hotel. He had worked a grid pattern from the hotel back towards the *Plaza de Paris* at the back of the town, through the shopping areas and markets into the main street *Marco de Campo*. Then on into the narrow streets of the old quarter and around the ancient castle that dominated the town. Finally he made his way back along the waterfront stopping to search every café and bar. He felt dead on his feet; he could feel his face burning from the heat of the afternoon sun and his shirt stuck to him like glue. He wished he had a photograph of Emma to show people. The town was much bigger than he had imagined and as each hour went by he realised the futility of his efforts, and yet he had to be doing something. He could not sit still.

Dispirited and feeling very tired he was now walking back to the hotel, passing the yacht club and the newly extended marina. He was hot, parched and every part of his body ached. He longed for the bath and change of clothes that he had promised himself. The hotel now came into view and he could see a red car parked at the entrance. Two people, a man and a woman, were standing by it holding a conversation. The woman looked like Emma but he was too far away to be sure. Despite his tiredness he quickened his pace. Now he was sure it was Emma and he glanced round looking for a gap in the traffic. He found it quickly and sprinted across the road. He was running now, but the couple was separating, the man was climbing into the car. Emma was waving as he drove off and turning to go into the lobby.

'Emma, Emma, Em,' he shouted above the traffic. He was panting now, near to collapse but just a few yards left to go. He called again and she turned, a puzzled look on her face and then recognition.

'Ray, what are you doing here?'

'I was concerned for you, you didn't telephone last night,' he gasped, 'I've... been... searching.'

She saw the look of anguished concern on his face, 'Oh Ray!' she cried, and threw herself towards him. 'Thank you for coming.'

Holding him tightly she buried her head deep into his chest.

Chapter 21

Ray Brooks sat by the table in Emma's room. His face looked dazed and the colour of the afternoon sun had drained from his cheeks. He was stunned by the news that she had just broken to him.

'Jane was Darren's sister, Robbie Wilson's daughter?' He repeated, 'And all this was a sham, a ruse, just to get near to your mother and you to extract information from you... But why?'

'Well I think originally it was just to make contact with Mother to try and get her to speak about the past. Hoping that she would let something slip that would give them information about my father and the whereabouts of the proceeds of the robbery.' She replied quietly.

'But she seemed so sincere, so caring when I met her. She was warm and friendly and made me feel good to be with her, I can't believe she belonged to the same family as that scum.'

'I don't think she knew how ruthless her brother and father were. If she did I don't think she would have gone along with their scheme. I am sure she was genuinely upset when I was kidnapped. Valerie said she was frantic with worry. Ask yourself, why did she go to the warehouse in Bermondsey that day? If it was just to report in to her father she could have used her mobile phone like we now think she did on several other occasions. No, I think it was to confront them, I think she realised how deep and nasty it was all becoming. Somehow they had convinced her that killing my mother had been a tragic accident but with my kidnapping...well I think she wanted it all to end. Emma paused, 'She was not all bad Ray; you must hang onto that.'

They sat in silence for a while then Ray spoke. 'There's a lot you haven't told me isn't there?'

'Yes,' sighed Emma, 'But I don't think I'm ready to share it just yet, I need to clear some things in my own mind first.' She said looking away, and the events of the afternoon and Juan's revelation came flooding back into her mind and she stifled a sob and dabbed her eyes with a tissue. She composed herself and looked up, 'You really are a kind man Ray, I do so appreciate you coming over here and showing so much concern for my safety.' She stood up and walked across the room and took his arm, 'Now I think I need to be alone for a while; it's been a very traumatic twenty-four hours. I'll see you in the morning.' She reached up and gently kissed his cheek as he left the room.

Emma closed the door and leant against it as the enormity of what she had learnt began to sink in. How could Mother - was it right to call her Mother? - have been party to such a deception? And how could she have so callously disregarded the plea from Juan in the letter he had sent? Mother had often seemed cold and hard at times but now Emma was overcome with a mixture of incredulity, bitterness and disbelief. She flung herself on the bed, her body, heart and mind racked with the pain this knowledge had brought. How she longed for someone close to comfort her, to put their arm around her, to hold her, but there was no one.

++++++++

Emma awoke, the pillow below her head damp from tears, her hair a tangled mess. She must have cried herself to sleep from the exhaustion of the day and all that she had learnt. She forced herself to get up and run a bath and as she lay in the warm water she found it best not to dwell too much on the knowledge she had so recently gained. It was still too painful to contemplate.

Shortly after she had finished dressing there was a knock on the door. She opened it gingerly. It was the hotel manager. 'I am sorry Senorita but this message was delivered before you got back this afternoon and the clerk was supposed to have given it to you straight away but he forgot and went off duty. He has just telephoned me and apologised.' He handed her a small sealed white envelope with her name and that of the hotel neatly written on the front. Emma thanked the man and locked her door. She walked across to the table carefully tearing open the envelope as she went. A sense of unease crept into her mind. Juan and Ray were the only two people in Spain to know she was staying at this hotel, so who could the note be from? Inside was a single folded sheet of paper; she extracted and opened it.

'I know what happened today. Do not say anything to anyone, especially the police. There will be no evidence to show that you were ever there or in the camper van, nor that your Spanish friend did what he did. Make sure you tell him. I suggest you destroy this note now.'

It was signed, *Frank Cowton.*

'So Frank Cowton had been there. He must have witnessed

everything.' she thought.

She hadn't really considered the consequences of what had happened at Masters house this morning, of the police investigation that would inevitably follow and the links that would be made between Barry Masters, Robbie and Darren Wilson, and Doreen Bertram. The police in England would be informed, Smurdon would make further investigation and when he did he would discover that on the very day of the shootings, she was here in the very place where it had happened. Emma was too tired to think it all through; could her presence here be linked in anyway? Frank Cowton seemed to think not. She thought of Juan, what about him? How would he cope with a police investigation? After all he did work at the *finca* and was bound to be questioned at length. Despite the fitful sleep she had just had, Emma still felt tired and decided to forego the evening meal but first she wrote a note to Juan and took it down to the reception desk with strict instruction that it was to be given to the man who returned her car. The promise of a ten euro note to the clerk ensured this would be done, she just hoped he would get it before the police contacted him. Back in her room she changed into her nightdress and climbed into bed. As she laid there deep in thought, concern for Juan was uppermost in her mind.

++++++++

Juan Delgardo was in a sweat. It was early the next morning and he was driving as fast as he dared along the winding road. But he was not heading for Emma's hotel; he was travelling in the opposite direction towards Edwardo's place. The engine whined as he slipped the gearshift into second to take the steep hairpin bend.

After he had dropped Emma off at the hotel the previous afternoon he had returned to the house, prepared a meal for Juanita and then sat with her until she began to tire. He was concerned how the news about her father's death would affect her but she showed little emotion. 'He disowned my mother as soon as he knew she had become pregnant, he did not care when she was dying, he disowned me from birth. I have no father,' she simply said.

He had left her to sleep then and went and sat in the kitchen resting his elbows on the table. He dropped his head into his hands. The enormity of all that had happened in little over twenty-four hours began to register with him. He poured a large glass of red wine to steady himself. He kept seeing the face of the young man he had killed and poured another drink. He couldn't recall leaving the kitchen and going through to his bedroom but in the early hours of the morning the nightmare had unfolded. And then he had awoken from the dream. The rifle. He had left the rifle on the ground by Darren's body. Although the gun belonged to Edwardo it would have his fingerprints all over it. It would be obvious to the police that someone else had been there and only a matter of time before they knew it was him. He had looked at the clock. It was 5.40am and already light. He leapt out of bed and started to dress with the intention of going straight to the *finca* there and then, but then he stopped and thought. Edwardo lived like a recluse. He had to. He had so very few visitors that you could count the number that came in a month on one hand and thankfully Maria his housekeeper was away until next week. There was also Juanita to think about. He couldn't just leave without getting her breakfast and seeing to her medication. He forced himself to attend to her first and prayed that it would all still be as they had left it. That he would be able to recover the rifle and dispose of it, then check the scene and call the police himself. Yes, that is what he would do.

He hurriedly finished tidying the breakfast things and went into Juanita. 'I must go now, Anna will be here soon.' He paused and then forced a smile, 'See, I promised I would find your sister for you. Now soon everything will be alright.' He leant forward and kissed her forehead.

'We shall see.' She had replied quietly.

There had been little conviction in his voice and he hoped she hadn't noticed. Now as he sped along the road towards Edwardo's place he was feeling less confident that all would be well. He reached the turning to the plot and stopped to look around. The area was deserted and quiet. He shifted the car back into gear and turned sharply behind the rock that jutted sheer out of the ground for some ten feet at this point and then along the narrow track through the densely wooded land that bordered the road. To any passing vehicle on the main road the entrance was well hidden as it was intended to be. He drove on through the wood for just over a mile emerging at the other end into the bowl like valley that had almost sheer sides at the upper slopes rising some two hundred feet above the valley floor. Apart from the two steep zigzag footpaths on either side there was no other way in or out. It was the perfect hiding place. Edwardo had never said how he came by it, but the age of the *finca* suggested it had been here long before he had arrived in Spain.

Juan took the final turn into the parking area by the house. Apart from Edwardo's four-wheel drive there was one other vehicle parked there, an old white Fiat van. Juan's heart skipped a beat as he saw it and pulled up along side. The driver's door opened and an overweight man of about fifty with greying hair eased himself out and started towards him. Juan recognised him as one of the traders from the travelling market that worked Denia and the nearby towns on a weekly basis. Edwardo occasionally did business with him.

He spoke in Spanish, 'Juan, isn't it? You'd better prepare yourself for a shock! Your boss is dead, he's been shot. Carlos is dead too.'

Juan looked genuinely shocked, he stammered, 'I wasn't here yesterday, it was my day off, what has happened?'

The trader looked at Juan for a moment, puzzled by his response. 'Well there has been a gunfight, that's the only way I can describe it. I've never seen anything like it in my life. I don't know when it happened, I'm not an expert, but Edwardo is over there by the well, Carlos is behind that boulder at the edge of the trees,' he said pointing, 'And there are two more bodies, men I don't recognise, laying over there,' he said, turning and extending his arm first towards the tractor and then to the far wall of the tool shed.

Juan started forward but the trader held out his hand to stop him. 'Best not go over there; the police will want it undisturbed.'

'The police?' queried Juan without thinking,

'Of course boy, I've called them on my mobile, they should be here soon.'

The enormity of all that had happened in the last twenty-four hours suddenly hit him. Juan's knees began to buckle and he went white as a sheet. He felt the bile rising from his stomach and he began to retch. The trader grabbed his arm and steadied him. 'Here, sit on this rock for a moment and put your head between your knees, I've got some water in the van I'll go and fetch it.'

Juan sipped the water and took some long slow breaths to calm himself. As he raised the bottle again to his lips he was looking straight to where the body of Darren Wilson lay. He closed his eyes for a moment and relived the horror of seeing Emma and Darren falling together, not knowing if his shot had been accurate. He opened his eyes and studied the scene once more, it was exactly as he remembered it, but how was he now to retrieve the rifle? The rifle! It was no longer there. He sat more upright and leaned forward, there was definitely no sign of the rifle. He began to panic; his mind was racing, what could have happened. The trader interrupted his thoughts, 'What's up boy, have you seen something?' He said looking at him intently.

'No, er, sorry, I was just trying to see who they were ... thought I might recognise them as having been to the house before,' mumbled Juan still lost in his thoughts.

'That's possible I suppose,' replied the trader looking towards the bodies, 'They look like foreigners to me, maybe English like Edwardo.'

Juan looked at him, so he knew about Edwardo's background also. As if reading his mind the trader spoke. 'Sure, I have always know him as Edwardo and he has only ever spoken to me in Spanish, which incidentally he does very well, but I can tell, and,' he paused, 'I believe the rumours.'

'What rumours?' asked Juan.

'Well among us traders there is...'

His reply was interrupted by the wail of a police siren coming from the direction of the track. The trader stopped speaking and turned and made his way towards it. Juan saw this as his only opportunity and while the trader's back was turned he ran over to within a few feet of where Darren's body lay. He was right; there was no sign of the rifle. Juan began to panic, his mind racing, someone else had been here, but who? He surveyed the rest of the scene. Everything else was as he remembered it as best as he could recall what he had taken in, in those final moments before he had fled with Emma. If someone else had been here then why would they have removed the rifle? Had they perhaps witnessed the shooting and were even now making a statement to the police?

Juan began to sweat and for the second time his eyes began to lose focus and his legs felt weak under him.

'Hey!' One of the policemen shouted but Juan didn't register the call. The policeman called again as he approached him, 'Hey, you must come away from...' Juan's knees began to buckle and the policeman leapt forward and just caught him in time.

The rest of the morning was little more than a daze to Juan. He sat on a low stone wall away from the crime scene under the shade of a large rambling fig tree as the morning sun rose higher in the sky and burnt off what little hazy cloud there had been.

Crime investigating officers from Alicante arrived and surveyed the scene. Occasionally they would stop and ask him questions about his employer, how long had he worked for him, what did he know about his work or means of income. Who had called at the *finca* recently, had he noticed any strange happenings, did the housekeeper usually have these days off. The questioning went on and on but Juan gave only the briefest of details. He had known Edwardo Marcos all his life. Edwardo had been married to his mother's sister but she had died before he was born. They had a daughter, Juanita who was only a few months old when she died and his mother; Katarina had taken her in as her own. Edwardo had disowned Juanita from the day his wife died. She now lived with him over in the next valley; they had grown up together as brother and sister and he had cared for her when his own mother had died. Of the existence of Emma, he said nothing.

As the morning wore on more police, photographers and forensic officers came and went about the task of collating and recording every detail. Eventually at about three in the afternoon he was allowed to leave but with instructions to report to the police office in Denia in the morning to make a full statement. He drove slowly back to the house his mind still puzzling over the missing rifle and what the consequence of that could mean.

Epilogue

Emma sat on her seat again at the end of the garden looking out over the familiar vista. It had been three weeks since she had returned from Spain and the summer sun now bathed the garden with its warmth and light. The oilseed rape in the fields below added bright splashes of yellow to the scene like a large patchwork quilt. A lot had happened in that time, the Spanish police had found the camper van that among other things had contained the passports of Robbie Wilson, Darren Wilson and John Peters. They had contacted Scotland Yard and after fingerprints of Edwardo Marcos had been forwarded they were able to confirm that he was in fact Barry Masters, the believed mastermind behind what was then the biggest robbery in British history. When the *finca* had been searched a very large quantity of British and Euro currency notes were found hidden in a floor safe together with some papers taken during the robbery.

Smurdon had discovered that Emma was in Spain at the time of the shooting but there had been no evidence to link her with it. Emma remained silent as he had interviewed her and told her to her face that he knew there was more to it than the Spanish authorities had been able to establish. However he was content that a twenty eight year old crime had been solved and that following a search of Wilson's London night club there was sufficient evidence to suggest that it was either Wilson, Peters or Darren who had killed her mother and probably had a hand in her aunt's deterioration. She had suffered enough he said and would not be taking the matter any further.

At the other end of the bench seat sat Ray Brooks, in all the busyness of the last few days they had hardly seen each other since they had both returned to England.

'Thanks for coming Ray, I really haven't had a proper opportunity and I wanted to say how grateful I am for what you did in coming out to Spain after me. It was such a relief to see you there and I'm sorry that the news I had about Jane was such a shock to you, you really liked her didn't you?'

'Yes I did, but my emotions are mixed really, whenever I tried to take the relationship that little bit further Jane always held back and now I know why - that she was just using me to further her quest to gain information from you.' replied Ray quietly.

Emma looked at him and could see the pain in his eyes as he spoke.

'Why do you think she was killed? He asked.

'The police discovered from telephone records that Curtis the solicitor had been Masters contact in England. Kept him informed of events and of course told him about the killing of Mother. At first they thought Jane was an agent for the government or the security company trying to recover the money, and then they discovered she was Wilson's daughter. They think Masters came to England looking for Wilson and Peters to exact revenge but discovered Jane at the warehouse instead. How he knew about the warehouse the police aren't sure and exactly what happened they are not certain but I know of course from Darren's outburst that Masters killed Jane.'

They were silent for a while then Ray asked, 'Have you found all your answers yet? I don't mean to pry it's just that you were obviously very hurt by what you had learnt in Spain and I just wondered... well I don't like to see you hurt.' he said with an embarrassed smile.

'Thanks Ray, yes I think from what the police have told me and what I learnt from Juan I have all my answers now.' Emma paused and fiddled with the signet ring on her finger.

'Don't tell me if you'd rather not.' said Ray.

'No, it's okay I think I'd like to tell someone ... and I'd rather that be you.' Emma replied. 'It all goes back to the late 1960's, early 1970's. My father Barry Masters, he *was* my father, and Mother lived together in the east end of London. Then in 1972 Father along with Wilson and Peters carried out the Sureguard bullion robbery and stole millions in gold and cash. How they knew the date and route is still not known but it's believed the information came form the security guard who was killed in the robbery. He was probably silenced because of that. They had been involved in serious crime before and Wilson and Peters had done time for robbing a post office but although Father was suspected of being involved as well there was never enough evidence to convict him. Wilson and Peters were arrested after a tip off but at the trial they said that Masters, sorry I don't like to call him Father, had masterminded the robbery and that it was he who had beaten the one guard and killed the other.'

'Nice of them to mention it.' interrupted Ray.

'Well, Wilson and Peters were convinced that Masters had set them up and double-crossed them. They went to prison for fifteen years and Masters got away scott-free with the money. Suddenly from being good buddies, there was now no love lost between them. A nationwide hunt was mounted and there were several sightings but the police discounted them all. One such sighting was at Hastings, a man answering Masters description had been seen several times with a couple of fishermen who were rumoured to be involved in trafficking contraband and possibly illegal immigrants. The night before it got reported, they had set sail and never returned. Bodies of the two fishermen were eventually recovered and the boat was found at the bottom in mid channel with the sea-cocks open. Some said it was a suicide pact but there was nothing to prove that and the coroner recorded an open verdict. What the police didn't know was that my uncle Edward had been working with them regularly as well. He had no doubt been involved in the illegal activities with Masters and the fishermen. I have no doubt in my mind that Masters killed the two fishermen and scuppered their boat to make it look like a suicide pact. He did that because he had been using them to ferry himself to and from his new found hideout in Spain and didn't want anyone left to tell the tale.

Immediately after that happened Uncle Ted and Aunt Millie upped and left leaving no forwarding address. That left Masters with a problem, Ted presumably knew of his plan to live in Spain but he didn't know where Ted had gone and was afraid he would grass on him. All was quiet for several years and I can only guess at the next bit. I think Ted must have contacted Masters somehow, perhaps he was short of money and tried to bribe him but Masters was having none of it. He came to England and met with Ted in the pub at Failand. The next thing we know, Ted is knocked down and killed by a hit and run driver. Again I've no doubt that was the work of Masters.' Emma paused, 'You can see now why I can't call him father.' she said.

Pausing, Emma looked up, stared into the distance and swallowed. Ray noticed a tear forming in the corner of her eye. 'And now we come to Mother, if that's the right word to use,' added Emma quietly. 'Masters had told Juan once when he was drunk that he had wanted an English woman to join him in Spain when he first went out there but that she had refused. Mother was scared of boats and she would never have gone on board a boat in her life. She couldn't swim and she hated the water. Whether it was a reaction to Mother's refusal or what I don't know but Masters had an affair with a Spanish woman named Margarita Marcos, he even took her Spanish name. She quickly gave birth to twins girls but had a very difficult delivery and died a few weeks later. From that moment on Masters disowned the twins.' Emma sniffed and dabbed her eyes with the corner of her handkerchief.

Meanwhile he had another problem, Doreen Patterson, my Mother, his long time lover was still in England and I suspect she knew about the robbery. He couldn't bring himself to kill her so he bought her silence. Gave her a new identity, ensured she was financially secure and gave her the one thing she desperately wanted but couldn't have herself.'

'A child.' responded Ray quietly.

'Yes, me, I was trade like a piece of merchandise. Taken from my homeland, my culture, separated from my twin sister, to be raised in a country not my own. I despise her, the callousness of it all. You know I want to hate Doreen Patterson for all those years, I don't want to call her mother anymore.' Emma was quietly sobbing now and Ray moved along the seat, put his arm around her and held her tight.

Emma dried her eyes, 'I wonder what my real mother was like, I will never know?'

'I think she would have been very beautiful and have a lovely personality and be strong and brave and courageous just like her daughter.'

She took his hand and squeezed it and nestled her head into his neck. 'Thanks Ray, you've been so very good to me.'

'What will you do now? He asked.

'*Tall Trees* will have to be sold and that along with Masters land in Spain, the money recovered at the *finca* and further monies recovered from Curtis the solicitor, have been accepted by Sureguard's insurers in settlement.'

'Won't you miss this beautiful house and how will you live?' asked Ray with concern.

'You know I don't think I will miss the house, there are too many painful memories here now, but I'm sure I'll miss this beautiful view.' she brightened and stood up walking to the boundary fence and looking out. 'I grew up here and this corner of the garden will always be special to me. Every time I look out there is something new to see, Nanny always used to call it Emma's corner.' she sighed and turned to face Ray. 'But now I have a new beginning, I have real family now who need me, Juanita has Leukaemia and being a twin they are very hopeful that my bone marrow will be a suitable match for her. I want to spend the rest of my life with her catching up on all the things we have missed together and caring for her.

And as for living, Aunt Millie's cottage is being sold and I shall have the money from that so I will not starve. You know Ray I feel so at peace about it all now, for years I had thought there was something missing in my life and now I know what it was.'

Ray stood and moved towards her 'Can I visit you in Spain?' he asked.

'Yes Ray, I'd like that, I'd like that very much.'

THE END

Printed in the United Kingdom
by Lightning Source UK Ltd.
112792UKS00001B/83